Sydney Effect

Here, within is a work of fiction. Names, characters, places and incidents are either the product of the author's imagination or are used fictitiously. Any resemblance to actual persons, living or dead, events or locales is entirely coincidental.

Ralph K Jones

Copyright © 2024 by Ralph K Jones.
All rights reserved. No part of this book may be reproduced or used in any manner without written permission of the copyright owner, except for the use of quotations in a book review.
First edition February 2024

Sydney Effect

Table of Contents

Chapter 1: Blood Debt 7

Chapter 2: Life of Pain 25

Chapter 3: Chaos 39

Chapter 4: St. Mary's 54

Chapter 5: Brutality the New Reality 66

Chapter 6: Rescue 79

Chapter 7: Empathy 86

Chapter 8: Catch 22 103

Chapter 9: Through the Flames 116

Chapter 10: Rotten 128

Chapter 11: Ambush 140

Chapter 12: Family 154

Chapter 13: Trial Separation 171

Chapter 14: Choices 180

Chapter 15: In the Lion's Den 189

Chapter 16: Cornered 200

Chapter 17: Caged 208

Chapter 18: Pain 218

Chapter 19: Last Leg 233

About the Author 251

CHAPTER 1:
Blood Debt

Team 21 pulls up to a wasteland swathed in impenetrable shadows in the heart of the forsaken industrial district. An intense mixture of tension and anticipation saturates the air as they weave through the warren of crumbling warehouses. Each forward step inches them closer to an unknowable epicentre of darkness where ominous secrets lie shrouded, and unseen threats lurk within every shadow. The police truck they ride in is a masquerade—an armoured beast garbed in the rusted skin of a forgotten relic, blending seamlessly into the desolate scene of decay. Graffiti and grime shroud its exterior, camouflaging it amidst the abandoned remnants of a bygone era. The warehouse, a raw and weathered sheet metal fortress corrupted by time and negligence, hoards its secrets behind a deceptive facade of dilapidation.

Maali and her comrades scrutinise their weapons in silent preparation, their resilience permeating the confined space. With masterful precision, she ejects the magazine from her trusted 10mm, verifying its readiness before securing it back into place. The reassuring click vibrates through her fingertips. A swift pat-down reconfirms her arsenal—a stockpile of spare magazines, a duo of flashbang grenades, and a formidable stun baton. Equally or more heavily armed, her squad forms a formidable phalanx, primed to confront the unspeakable horrors that lurk ahead.

Under typical circumstances, a tactical approach of caution and moderation would have been their strategy, avoiding excessive gear. But this operation was anything but routine—a cancerous lesion nestled within the heart of Sydney—an underworld hub of perverse and chilling atrocities. An insidious syndicate, known for its ruthless exploitation of the desperate, ran a covert body chop shop, their insatiable thirst for black-market organ harvesting sending shockwaves of terror across the nation. The team steeled themselves for an explosive showdown, acutely aware of the looming danger and potential casualties. Shrouded in secrecy and conducted off-grid for nearly a month, this raid came with the burden of an ominous suspicion. Assistant Commissioner Jeffries harboured a chilling theory that corruption had seeped into the very marrow of their law enforcement hierarchy. This revelation heightened the stakes of their mission, elevating the lurking danger into a daunting precipice of complexity. As the truck rolled forward, each member clung to a flicker of hope that the operation would not spiral into a cataclysmic clusterfuck.

"Ready, Maali?" Luca's voice pierces the heavy silence, shattering the veneer of tension that hung around them. He delivers the question with a cheerfulness that seems almost out of place amidst their gloomy setting. She pivots to face him, her dark eyes meeting his, and a smile flickers in response. Luca, an oasis of enthusiasm in their harsh reality, embodies a steadfast commitment to their cause. His hands, weathered from countless missions, methodically surveys his F88 Austeyr rifle, checking each part with an intimate familiarity. His routine is infectious, and the air fills with the metallic sounds of preparation as the rest of the team gears up for the looming operation.

Among the eclectic group of hardened individuals, Maali radiates an undeniable aura. Her striking features, the interwoven threads of her cultural heritage, are coupled with an indefinable depth – a wisdom passed down through generations and etched indelibly into her essence.

Returning her focus to the task at hand, she gives a firm nod, her voice steady and filled with conviction. "Yeah, good to go."

The mission had been drilled into them; each step rehearsed until it became second nature: infiltrate, neutralise any potential threats, apprehend survivors, and safeguard the scene to maintain the integrity of the evidence. In a world where bringing even the vilest criminals to justice hinges on incontrovertible and unblemished proof, the stakes are sky-high, leaving no room for error.

Once they are sure of their arsenal and primed for the looming battle, Luca communicates their readiness through a quick thumbs-up. The team manoeuvres like professional fighters in a ring of treachery, threading through the shadows, their footfalls reduced to mere whispers to ward off premature discoveries. Trust is a scarce commodity in this perilous world, and caution is their only ally. 'Better safe than shot' is Maali's sombre mantra as they near one of the side entrances. Maali and Luca approach the weathered door with a blend of caution and precision honed from years of experience. The door, a relic from a bygone era, stands as a silent guardian of the secrets within. Its surface is a fusion of rust and peeling paint.

Luca pulls out a compact, electronic lock-picking device, a sleek tool of modern technology contrasting starkly with the decay around them. He deftly inserts its slender probe into the keyhole, his fingers dancing over the controls with practised ease. The device whirs softly, its internal mechanisms engaging with the ancient lock in a delicate dance of old and new. Meanwhile, Maali focuses on the hinges. She retrieves a small tube of high-grade lubricant from her utility belt, a necessity in their line of work. With careful movements, she applies a few drops to each hinge. The oil seeps into the neglected metal, breaking down years of grime and rust.

Together, they stand ready. Luca gives a subtle nod as the lock-picking device emits a triumphant vibration, signalling the lock's release. With a gentle push from Maali, the door swings open gracefully, betraying none of its age or decrepitude. The absence of any creak or groan from the hinges feels almost unnatural.

Stepping forward, they cross the threshold, and Team 21 ventures into a space that defies expectations. The warehouse, akin to a TARDIS in its deceptive vastness, sprawls before them in a web of neglect and hidden danger. Weapons are clutched not with trembling hands of fear but with the readiness of seasoned warriors. Each corner is scrutinised, gazes penetrating the gloom, seeking the criminal vermin they've come to eradicate. An eerie silence envelops them, a heavy, thunderous hush that seems too quiet, too still. It's a calm that feels peculiar, like the deceptive lull before a storm.

Luca forges a path ahead, navigating through the labyrinth of cast-off junk and debris. The ground is littered with rust-stained mounds, remnants of a world long forgotten. Broken down forklifts, their metal bodies warped and decayed, lay abandoned. A row of old Commodores, each in various states of disrepair, tells a story of times past. The air is thick with an indescribable, pungent stench—a nauseating cocktail of blood, decay, and chemical fumes so potent it seems to claw at the back of Maali's throat.

Containers, stacked haphazardly, create a maze of steel and mystery, their contents unknown yet undoubtedly sinister. The warehouse feels less like a building and more like a rabbit warren, a place designed to trap and disorient. Stifling the bile rising in her throat, Maali steadies her grip on the trigger, a cold realisation dawning that their opposition is likely as fierce as they'd predicted. Her gut churns with unease, an instinctual warning that something is amiss. She glances at Luca, her unease mirrored in her eyes.

Luca, sensing her discomfort, flashes a brief, wry smile in the dim light. "They say every journey starts with a single step. They never mention it's off a cliff," he jokes in a hushed tone, attempting to cut through the tension with his usual humour. As they approach the source of the distant, thrumming Drap music, the atmosphere grows increasingly oppressive. Muffled voices intertwine with the rhythmic bass, heightening their anticipation. The door before them stands as a final barrier to the battle to come.

Luca positions himself at the door, his eyes sharp and resolute. Beside him, Donald, the grizzled veteran with a face that speaks of countless past confrontations, stands prepared. His gaze meets Maali's, conveying a silent pledge of solidarity. With a nod from Luca, Donald primes a flashbang, his hands steady despite the adrenaline surging through his veins. The team, on the brink of action, brace themselves for the breach. Luca's hand reaches for the door, ready for the swift, decisive move.

As Luca readies to thrust the door open, the tense air is shattered by a sudden, bone-jarring crack—a high-calibre round, fired with chilling precision, tears through the moment. The bullet finds its deadly mark, striking Donald's hand just as he's about to release the flashbang. The grenade slips from his grasp, falling back onto the team.

In an instant, the world erupts into chaos. The flashbang detonates in a blinding burst of light and a deafening roar, disorienting the team. Maali's vision whites out; her ears ring with the aftermath of the explosion. The team, caught in the unanticipated blast, scrambles blindly, their senses overwhelmed.

Donald, despite his severe injury, stumbles forward, his other hand instinctively reaching for his weapon. But it's too late. Another shot rings out, this one delivering a fatal blow. The bullet strikes him in the back of the head, his cerebral matter spraying across Maali and Luca in a grisly display. His body crumples to the ground, a final act in a career marked by danger and bravery.

The team, momentarily incapacitated, finds themselves in a desperate struggle. Blinded and disoriented, they fire sporadically, their shots more reflexive than aimed. The warehouse, once a silent maze of shadows, now echoes with the chaos of the ambush. Their adversaries, seizing the opportunity, unleash a barrage of gunfire towards the disoriented officers. Maali, blinking furiously to clear her vision, feels the cold grip of dread.

The room transforms as if caught in the grips of a terrible nightmare, with shadows taking on sinister shapes and every sound a potential threat. A sudden eruption of noise, like a beast's roar, Fills the air as grimy figures emerge from the darkest, most hidden corners of the room. Their appearances are ragged and wild, but their weapons gleam with deadly intent, and their movements are those of hardened killers.

Drake and Danvers react instantly, but not quickly enough. They're caught in the open, and the gunfire comes in too fast, too furious.

Drake is the first to fall, his face a mask of disbelief as bullets tear into his chest. He lets out a grating cry, his voice filled with surprise and pain, as his body jerks in a gruesome ballet before collapsing to the floor in a crumpled heap.

Danvers has just enough time to let off two wild rounds before a bullet finds its mark. It's a precise shot, aimed with cruel efficiency, which rips through his throat. The light fades from his eyes as he staggers back, clutching at the wound, blood bubbling between his fingers. His legs give way, and he slumps to the floor, his life extinguished in a matter of heartbeats.

Maali, Luca, and Cam are momentarily frozen, their minds struggling to comprehend the swiftness of the violence. But survival instinct kicks in, propelling them into action. They dart for cover, dodging and weaving as bullets shred the air around them, each shot a lethal reminder that death is only a moment away.

The room echoes with the sounds of gunfire, screams, and the relentless pursuit of those who have turned this well-planned raid into an ambush. The stench of fresh blood and gunpowder fills the air, a sickening declaration of the brutal reality they now face.

Finger coiled around the trigger, Maali retaliates, her weapon spitting bullets at the nearest threat. Driven by her survival instinct, she dives behind a crate reeking of the workshop's nauseating by-products. Luca finds sanctuary amidst the scattered remains of an aged forklift while Cam hunkers down behind a putrescent vat, its contents frothing and sizzling as they spill over.

As their adversaries close in, bent on eradicating them, Maali lifts her radio, pressing down on the transmit button with shaking fingers. "Dispatch, this is Team 21. We're under heavy fire, authority code 4-3-5-6. Send everything. Repeat, send everything! Over." Her voice cuts through the anarchy, carrying a desperate plea for help.

In response, the dispatcher's voice crackles to life over the raging gunfire. "Team 21, this is Dispatch. Help is on the way. Hold your pos...," the voice stipulates before the connection is abruptly severed, leaving them stranded in the midst of a deadly onslaught.

Within the barrage of returned gunfire, the crew's shooting skills prove as pitiful as their bravado, their errant bullets resembling a botched circus act more than a disciplined firing squad. Sensing a window of opportunity, Maali dares to step out from cover. With steely concentration, she aligns the sights of her pistol on an unseemly silhouette looming on the catwalk—a bloated horror, half of his face savaged by chemical burns. Her first shot grazes the hand gripping his rifle, wrenching a bestial scream of pain from his throat. Without faltering, she fires again, this round drilling into its intended target between the creature's unseeing eyes. As his lifeless form tumbles down, she retreats to her precarious cover, drawing the livid attention of a number of gang members.

As bullets pummel the crate, the odour of death intensifies, verifying her ghastly suspicion. Amid the pandemonium, however, Luca and Cam execute a retaliatory strike, each bullet finding its mark and bringing down four more foes—a fragile spark of hope flickers amidst the despair. But the momentary reprieve is shattered as the door they were planning to breach swings open violently. From within, six more gun-toting marauders pour out, their firearms belching a deluge of bullets, filling the confined space with a melodious portrayal of ruin.

Maali swiftly pivots, her pistol finding its mark with deadly accuracy as she takes down the first thug to emerge, his life extinguished by a single shot that pierces his neck, severing his spine. With methodical accuracy, she dispatches the second assailant with a pair of gut shots while a bullet finds its way into the eye of the third, ending his reign of terror. However, as she takes cover to reload, a sense of dread washes over her as the remaining gang members converge on Luca and Cam. They appear to be in a drug-induced fog, their lack of self-preservation apparent as they make little attempt to protect themselves.

Cam peers out from behind cover, his eyes scanning for the remaining gang members. Sweat trickles down his forehead, his breath coming in ragged gasps. He shifts slightly, trying to get a better angle, and that's when it happens.

A sudden, deafening blast resonates through the room as the last man on the catwalk fires his shotgun. Cam's face registers shock and disbelief before he's violently thrown back, blood and fragments spraying from the impact. He falls to the ground, his body lifeless, his eyes still wide with the terror of his last moments.

Luca's reaction is immediate. Driven by adrenaline and anger, he swings his weapon towards the catwalk, his aim steady and true. A single shot rings out, and the man with the shotgun falls, his body jerking as Luca's bullet finds its mark. But the triumph is short-lived. An unexpected shot from a hidden assailant finds an unforgiving gap in Luca's armour. The impact spins him around, and he collapses to the ground, his face contorted in agony—blood seeps from the wound, staining the floor a dark, menacing red.

Maali's heart pounds in her chest, the world narrowing to the threat charging towards them. Her hands grip her pistol tightly, every sense honed to the task at hand. With a committed cry, she unleashes a flurry of shots, the gun's recoil jarring her arm, the smell of gunpowder filling her nostrils.

One of the chop crew members falls, her bullet clipping him in the shoulder, sending him sprawling to the ground, his screams echoing through the room. The others falter; their advance momentarily halts as they glance around at the fallen bodies, uncertainty and fear flashing fleetingly across their faces.

The room seems to hold its breath, a pause in the relentless violence, a moment frozen in time. But Maali knows it won't last. Her eyes are steely, her body coiled like a spring, ready for whatever comes next. The taste of fear and tenacity is bitter on her tongue, and she knows that every second counts in this game of survival.

Galvanised by an overwhelming flood of resolve, Maali momentarily exposes herself to grab a strap on Luca's armour, fiercely pulling him towards cover. Acting swiftly, she retrieves a grenade from her gear, yanks the pin, and hurls it high into the air. Luca, shielding his eyes and ears, braces for the explosion as the grenade detonates, releasing a blinding flash that disorients the chop crew, buying them a precious moment of advantage.

"Come on!" Maali quickly injects Luca with a combination of coagulant, analgesia, and adrenaline before extending a helping hand to Luca, pulling him to his feet as they hastily make their way towards one of the side doors. They burst through the door with a powerful collision, sending it flying off its hinges. "Dispatch confirmed help is on route. We just need to..."

Luca raises his rifle reflexively as a single shot echoes from the ominous obscurities before them. With stanch aim, he pulls the trigger, but as his bullet finds its target, another round tears through his oesophagus. Maali's heart sinks as her partner crumples to the ground, lifeless, before he even hits the floor.

Maali's eyes dart to the fallen gang member, whose life quickly fades away as he clutches his grievous wound. Without a moment's hesitation, she dispatches him with a cold and calculated shot to the skull. The remaining gang members begin to regain their senses, their confusion turning into malicious intent. Knowing she must act swiftly, Maali's high-octane dash carries her towards the next door in her desperate bid for survival.

The relentless gang members taunt and threaten Maali, their voices echoing through the dimly lit warehouse. "Gonna skin you, sow! You Oinkers, come in here, try stealing our shit! Fuckin' bastards never learn!" Their sadistic pledges to torture and mutilate her only fuel her fortitude to escape. Despite their relentless assault, Maali holds her ground, skilfully returning fire with calculated precision. Her shots keep them at bay, momentarily halting their advance. However, amidst the mayhem, she realises a disturbing pattern—she's being herded, cleverly directed away from the potential exits of the warehouse.

Maali makes a desperate beeline for what appears to be an exit, but her hopes are dashed as a leering thug steps into her path, brandishing his weapon like a child with a new toy. The air erupts in a lethal percussion as he unloads his magazine, each bullet a thunderous roar punctuated by the wicked hiss of displaced air. Her retreat is erratic, each pirouette accompanied by the explosive detonation of concrete as bullets strike the wall, ripping it apart with shocking violence—fragments of grey rubble and dust rain around her in a devastating downpour of toxic filth.

Another dash for freedom, another thug appearing as if summoned by her desperation. He lobs a crudely made grenade. The wall it strikes erupts, shrapnel whizzing through the air. Maali feels a sharp sting in her arm, glancing down to see a small metal fragment lodged in her flesh. She grunts, pushing back against the pain as she wraps a cloth around her bleeding arm. Blood stains the fabric a dark red, painting a bleak picture of her predicament. The reality slams into her like a runaway freight train; these thugs are toying with her-. "Well, Maali," she mutters to herself, "You've really landed yourself in one hell of a pickle, haven't you?"

After dispatching yet another gang member and desperately attempting to establish contact through the radio, only to be met with a stubborn wall of static, Maali finds herself inexorably drawn back to the haunting scene where her world shattered. A wave of sorrow washes over her as she locks eyes with Cam's lifeless face, a stark reminder of the sacrifices made in this nerve-wracking pursuit.

Sliding her last magazine into place, the weight of the dwindling ammunition settles heavily upon her. Only seven rounds remain—a meagre arsenal against the relentless onslaught before her. Dread clenches her gut, threatening to undermine her backbone. Yet, unwavering, she squares her shoulders and steadies her aim at the first gang member to emerge from the shadows.

Standing tall, a hulking figure with a visage disfigured by countless battles, the deformed giant presents an intimidating challenge. His broken nose, like a badge of honour to a life immersed in violence, bears more angles than a cut diamond. But Maali, resolute in her purpose, squeezes the trigger with dogged conviction. The bullet finds its mark, piercing his heart with gory exactness, extinguishing his life in an instant.

As the lifeless body crashes to the ground, Maali swiftly redirects her attention to the greasy figure lurking behind him. Her fingers move precisely, delivering another lethal shot that ends his menace. Four more rounds erupt from her weapon, a controlled burst of firepower that temporarily holds the remaining adversaries at bay.

The room seems to close in around Maali as the drug-crazed thugs draw nearer, their faces twisted with wicked expectation. The walls pulse to the rhythm of her pounding heart, knowing each beat could be her last.

Her team and her friends were all gone in a torrent of violence and blood. The memories flash before her eyes, their last moments imprinted into her mind, a haunting recollection of loss and regret. They had fought bravely, but it hadn't been enough. The harsh reality settles like a crushing weight on her chest: she's outnumbered, cornered, and her gun is the only barrier between her and a fate worse than death, holds just a single, solitary bullet.

Time seems to stretch and warp; seconds feel like an eternity as she raises the indomitable metal of the pistol to her temple. Her hand trembles, not with uncertainty, but with the sheer terror of the decision she faces. The cold barrel presses against her skin, an unfeeling kiss of steel, its presence a stark promise of oblivion.

Memories flash unbidden through Maali's mind - haunting images of comrades who had been taken before, only to be returned as mere shadows of themselves. She remembers their hollow eyes, their silenced spirits, moving through life like ghosts, forever altered by the unspeakable horrors they endured. They were living shells, walking embodiments of death, their souls seemingly left behind in the hellish depths of their captivity.

As the chill of the metal imprints its finality upon her skin, Maali's mind, in a desperate grasp for solace, retreats to an untainted fragment of her past. She finds herself transported to a sun-drenched meadow of her childhood, where the world is vast and unscarred. She's a little girl again, chasing the whims of the wind, laughter bubbling from her lips like a pristine stream. Around her, the air is alive with the dance of butterflies, their wings painting fleeting masterpieces against the canvas of the sky. Her mother's voice, warm and melodious, calls out to her, weaving through the tall grasses, a lullaby of safety and love. In this fleeting sanctuary of memory, Maali's heart unclenches for a moment, basking in the innocence and wonder of a life unburdened by shadows. Yet, as the vision starts to fade, the harsh grip of her reality seeps back in.

The thugs' taunts grow louder, their footsteps thundering in her ears, but all she hears is the deafening roar of her own thoughts. Captivity, torment, degradation – these are the horrors that await her if she's taken.

The thought twists in her stomach, a nauseating cocktail of dread and revulsion.

Tears sting her eyes, blurring her vision, but she fights them back. This is her choice, her control, the one shred of power she has left in this nightmare. She refuses to become another lifeless husk, a puppet walking through life with a damaged soul.

"From the earth to the earth, I write my own story," Maali whispers, her voice defiant.

Her finger brushes against the trigger, its cool surface starkly contrasting with the hot, frantic pulse beneath her skin. Within Maali, a desperate yearning for release battles with a primal fear of the end of her human journey.

The moment hangs, suspended in time, a chilling display of despair and willpower. And through it all, the terror, the loss, the unbearable weight of her decision, Maali stands strong, her spirit unbroken, her eyes clear and focused on the path she must take. Her decision, a harrowing crossroads between life's fragility and the strength of the human will, shimmered with a profound truth: within the heart of chaos, there is always a choice.

And so, Maali chose, not just for herself but for every silent voice that had ever stood at the edge of despair. Her breath comes in ragged gasps, each one a painful reminder of the life she's leaving behind. But there's no turning back now. With a fierce whisper in the face of the abyss, the decision is made.

She squeezes the trigger.

But instead of the anticipated deafening bang and ensuing peace, there's a hollow click. The cruel irony of the misfire lands like a punch to the gut, a merciless demonstration of the wicked games fate enjoys. With the failing of her pistol comes an avalanche of nightmarish recollections—

haunting images of her female comrades enduring unthinkable atrocities, unnerving visions birthed from her darkest fears. The monstrous reality of the chop crew, their corrupted desires, and perverse glee come crashing down on her.

Tossing aside their spent firearms with disdain, the fiendish crew swarms in like ravenous wolves. Their faces twist in an awful parody of excitement, revelling in their forthcoming debauchery. Their presence is an assault, violating her space with their grimy hands and predatory eyes. And within those eyes, the unmistakable traces of the illicit SPICE drug—the intricate network of black veins tainting the sclera—serve as chilling proof of their complete and utter moral decay.

Energised by a dogged ferocity, Maali clashes brutally against her advancing tormentors, their cruel intentions manifested in their grotesque visages. As one monstrous gang member launches himself onto her, slamming her against the unrelenting floor, a torrent of loathing ignites her defiance. Struggling to retain her gear as the gang members claw at her protective armour and tear away patches of her clothing, her primal survival instinct takes over. Amidst this savage assault, she's left with no choice but to shed the vestiges of her identity, baring only the unconquerable spirit that pulses through her veins.

"We're gonna have a good time, girly. Time to party," the assailant sneers, his lewd words punctuated by the repugnant trace of his tongue along her cheek. With his knees trapping her legs and one hand wrestling with hers, he fumbles to undo his pants. Amidst this dire moment, Maali's resolve hardens. With a burst of focused rage, she drives her thumb deep into his eye socket, viciously twisting until the fragile orb ruptures, the sensation akin to squashing an overripe grape. His agonised screams fill the air, his frenzied thrashing escalating as torment and terror seize him.

In the midst of this harrowing confrontation, the air is punctured by a thunderous blast from outside—a deafening explosion of a heavy-calibre weapon resonating with lethal intent. The sheer force of the shot sent shockwaves through the darkness, shaking the very foundation of their malevolent gathering. Startled screams erupt as their depraved harmony is shattered by the unexpected hell that has descended upon them.

The chop crew members hit the deck, their bravado shattered by the unexpected turn of events. One of them hisses, "What the fuck was that? We cancelled the pigs' backup!" The question hangs in the air, unanswered, as two rapid gunshots ring out, delivering swift justice. The bullets find their mark, striking down two of the gang members. The now one-eyed brute atop Maali momentarily loses focus, his attention diverted by the sudden ruckus. Seizing the opportunity, Maali swiftly retrieves a stun baton from the remnants of her gear harness and thrusts it into the brute's neck, forcing him off her. With her assailant defeated, she quickly scans her surroundings, spotting a rifle discarded on the floor nearby. She grabs it, seeking cover as her stare locks onto the sight of two figures charging in—a man and a woman, both displaying badges hanging from their belts.

Not willing to surrender to despair just yet, Maali sets her sights on a gang member targeting the new arrivals and pulls the trigger. The shot strikes true, felling the assailant and giving the newcomers a clear path towards her. With focused strides, they sprint over, pausing only briefly to unleash a hail of bullets at the surviving chop crew members. The pair reaches her, their faces etched with doggedness and urgency. The man extends a helping hand, introducing himself, "Noah Thomas. This is Maria," he says, indicating the woman who deftly slides a new magazine into her weapon and returns fire towards an unseen adversary. "We heard your call. Is anyone else alive?"

Her head snapping to each side, Maali's wide eyes sweep their surroundings for potential threats. Noah mutters a string of expletives, the leather of his grip audibly creaking under the pressure. Maria's voice slices through the dense tension, crisp and imperative, "Footsteps, lots of 'em. It's time to move; let's go!"

With a rough tug, Noah corrals Maali into formation behind him, Maria sliding into the rear. Their escape mirrors their entrance, retracing the web of debris and discarded machinery. Breathless but heartened by their timely arrival, Maali manages to rasp, "Glad you got the memo."

"Caught your SOS and put ourselves forward," Noah says, his voice as solid as granite. "A stand-down order came through—some 'health and safety' crap. But we don't leave our own out to dry. If one of us bleeds, we all bleed."

His words are cut short by the ferocious roar of fresh gunfire. Maria, a storm in motion, whirls around, her weapon rising with fatal intention. She uncages a volley of controlled shots, dispatching the advancing gang members and forcing the rest to scurry behind whatever cover they could find.

The air crackles with continuous gunfire as they make their way towards the edge of the district. Noah's eyes light up with relief as he spots a beat-up car nearby, its engine humming with anticipation. "There's our ride! Let's move!" he exclaims, gesturing towards the vehicle. Maria stands at his side, ready to spring into action.

Yet, Maali's sharp instincts detect movement on a nearby rooftop. She quickly raises her stolen weapon, her finger tightening around the trigger, just as the rooftop assailant unleashes a torrent of bullets from an enormous rifle. In a split second, their bullets find their marks simultaneously. The gang member collapses lifelessly, a victim of Maali's precise aim, while Maria's fate takes a cruel turn. The shell from the massive rifle tears through her chest, obliterating her ribcage and showering Noah in a gruesome spray of blood and bone.

Caught in the throes of shock and horror at the sight of his partner's gruesome end, Noah's situational awareness plummets. A white-hot burst of pain blindsides him, shooting through his leg as he's hit, forcing him to crumble onto one knee with an animalistic cry. Yet, amidst the whirlwind of terror and turmoil, Maali's instincts remain lethally acute. Harnessing a cold-blooded willpower, she efficiently dispatches the ambush predator, her bullets delivering swift retribution. The resounding chorus of weapon fire momentarily fades away, leaving a chilling silence punctuated only by pained wheezes and the punctuated cadence of Maali's thumping chest.

In a gruelling display of inner strength, Maali and Noah stagger towards the waiting vehicle, with a monstrous echo of gunfire relentless in their ears. Each footfall is an epoch of agony, with the spectre of sporadic bullets snapping at their heels. Their rescuer, still an enigma behind his badge, doesn't waste time with formalities. With a burst of energy, he wrenches open the back door, unceremoniously shoving them inside before vaulting back into the driver's seat.

Time dilates, each tick echoing with deafening urgency as the engine snarls to life. With a stomp, the officer mashes the gas pedal, forcing it to submit to his command. Rubber screams against asphalt, with the car launching forward in a surge of raw horsepower. The high-pitched strain of the engine becomes an audible manifestation of their surging adrenaline as they tear away from the lawless territory, leaving a turbulent wake of disarray and uncertainty trailing behind them.

CHAPTER 2:

Life of Pain

10 Years Later...

"**M**aali!" The voice slices through the fog of her haunting reverie, yanking her back to reality. She swivels to face Noah, his brow furrowed, a question mark etched into his concerned look. "You with us? You seem miles away."

She presses the pads of her fingers against the bridge of her nose, ushering the lingering demon of their first encounter back into the shadows. A mental clearing for the pressing challenges at hand. "Yeah, just... basking in the last of the sun's warmth. You know, before the ice-cold night sets in. It's not how winters used to be."

Noah, now a grizzled veteran officer in his forties, expels a soft sigh, his countenance a complex display of doggedness and hard-earned wisdom. A hint of a smile flits across Maali's face as she prods him playfully on the shoulder, their shared history reflected in her eyes. He responds with a wry grin, his tousled, greying locks lending an air of rugged charm to his usually stoic demeanour. The gravity of their impending mission presses down on them like the thickening air before a storm. His voice, streaked with a trace of urgency, breaks the weighty calm. "Well, cut it out. This isn't a small-time gig. We are getting a 1.5 per cent cut, all in Zytro. You're up to speed, right?" Maali's responding smirk and confirming nudge weave a silent pact between them, the tapestry of their decade-long bond woven on the battlefield. "That's it, Sis. Get ready. The package is about to arrive."

Her exasperation barely masked, Maali wrangles her riotous curls into a neat bob, deftly tucking them away. She sinks into position behind the intimidating .50 calibre rifle, a sentinel mounted on the rooftop. Her sharp watch sweeps over Darling Point like a lighthouse beam, quickly homing in on an elderly cargo ship in the distance and a diminutive vessel closing in. The unassuming facade of the approaching boat belies its true significance; it's the treasure chest, not the vessel, that matters. Nestled within its rusty belly is a trove of D.TEM, a substance promising the coveted boon of near-unending youth and vitality. Due to overpopulation fears, its illicit nature only inflates its value, except for those with the right contacts. A solitary vial is a small fortune; rumour has it the boat harbours a stash of over a hundred.

As she goes through her final checks, Maali's scope sweeps across the Sydney skyline in a subtle art of observation and reverence. 'Once upon a time, this was a city that sparkled with unrivalled beauty,' she muses silently. From their aerial viewpoint, it's almost easy to lose oneself in that faded vision. Skyscrapers pierce the heavens, their faces glazed with glass, crowned with verdant rooftop gardens like earthbound stars.

But a keener inspection reveals the less palatable truth. Much like countless other urban jungles across the globe, Sydney has not been spared the slow rot of time and unchecked human greed. It's swollen with an excess populace; its arteries clogged with unceasing crime, its soul steeped in a pervasive miasma of decay. The reality is a poignant stab of melancholy, a stark illustration of how even the most resplendent cities can falter under the merciless weight of a declining civilisation.

"Jesus Christ, Maali! Keep your damn head in the game!" Noah's voice slashes through the tranquillity, the veneer of rough chastisement unable to veil the desperation pooling in his gaze. "I need this gig, damn it. The child support is bleeding me dry!" An engineered chuckle breaks from him, but the undercurrent of strain in his timbre can't mask the reality of his fiscal battle. In a world where their once-noble profession is being stripped and supplanted by corporate mercenaries, these paid side jobs have become more than just additional income—they're lifelines. The air is pregnant with their gritty desperation, a stinging reminder of the depths they're willing to plunge to stay buoyant in a system haemorrhaging its morality.

With a mental shake, Maali blinks away her daydream, subduing the hullabaloo of her emotions as the guttural rumble of the approaching boat swells in volume. Her eyes narrow into piercing slits, her focus honing in on the deck's inhabitants—three towering figures and a pair of seated ones. Noah disrupts her surveillance with an audible throat-clearing, "Seems we've got more company than expected."

A hint of a smirk tugs at Maali's lips, her amusement echoing in a snort. "So what? We're packing this behemoth," she murmurs, her fingers tracing an affectionate path over the colossal weapon nestled against her shoulder. "With the high ground and the element of surprise, we're golden. Plus, Earl has a reputation that precedes him. These pricks aren't foolish enough to cross him." Her rough chuckle breaks free. Earl, the dirtbag who commissioned them, might be a hard nut to crack, but that's precisely why he's managed to survive in this pitiless world.

Noah was on the brink of a reply when Maali's eyes snapped wide open, a sharp intake of breath cutting through the silence. "What the actual fuck... do you see that?" she breathed out, her voice a mix of awe and fear. Her gaze was fixed on the horizon, transfixed by a spectral glow pulsating from an enigmatic source. The air around them seemed to quiver with a strange, ineffable energy, sending a shiver down their spines and causing the hair on the back of their necks to stand on end.

Once a picture of tranquillity, the harbour waters now roiled and churned as if agitated by an invisible leviathan lurking beneath. Unnaturally high and erratic waves crashed against each other with a ferocity that defied nature. It was as if the sea itself was rebelling against an unseen invader, its surface a wild canvas of swelling, heaving water. The once rhythmic lapping of the waves had turned into a vortex of motion that hinted at a deep, unworldly disturbance.

The water swelled in bizarre patterns, forming towering columns defying gravity before collapsing into the frenzied depths. Shadows seemed to dart just beneath the surface, giving the illusion of something vast and unknowable moving with purpose. The sea appeared alive, animated by a force that was both mesmerising and terrifying.

Noah turns in bewilderment at her sudden outcry, his retort dying on his lips as his gaze trails hers. His eyes, mirroring hers, stretch wide in stunned incredulity. "Sweet mother of... what the hell is that?" The vision unfolding before them defies rational understanding. A titanic vortex of perplexity has materialised in the sky, its unexpected presence burgeoning in size and intensity with every passing heartbeat.

Mayhem breaks loose on the docks as Earl's crew abruptly abandon their posts, their attention violently commandeered by the alarming spectacle in the heavens. Exploiting this diversion to their advantage, the crew from the boat disembarks swiftly, their movements eerily silent and coordinated. With purpose, they manoeuvre to encircle the unobservant hired guns, who remain blissfully oblivious to the burgeoning danger.

Maali, jolted from her stupefied trance by the unexpected activity, shakes Noah with a sudden urgency. "Look," she presses, her voice thick with impending dread.

Bracing herself behind the mounted rifle, Maali is poised to unleash a hailstorm of bullets. But Noah's hand, urgent on her shoulder, signals for her to bide her time. "This is a complete clusterfuck, but... let's just watch and wait for now," he suggests, his tone rife with hidden purpose.

Indignant, Maali snaps back, "We had a goddamn agreement, Noah." Unpaid debts and unspoken gratitude weave together, stoking the furnace of her torn emotions, leaving her in a quagmire of conflicting obligations and unforeseen repercussions.

"Maybe," he points into the sky, "but this might be our golden opportunity. Let them tear each other apart while we claim it all. Screw the measly 1.5 per cent, we're talking about 100 per cent. And we'll ensure it goes where it can make a real impact." When she attempts to object, he gestures more forcefully into the sky. "I don't know if you've noticed the colossal son of a bitch—"

Before he can finish his sentence, the ear-piercing sound of gunfire erupts below. The smugglers, on the verge of surrounding Earl's men, are taken by surprise as a fierce counter-attack begins. Bullets tear through the air with deadly precision, creating a chaotic symphony of devastation. Earl's crew fights back valiantly, their mettle driven by desperation. Despite being outnumbered, they refuse to yield.

Just as a glimmer of hope begins to sear through the bleak horizon, the boat's cargo hold belches forth an ominous trio concealed amongst the darkness. Their deadly arsenal glimmers ominously under the purple glow of the setting sun, automatic rifles held in a deathly grip that tells tales of their ruthless efficiency. They fan out, a phalanx of devastation armed and ready.

The new arrivals waste no time. A savage waltz of firepower explodes across the dock, their automatic rifles spitting death with methodical precision. The carnage is instantaneous, Earl's men dropping like felled trees, their lifeless bodies sprawled unnaturally across the concrete. Amid the gruesome exhibition, Earl's voice cuts through the bedlam, laced with rage and the sour tang of betrayal. "Noah! You duplicitous snake! You godforsaken son of a bitch!"

Ignoring the bellowed accusation, Noah leans towards Maali, his words barely above a whisper, yet cutting through the chaos with sharp clarity, "You ready?" Maali's gaze locks onto his, a wordless pact of shared resolve. Without missing a beat, they both lean into the storm, pouring forth their lethal counter-attack.

The .50 calibre rifle nestled in Maali's grip roars to life, its muzzle flash briefly illuminating her sombre face. The boat's engine block detonates under the onslaught, followed swiftly by the wheelhouse, the concussive blast throwing shrapnel and debris in all directions. The hapless helmsman caught off guard, is instantly reduced to a disfigured, still form amidst the splintered remains of his post.

Together, they become agents of chaos and death. Noah, with methodical calmness, selects his targets with a surgeon's deliberation. Each pull of his trigger crafts a terrifying exhibition of destruction, scattering lethal kisses that systematically incapacitate their adversaries. The evening air resonates with the deadly percussion of his firearm, forming a horrifying harmony with the rising upsurge of pain-filled cries.

"Another fine day in hell," Maali's words cut through the fray, a dark mirth twinkling in her eyes. She steadies her weapon, laying the crosshairs over the bridge of the distant vessel. Holding her breath, she gently squeezes the trigger. The bullet screams across the 1200-metre gap, hammering into the ship's clear view screen. The impact point, where the bullet pierced the glass, forms a distinct, spiderweb-like pattern. At the very centre, there's a small, round entry point, deceptively neat, surrounded by radial cracks that emanate outward. These cracks resemble thin, jagged veins of ice, branching and intersecting in a chaotic yet almost artistic display. Recognising the danger, the smugglers aboard quickly reposition, their ship retreating into the shadowy shroud of the vast sea.

With a grin of satisfaction tugging at her lips, Maali secures her beast of a rifle and readies her smaller but potent .233. Adrenaline pulses through her like a thunderous rhythm, electrifying her senses. "What a way to spice up a Sydney evening," she muses, the aftermath of the clash lingering palpably in the air. Bracing herself for whatever comes next, she advances her weapon at the ready.

Before she can make a move, Noah extends his arm, obstructing her. "Easy, sis. Looks like our friend still clings to life," his voice is a gravelly note of caution, his eyes fixed on the corpulent figure of their injured employer. Earl, the man they betrayed, drags his bloodied form across the dock, trailing a gruesome stream of lifeblood behind him.

"And what about our little light show?" Maali retorts, her gesture cutting through the twilight to the ominous spectacle illuminating the sky.

"We'll cross that bridge when we come to it," Noah responds, his voice steadied with a tempered caution. They move slowly but deliberately, eyes sweeping across the carnage to ensure their enemies lay silent and defeated.

Closing the distance, they find Earl gasping and writhing, pain and desperation etched in his eyes. Blood seeps from a gunshot wound in his abdomen, each laboured breath a struggle against the Grim Reaper's call. "Why, Noah?" he chokes out, his voice a desperate croak. "You and Maali... you two were always straight shooters."

Noah descends to kneel beside the wounded man, a bitter smile tugging at the corners of his mouth. "Old mate," he intones, an echo of regret colouring his voice. He pauses, his gaze distant and heavy with unspoken sorrow. "It's not that complicated; I saw an opportunity and took it without a second thought. We thought all we had left was loyalty, but... sometimes, loyalty has to change direction, find new horizons." His voice is a mix of resignation and a hard, sad truth.

Noah jerks his head upward, indicating the colossal entity casting its monstrous shadow across Sydney. The vessel, an inverted pyramid radiating an uncanny luminescence, hangs precariously in the skyline, dwarfing the city's skyscrapers by hundreds of feet. Its multilayered structure, a menacing labyrinth of metal and lights, imbues the city below with an almost ethereal glow that chills the onlookers to their cores.

With a wane nod, Earl manages a feeble chuckle, his voice barely above a whisper, "A game-changer indeed." As Noah rises, Earl's hand makes a pitiful lunge to seize his, "Don't leave me, fella," he implores, his voice laced with desperation.

Noah's response is devoid of emotion, his voice as detached as his gaze, "Nothing personal, Earl. Just business." With those words, he pivots away, heading towards the docked vessel.

Earl's stoic words echo in the air, his voice fading into resignation, "It never is."

Upon witnessing this, Maali's eyes morph into slits, a spark of rebellion igniting within her. She resists Noah's decision vehemently, "We're not leaving him to die alone," she declares, her voice a rough blade of defiance.

As she hunkers down beside the fading Earl, her hands instinctively applying pressure to his ghastly wound, Noah's gaze locks with hers. "He's a goner, Maali," he calls out, a delicate balance of urgency and purpose echoing in his words. He motions towards the looming spectacle in the sky, "Our families, the cargo—they're our priorities now."

Maali's hands press firmly against Earl's wound as his voice, barely a whisper, grapples with the silence. "The D.TEM...it's not just for longevity," he forces out.

Maali, attributing his words to delirium, dismisses them, "You're okay, mate. Just hold on," she soothes. Her voice drops to a whisper, her tone carrying the warmth of a shared history, "We'll honour you right, brother. Your spirit will return to the country."

Wrestling against the debilitating agony gripping him, Earl drags himself slightly off the ground. A glimmer of zeal shines through the pain etched onto his face. "No, Maali, listen. It's a rapid cellular regenerator. Understand? It can practically mend anything." His voice trembles, choked by a surge of blood welling in his throat. A momentary gathering of strength allows him to continue, "Grab me one vial from the package. There are a hundred of them and some H3 power cells. I need just one; the rest is yours." His plea hangs heavy in the silence, the profound implications of his revelation taking hold.

Earl's admission is punctuated by Noah's return from the boat, a neoprene-clad package in his grip. It promises a glint of hope in their morose predicament. With calculated casualness, he places the container beside Earl, the magnitude of their future hinging on its contents. Slitting the seal, he opens the package. A mirthless chuckle slips from his lips, commingling with the harsh reality sprawling before them. "You said there'd be a hundred... we've got a meagre ten," he comments, tilting the case so Earl can perceive the deception. Among the perfectly lined vials, only a tenth are filled, the rest hauntingly empty—a bitter homage to the betrayal. "Seems like your mates were already planning a double-cross," Noah's voice carries a blend of cynicism and acceptance.

Amid the irony and the pain, Earl lets out a strained laugh, the taste of his blood an unwelcome companion, "Well, no fucking surprise!" His blood-streaked figure, revelling in the absurdity of their circumstances, prompts a reluctant smile from Maali.

Snatching the case, Maali seizes a vial, her gaze locked onto Earl's rapidly fading one. "And now what?" she repeats, her voice fraught with a dire urgency.

With a feeble motion, Earl tugs her closer, murmuring into her ear, "It's a suppository."

Maali recoils in horror, aghast at the prospect of shoving the small vial into Earl's bloodied, sweaty ass.

Basking in Maali's disgust and disbelief, Earl's grin unfurls, "Just messing with ya. Just get it under my tongue, and it'll do its magic." The flicker of mischief in his eyes reinforces the playful absurdity of his prank. With a strange cocktail of relief and uncertainty, Maali gently cradles Earl's head, coaxing his mouth open. The substance within the vial, akin to liquid gold, drips onto his tongue. Almost instantaneously, a miraculous transformation begins to unfold. Earl's wounds, once gaping and near-fatal, start to close with an astounding speed, as if he's being rejuvenated from within. Both Maali and Noah watch in disbelief, the extraordinary capabilities of the vial standing as a confirmation of the revolutionary power they have just discovered.

As an added layer of insurance, Noah forcefully heaves Earl upright, directing him towards his own vehicle. With the fluidity of someone accustomed to such manoeuvres, he snaps a handcuff around Earl's substantial wrist, securing the other end to the sporty carbon fibre spoiler jutting from the trunk. "These cuffs are on a half-hour timer," Noah announces, his voice imbued with authority. He punctuates his declaration with a tap of his pistol against Earl's brow, a hostile reminder of the stakes. "Stay put, fella. We'll be dust by then." His words seethe with a silent warning - Don't make me regret showing mercy.

Earl distorts his features into a pleading pout in a final, desperate bid. "Noah, one more vial, please. It's my kid, she's really sick, and this cargo was her only hope. I'll do whatever; you can take the lot in my truck, just please!" His voice wavers between urgency and fear, a desperate attempt to shake Noah's hardened exterior.

As Noah considers Earl's plea, Maali has already begun plundering the truck's contents. She emerges, the spoils of her search - a remarkably well-preserved pulse rifle and a pair of pristine H3 cells - cradled in her arms. At the sight of Earl, Noah's expression turns glacial. "I'm afraid that's a no," he states, his voice cold and devoid of empathy.

Earl's futile act of defiance goes unnoticed as Noah and Maali coolly retreat, his middle finger jutting out as a powerless symbol of rebellion. Their attention is promptly captured by a rapidly unfolding spectacle in the skies over Sydney.

A fleet of military aircraft slices through the oncoming twilight, their synchronised movements transforming them into a swarm of deadly hornets buzzing towards their target - the inscrutable vessel that looms ominously over the city. Close to a hundred G9 Pemulwuy jets, the pride of the military's air force, cut through the sky, their engines roaring in a fierce, deafening chorus that echoed across the city. Each aircraft was a mechanical beast, a marvel of human engineering, armed to the teeth and powered by the sheer force of burning hydrogen and ignited ambition.

As they neared the alien monolith, they moved as a single entity. Their noses dipped simultaneously, the air around them crackling. Suddenly, the underbellies of the jets released their payloads. Missiles, sleek and deadly, rocket towards the vessel, their trails of smoke drawing angry lines against the serene canvas of the evening sky. The city held its collective breath as they watched the missiles hurtle towards their target.

Without warning, the steady roar was shattered as the missiles struck the vessel's hull. A series of explosions erupted in rapid succession, a boom that reverberated through the city. The hull of the vessel was bathed in a blinding light, each blast blooming like fiery roses upon its surface. The vessel bore the assault, its silhouette stark against the backdrop of the incandescent onslaught.

The spectacular display lights up the evening sky, casting long, dramatic shadows throughout Sydney. The violent bursts of light and the hectic flurry of destruction paint a scene that rivals and perhaps even surpasses Sydney's famed New Year's Eve display. The city stands in the shadow of this violent show, humanity's display of defiance against the alien presence.

As Noah and Maali hasten towards their vehicle, their eyes are involuntarily drawn back to the unfolding spectacle. The roar of the G9 Pemulwuy jets reverberates in their chests as the aircraft execute their manoeuvres with lethal grace. The spectacle is both awe-inspiring and terrifying, an expression of the boundless potential of human technology. "Why are they attacking? What in God's name is happening?" Noah's gaze meets Maali's, and she shakes her head in mutual disbelief. Against the backdrop of the radiant vessel, the scene takes on an almost surreal quality, humanity clashing against an unknown cosmic entity.

As the smoke from the bombardment disperses, a chilling sight reveals itself. The alien ship remains unscathed, defying the military's formidable onslaught. The city beneath descends into anarchism - horns blare, sirens wail, and civilian screams punctuate the air, adding to the panic. Plumes of smoke from missile wreckage rise, blanketing the city under the shadow of the strange vessel.

Suddenly, the alien vessel emits a blinding burst of light, muting the city's noises. The G9s charge again, launching another volley of missiles, but an eerie silence envelops the scene. All lights in Sydney snuff out, leaving the city at the mercy of the dying twilight. The propulsion systems of the airborne missiles stutter and fail, and the crafts that launched them soon follow suit. As the city plunges into terrified disarray, an unsettling hush blankets the landscape while the radiance from the UFO retreats to its initial glow. Maali's whisper pierces the silence, "Seems like that's their way of fighting back."

A newfound urgency laces her voice, "Noah... We need to get to your children. Your ex-wife's apartment isn't too far, right? One of those towering blocks?"

Noah and Maali dive into the battered car they had waiting, slamming the doors behind them. The old Falcon XR8 interior is a dim, claustrophobic space filled with the smell of oil and worn leather. Noah jams the key into the ignition, twisting it violently. The engine coughs and sputters but refuses to roar to life. Frustration bubbles in his throat as he pumps the gas pedal.

"Old petrol engines, our silent rebels against the all-seeing electric grid," Noah whispers with a hint of irony. "Come on, you stubborn piece of junk!" he growls, teeth gritted.

Maali's eyes widen in realisation, her mind connecting the dots. "The EMP," she breathes, her voice calm and deliberate. "From the alien ship. It must have disabled the car."

With a furious yank, Noah pulls the door open, the hinges screeching in protest. "Damn it! Damn it! Damn it!" Noah curses before regaining his composure. He points towards Kings Cross, his finger steady. "Route alpha it is!"

Maali hesitates for a heartbeat, then gives chase, her pulse rifle gripped tightly, the cool metal a reassuring presence in her hand. Her breath comes in sharp gasps, each inhale a struggle, each exhale a prayer. The world around her seems to blur, the edges softening, reality-bending, and all that remains is the thunder of her heart and the burning in her lungs.

She sneaks a glance at the magnificent alien ship, her anxiety mirrored in her face. "Christ... Sydney's already on the brink. This might just tip it over."

Noah's footsteps pound the asphalt beside her, "No matter how this pans out," he snarls out, the steely drive in his voice defying the madness, "It's going to end ugly."

CHAPTER 3:
Chaos

'The city has tipped over the edge of sanity.' This singular thought dominates Maali's mind as she weaves through the disorder of the city, matching Noah's relentless stride despite the fiery protest from her exhausted muscles. They've been sprinting non-stop for over ten minutes, plunging headfirst into the wild heart of the city. With each passing block, they navigate a more severe level of disarray. Upended and ablaze, cars are strewn haphazardly across their path, their crooked frames creating a forbidding attestation to the city's descent. The lifeless bodies that still occupy some of the wrecks send a cold shiver down Maali's spine, but she forces her eyes forward, focusing on the immediate path. There's no sense in absorbing the scenes of despair around them; Maali knows all too well they can't alter the past.

The populace is ensnared in a web of mental subjugation, where an omnipresent algorithm shackles minds. This insidious system dictates reality, warping truths until the absurd becomes the norm. Those daring to challenge the status quo, refusing to swallow the proverbial pill of conformity, find themselves ostracised and expelled from society into a void of hopelessness. They are denied jobs, benefits, and a place in the world, forced to exist on the fringes, invisible and forgotten.

For those who conform, life is a relentless mental acrobatics, a constant struggle to stay afloat in the ever-shifting tides of rules and regulations. Sydney, like the rest of the so-called free world, simmers in this pressure cooker, a society under the crushing weight of elitist control and hypocritical do-gooders. These feeble rulers, weak yet craving power, have orchestrated a world where crimes against the state are ruthlessly crushed. In contrast, crimes of human against human are often overlooked and used as tools to sow division and maintain a stranglehold over the masses.

This orchestrated division is a strategy as old as time yet hauntingly effective in this era. The elite pit the poor against the impoverished, ensuring a fragmented society where unity is a distant dream and control is effortlessly maintained. But beneath this tightly sealed lid of oppression, the pressure builds, steam escaping in fits and bursts.

A litany of colourful expletives tumbles from Noah's lips, each curse punctuating the rhythmic thud of his footsteps. "Godforsaken bastards! If they lay a finger on my kids, I'll rip out their guts and strangle 'em with 'em!" His threats become increasingly graphic as they dart past a string of ravaged storefronts. Amidst the upheaval, opportunistic looters are revealed, clutching their ill-gotten gains close to their chests. With his children as his singular focus, Noah bypasses direct confrontation. However, his path veers just enough to allow him to deliver a solid shoulder check to a nearby thief. The resulting collision sends the looter sprawling, his skull meeting the pavement with a gruesome crunch. In a fluid motion, Maali vaults over the fallen looter, maintaining her relentless pace.

Each demolished shop was a glaring reminder of the monolithic corporate dominance that had devoured the city's once vibrant landscape of small businesses. No quaint boutiques or family-run cafes remained; only the cold, impersonal facades of massive conglomerates stood, their logos a symbol of an oppressive monopoly. Amidst the ruins of individual enterprise and the rise of omnipotent corporations was a stark illustration of the dire consequences of a society stripped of its economic freedom and personal autonomy.

In this oppressive landscape, where digital transactions dominate, the intangibility of paper money has left those marginalised by the system in a relentless struggle for survival. The streets, cluttered with the remnants of consumer indulgence, mirror the desolation of a society under the iron grip of total corporate rule. In this merciless world, every transaction and interaction is scrutinised, obliterating any semblance of privacy or independence. For the hopeless, there remains no choice but to resort to bartering whatever they can salvage, including their own bodies, for mere sustenance. This harsh reality underscores the extreme desperation and degradation experienced by those abandoned by the digital economy.

As they penetrate further into the city's core, they bear witness to society's rapid unravelling. Years of resentment and simmering anger erupt in a volatile display of anarchy. Bands of malcontents take over the streets, venting their pent-up rage on anyone and anything in their path. Weaving their way through a maze of alleyways, Maali and Noah navigate a cautious path, evading the pulsating waves of violence that flood the main thoroughfares. Pausing momentarily in the safety of a shadowed alley, they watch as a violent skirmish spills onto the street mere feet from their hiding spot.

With a gaze brimming with a potent blend of hopelessness and vigour, Maali silently absorbs the disorder unfurling before her. "This city has been smouldering for years, but now, with a single blow of the bellow, the flames are visible for all to see," she murmurs, her voice burdened with the raw taste of sombre realisation. Fear, tangible and pungent, hangs heavily in the air, underscored by the piercing terror-filled screams echoing off the city's buildings.

As Maali watches the raw brutality unfold, a potent cocktail of powerlessness and rage seizes her. A figure, swathed in black and with its face obscured, is brutally knocked to the ground by an imposing beast with a hundred pounds of brute force advantage. The thunderous impact resonates through the air, followed by a nauseating crunch as the aggressor's mammoth boot finds purchase on the defenceless figure's teeth. The black-clad victim succumbs, their body going slack. The echo of the gruesome impact reverberated through the alley, a signal unbeknownst to the aggressor, awakening the vengeance lurking in the glooms. Two shadowy figures, sharing the attire of the fallen, spring from their hiding places, launching an ambush on the brutish victor with a bike lock and a crowbar. The dynamics of power shift as quickly as lightning - the predator becomes the prey. Yet, their moment of triumph evaporates almost instantly in the ever-escalating frenzy. A sea of broken glass carpets the streets, reflecting the lunacy in its fractured medley, while each storefront stands as a witness to rampant looting, some licked by the ambitious tongues of arson flames.

Noah's voice, ripe with frustration, slices through the noise, his eyes scanning their turbulent surroundings with steely resolve. "We need to reroute. There's too much heat ahead." Without a beat of hesitation, he assumes the lead, traversing the anarchy-laden streets. Maali's gaze, a whirlpool of concern, lingers on the brutal scene for a moment longer before she tears her eyes away and refocuses on Noah, matching his unwavering stride through the seething cityscape.

With a voice fortified by duty, Maali breaks the silence, "We're cops, Noah! We should be stepping in."

Noah spins on his heel at the alley's mouth to face her, a finger pressed urgently against his lips, demanding her silence. His voice is charged with raw emotion. "Are you out of your mind?! We're two people in a city unhinged. If we throw ourselves into this madness, one of two outcomes awaits." With calculated caution, he peeks out from their alleyway refuge, eyes scanning for immediate threats. Seeing nothing more hazardous than a handful of looters and a few ablaze trash cans, he pivots back towards Maali, his eyes broadcasting a frustration. "Look around, Maali. Our identities are lost in this mayhem, our badges... they've lost all their meaning."

As they push onward, he continues, "I get it; the desire to help is powerful. But the moment we reveal who we are, we'll be engulfed by terrified mobs, pleading for salvation from this hellhole." He waves a dismissive hand at the surrounding hell, the haunting backdrop of screams and sporadic gunfire echoing through the air serving as ample explanation. With a solemn acceptance, Noah confesses, "We have to stifle the instinct to play the heroes in a city where sanity has been discarded. If they see us as the last vestiges of law and order, we'll be inundated with desperate souls seeking deliverance. And in the end, we'll be swallowed whole by the very inferno we're trying to escape."

Two booming ACCO C1800 trucks rip through the intersection before them, their engines bellowing roars of mechanical mayhem. One, losing its grip on the slick road, veers violently, slamming into a body slumped against a lamppost. The collision is a violent ballet of shattering glass, bone and metal, leaving a debris storm in its wake. Miraculously, the driver wrestles the truck back from the brink of disaster, narrowly averting a more disastrous crash. The injured truck strains to catch up with its partner, its transmission wailing in protest as it pushes its engine beyond its limits. In a flash, both vehicles disappear around a corner, leaving only the shrill echo of their tires squealing against the asphalt, a noxious blend of bitter diesel fuel, burnt exhaust, and metallic decay in their wake. Maali cuts across the road, resolutely averting her gaze from the grisly smear of crimson now marking the previously pristine lamppost.

"Idiots," Noah mutters under his breath. "Begging for a fast track to the Grim Reaper with that kind of recklessness."

Suppressing a chuckle, Maali finds a glimmer of humour in Noah's irritable disposition. 'Ah, the endless grumbling of a grumpy old man,' she thinks to herself.

"No more dawdling; we need to push on!" Maali can't help but admire Noah's boundless stamina, especially considering his affection for cigarettes and alcohol.

"Right behind you." Sticking close, she has no intention of losing sight of one of the only people she trusts in this free-for-all. "You never mentioned the second reason."

"Huh?" Without looking back, Noah questions, "What the hell are you talking about?"

Intrigued, Maali elaborates, "Earlier, you mentioned two outcomes if people discovered our true identities. What's the second?"

"Ah," Noah sighs, a thread of fatigue lacing his voice. "If the wrong sorts identify us... we won't be going anywhere except in a body bag. Even in the best of times, there's too few of us to maintain order, and with those corporate enforcers from SorrowStar tarnishing our reputation, being part of the force ain't as respected as it once was."

Pausing briefly, he rummages in his pocket, pulling out the GPS tag from his badge. Given the intermittent power outages sweeping across the city, Noah expects it to be as useless as most other electronic devices. Yet, as he glances at the small screen, surprise flickers across his face. "Well, I'll be damned," he mutters a note of unexpected pleasure in his tone. "The GPS is still operational." With the street signs demolished or defaced and the convoluted detour they've been forced to navigate, it's their only assurance they're heading in the right direction. "Seems we're still on track. There must be some emergency power grids still online."

Maali's response comes with a gravely concerned tone. "Kings Cross. It's not exactly a place of hospitality, especially now. I hope—" Her voice is brutally severed by the harsh retort of a shotgun blast nearby, causing both of them to tense, their hands moving to ready positions near their weapons. Yet what unfolds before them is less of an immediate threat and more of a frantic demonstration of disorder.

A panicky cluster of dishevelled figures stumble from a blasted-open storefront, burdened by the limp form of one among them who has taken a devastating shotgun hit to the chest. The maimed man is saturated in crimson, leaving a gruesome trail in their wake. The disturbing sight stirs Maali's instinctive urge to help. "Jesus... we can't just stand here, Noah," she entreats.

"No, Maali!" Noah's voice cuts through her plea, a sharp edge of frustration in his tone. "We can't rescue everyone. Charging in there will only paint a target on our backs. And that store? It's a killing floor just waiting to happen, laid out by the bastard with the shotgun." The echo of another blast punctuates his words, forcing them to dart into cover.

The cruel reality gnaws at Maali's conscience, her innate desire to help clashing with the stark reality of their situation. Yet halfway through the oppressive slums, the burden of standing by grows unbearable. As they exit another shadow-haunted alley, they are met with a chilling scene—an innocent family encircled by a rabble of merciless thugs. As the father brandishes a tire iron with unshakeable grit, one of the brutes takes a swing at him, only to be met with a savage counterstrike that sends him sprawling, his face disfigured by the force of the blow.

The sight of the father's fierce resistance ignites a catalyst of resolve in Maali. She is habitually an embodiment of firm resilience, but the plight of the innocent gnaws at her. As the outer chaos mirrors her inner turmoil, her eyes kindle with a renewed fortitude. In this crucible, her duality finds harmony, forcing her to step up in the face of the enveloping darkness.

The thickened air seems to hold its breath, the hum of distant commotion shrinking into an eerie hush. The mocking jeers of the gang members dwindle into an ominous quiet. Like wolves closing in for a kill, they collectively draw in, tightening their circle around the family. The father, his sinews taut with firmness, stands as the only barrier between them and his family. The tire iron in his hand traces menacing arcs through the dim light, each swing a potential last stand.

His wife, fuelled by a maternal desperation, throws herself into the fray. She lunges at their tormentors, her fingers clawed and seeking, transforming from a mere mother to a wild, cornered beast fighting for its brood. Eyes, throats, anything vulnerable - she scratches and strikes, the only rule of her combat being survival.

The surrounding gloom, cut sporadically by the harsh glares of stray flames, does little to soften the menace of the scene. The cruel grins, the anticipatory gleam in the gang members' eyes, and the oppressive weight of impending violence fill the narrow alley with a sense of dread that crawls under the skin and freezes the blood. It is a spectacle not of a simple confrontation but of raw, primal fear battling against the instinct of survival in its purest form.

A shrill cry pierces the violent night, rending the shroud of chaos, bouncing off the brick walls of the constricting alleyway. It's a beacon of vulnerability seeking a saviour amidst the tempest of terror. A terrified girl, her eyes, wide pools of raw fear, lock onto Maali's. "Please, Miss, help us!" Her voice, a desperate scream, echoes hauntingly, carrying the dread of a prey cornered by predators. "We can't keep them off... Save us!"

Her plea snags on Maali's heartstrings, rumbling through her being, rousing the sleeping empath within her. It gnaws at the edges of her steely determination, whispering, daring her to challenge the engulfing shadows, to illuminate the darkness with a torch of hope this petrified family seeks.

The tension within her snaps. Propelled by the child's inner light, she steps forward, the pulsating hum of her rifle filling the silence. She stares down the menacing gang with an icy gaze that challenges their bravado. Her voice slices through the air, cold, unwavering steel. "This is it. Retreat or be reduced to ash. The choice is yours."

Her audacious ultimatum triggers tremors of apprehension among the gang, unsettling their cocksure smirks into flickers of indecision. Yet, the gang leader, emboldened by his human shield—the girl—refuses to yield. Maali's gauntlet has been thrown.

Seeing no alternative, Noah strides up next to her, his pistol mirroring her weapon's silent threat. His whisper cuts through the tension like a razor's edge. "In this together. But remember, Maali..." His grip on the pistol tightens, his knuckles pale under the strain. "We can't save them all."

Maali's gaze doesn't waver from the gang. "A bit too late for second thoughts," she shoots back, her voice stanch, full of steel. Noah grunts in reluctant agreement, the sound disappearing into the tense silence that swaddles them. Maali's weapon, humming ominously, becomes the only dialogue they are willing to entertain with the gang as a showdown looms in the beleaguered alley.

The gang leader, maintaining his hold on the girl's throat, sneers at them. "Back off! This ain't your business, assholes! We found 'em first, and they're ours!"

Noah, a figure of steadfast defiance, steps into the theatre of menace, his stature radiating a challenge the gang members cannot ignore. "So, this is your game?" His voice, a concoction of contempt and provocation, sends ripples of unease, skittering through the ranks. The shadows flit in his eyes, reflecting a dangerous glimmer of exhilaration. "What's the next move, boys?"

The gang leader remains resolute, his predatory gaze locked onto the terrified girl. He inhales deeply, a perverse pleasure taken from the scent of her fear-soaked hair. A wicked sneer curls his lips, his words slithering through the night air, venomous and vile. "The next move, you dogs, is you running off with your tails between your legs. We've got some... playtime to catch up on." The air becomes heavy with the girl's wretched sobs, her parents' futile struggles a desperate waste, as the gang members' collective might clamp down on them like a vice.

The wave of fury surging within Maali threatens to burst its banks, her finger itching on the trigger, an unbridled tempest barely contained within the pulse rifle. The potential havoc it could wreak on the innocents holds her back, trapping her in a cauldron of indecision. But her turmoil is suddenly sliced through by the sound of Noah's laughter. It rings through the alley, laced with an incongruous cocktail of derision and defiance. 'What's he laughing at?' she wonders, her simmering fury momentarily eclipsed by bewilderment.

Noah strides forward, his approach steady and commanding, the dangerous aura around him pulsing like a storm's heart. "Oh, so that's all it takes to claim a turf?" He brandishes his pistol, the icy sheen of steel catching the scant light, as he cocks the hammer back, its metallic click echoing a deadly promise. "Well, in that case... welcome to our house." His finger curls around the trigger, the latent threat in his stance poised to erupt.

The deafening crack of the pistol shatters the air, and the gang leader collapses to the ground, his knee torn apart by the bullet's impact. His agonised screams pierce through the silence, filling the block with raw terror. A few of his thugs hesitate, their bravado waning in the face of such merciless retribution. Maali fires a warning shot, the searing blast racing above their heads, forcing them to retreat. Amidst the bedlam, Noah's laughter echoes once again. "Well, does that mean all this," he lazily waves to the block, "belongs to me now?"

An ominous quiet blankets the scene, punctuated by the terrified thumping of hearts, each beat resonating with the looming dread. Maali matches Noah's stride, her words biting through the silence like shards of ice. "Nah, I think you need to wave your dick around a little more."

Noah's laughter, once defiant, now morphs into something more chilling, a ghoulish murmur that twists the blood in their veins. His grin, spiteful and cruel, casts a terrifying reflection of the dark battleground of his soul. Without missing a beat, he squares his pistol once more, his eyes sparking. "As you wish!" The ensuing gunshot rips through the night air, a searing bullet tearing a bloody path through the gang leader's calf. His agonised shriek is swallowed by Noah's sinister guffaws, a sickening serenade to the fear seizing their adversary.

As Noah reloads, each click and slide becomes an echoing pronouncement of the nightmare unfolding. With a gleeful smirk, he pockets the loaded magazine, the heaviness of potential death a morose delight. He raises his weapon once more, its deadly silhouette cutting through the trembling fear that binds the gang. "Who's next in line?" His voice drips with a tantalising promise of doom, counting with morbid glee, the pistol swinging ominously from one face to another. "Nine... eight... Ah, to hell with it!"

Without preamble, he squeezes the trigger, the roar of the gunshot slicing through the tension-ridden air. A thug's hat is ripped from his head, the near miss sending him scrambling to escape, his panic a contagious virus. As if propelled by a surge of dark amusement, Noah fires again, the bullet grazing another punk's arm. The sharp wail of pain and subsequent flight further stoke the mayhem. Basking in the pandemonium he's wrought, Noah taunts his remaining opponents, "Plenty more where that came from, boys!"

With sanity fraying on all sides, the unsettling hum of Maali's pulse rifle buries a plasma charge into the earth. The seismic boom echoes their defiance, paving the way for Noah's relentless advance, his laughter no more than a sinister echo of the lunacy consuming him. The gang's bluster shatters, dissolving into frantic flight as they carry their whimpering leader from the onslaught. Gunshots crackle through the air, their harsh staccato a brutal declaration. When the echoes finally recede, Maali and Noah stand amidst the fleeting stillness.

As the last remnants of the gang disappear, Maali turns to Noah. "Having fun with your new block?"

He shoots her a scathing look, his lips curling into a cynical grin. "Too many damn bullet holes for my liking." Their attention shifts back to the family, the mother and father slowly picking themselves up.

Bloodied but unbowed, the father brandishes his tire iron, positioning himself as a staunch bulwark between his family and the unexpected saviours-turned-potential-threats. His wife's arms envelop their daughter in a fierce, protective embrace, her gaze never leaving the two strangers. The father raises the iron, the weapon reflecting desperation in his eyes. His voice, strained and guttural, commands, "Back off! Get the hell away!"

Noah holsters his gun, his hand coming up in a pacifying gesture, and Maali lets her rifle hang loosely from her shoulder, her hands raised in a placating manner. "We're not your enemies," she assures them, her tone soothing in its sincerity.

The mother, her protective embrace steadfast, eyes them warily and asks, "So, you're the good guys?"

Maali meets her gaze, a hint of sorrow in her eyes. "It's complicated," she replies, her voice tinged with a sombre realisation of their own moral ambiguity.

Noah's retort is curt, his gaze tenacious. "But you can't stay here. Find safety. Go home."

From behind the protective shield of her husband, the mother her tone fragile yet resolute. "We were visiting a friend... when everything went to hell." Her trembling hand points skywards towards the looming vessel that hangs like a harbinger of doom.

A sense of urgency pulses within them, prompting them to abandon the fractured sanctuary of their brief respite, yet Noah finds himself tethered by a gnawing concern. "Your home... can you reach it alone?"

The father, pride vying against reality, steps forward, only to falter, buckling to the ground with a choked gasp of pain. Instantly, his wife and daughter are at his side, their desperate need now starkly revealed. The mother's plea is a haunting refrain that echoes through the charred ruins of their city. "Help us... Michael is badly hurt... and I... I'm not faring much better."

The strangled cry for aid weaves its way into their conscience. Maali turns to Noah, seeking his decision. A scowl etches deep lines on his weathered face, but finally, he surrenders. "Alright. We stay with you till Kings Cross. Beyond that, you're on your own." While still brusque, his words bring a wave of relief over the beleaguered family.

With the addition of wounded civilians, their pace grinds down to a crawl, every step punctuated by their laboured breaths. However, the heart of their struggle lies not in their burdened journey but in the harrowing spectacle of the city's succumbing to mayhem. Normalcy, replaced by bedlam, becomes a distant memory as citizens scramble over scraps, brawling savagely for the remains of dwindling supplies, their desperation resulting in the spoils of war being trampled underfoot. Inebriation becomes a common refuge, with alcohol consumed in careless abandon, and drugs, once confined to the fringes, are now openly consumed on the city's ruined sidewalks, the public spectacle heightening their sense of desolation.

What churns Maali's insides is the absence of any law enforcement and the lack of any sense of order. Not a single fellow officer is in sight, nor are the ominous SorrowStar-affiliated corpo-cops that have become a common sight in recent months. Once a symbol of vibrancy, the city has plunged into anarchy far quicker than any of their worst-case scenarios had predicted. The devastating tide of lawlessness has swallowed the last vestiges of order.

A disquieting tremor snatches their attention, drawing every gaze upward to the formidable vessel hovering ominously overhead. Suddenly, a beam of brilliant blue light bursts forth, slashing the pitch-black canvas of the night sky with its ethereal luminescence. This celestial lighthouse begins to sweep across the cityscape, its divided sections spreading like the rays of blue moonlight, searing through the murky darkness.

Like a watchful sentinel, the beam scrutinises the sprawling urban landscape beneath, its invasive gaze unflinchingly dissecting the turmoil below. The luminary shaft moves with methodical precision, its glow casting an eerie pallor over the riotous streets and towering edifices. Its rich, azure hue stands in stark contrast to the maelstrom under its watch, offering a bizarre spectacle of unearthly tranquillity amidst the brouhaha.

With each calculated sweep, the beam stitches a vivid spectacle of light and shadow, marking its path with radiant trails that linger in the wake of its exploration. The unsettling spectacle renders them immobile, the piercing beam instilling a collective sense of apprehension that outweighs the terror sown by the anarchy at ground level. The silent question now echoing in their minds - what is it searching for?

CHAPTER 4:
St. Mary's

Just as suddenly as it started, the light display ceases, the eerie blue beam retracting back into the looming vessel, leaving the city again plunged into an uncertain flickering darkness. A palpable sigh of relief echoes through the group as the city's newfound sentinel seems to recede, its watchful gaze retreating from their world.

Respite, however, proves short-lived, as the echo of the riotous situation quickly fills the quiet left behind. Despite the delay caused by assisting Michael and his family, Maali and Noah manage to navigate through the turmoil of King's Cross, avoiding further conflict.

As they edge away from the chaos, Maali casts a glance back at Michael, her eyes filled with concern. She asks, "Are you sure you'll be okay?" Her voice, despite its strength, betrays her worry.

Michael returns her gaze with a firm nod and a reassuring smile. "We'll be fine, Ma'am. I appreciate your help. You two, just keep yourselves safe out there."

Acknowledging his words, Maali gives a reluctant nod, her gaze lingering on Michael and his family. Noah, recognising her hesitancy, gently nudges her, his hand firm on her arm.

"Maali, we need to keep going," he urges softly.

The implacable landscape that stretches out beyond King's Cross gnaws at the senses. Maali trudges through the wreckage-strewn streets, each step revealing more catastrophic aftermath of the city-wide EMP and the ensuing riots. Abandoned cars, their metal skins warped and blackened, are strewn haphazardly across their path. Flames lick the night air from the ruins of some vehicles, painting a picture straight out of the mind of a future serial killer, their eerie glow illuminating contorted shapes of human remains within.

The sight sears itself into Maali's memory, sparking a surge of revulsion and sorrow. She stammers out, "Noah..." Her voice is a mere thread of sound, brittle under the weight of the ugly reality.

Noah's gaze lands on her, his eyes echoing the unspeakable horrors they witness. "Maali," he says, his voice bearing the mark of shared pain, "I understand... it's unbearable." His words hang in the air, like an obituary to the world they once knew. "But we can't allow it to engulf us. We have a mission."

Without looking away from the uninviting panorama, he adds, "Try not to focus on the details... especially the children..." His voice breaks on the last word, his vulnerability laid bare. Swallowing hard, Maali steels herself and hastens her steps, pressing onward through the field of desolation.

Fatigue weighs heavily on Maali's body, but as St. Mary's Cathedral looms on the horizon, a symbol of steadfastness amidst destruction, a spark of hope ignites within her. The church, once surrounded by open grounds but now hemmed in by the city's unrelenting growth, retains a hint of its former majesty. The congregation's unwavering belief that the cathedral can resist even the corporate might of companies like SorrowStar fans the flames of tenacity burning fiercely within her.

Just as Maali rounds a corner, Noah halts abruptly. He drops into a crouch, issuing a silent command to do the same. Maali sinks down beside him, her voice a hushed whisper, "What is it?"

His eyes, locked onto the cathedral, barely glint towards her. "See the rose window? Above the entrance?"

She follows his line of sight, her gaze drawn to the window. A dull gleam of blue flits across the stained glass, playing hide and seek with the surrounding moss-covered stones. "What...?" she murmurs, her words trailing off. Could it be a sign of life? A priest seeking refuge within the church's old walls?"

Noah grumbles in response, his voice laced with scepticism. "A priest with an EM-shielded flashlight? That's highly unusual." His gaze remains fixed on the window, the intermittent flashes of light intensifying his curiosity.

"We should check it out," Maali proposes, her tone resolute. Noah raises an eyebrow, intrigued by her persistence. "If it's just people seeking refuge, it might not be a big deal. But there's a chance there's something more to it. They could even have transportation. And since we're passing by the cathedral anyway, it won't take us off course."

Noah's glare deepens as he observes the continuing flickering lights within the cathedral. Letting out an exasperated sigh, he begrudgingly gives in. "Alright, let's do it. Stay low and stick close to me. We have no idea who these people are, and my gut tells me they're more than just frightened civilians." Gripping his pistol firmly, he proceeds with caution, his eyes sweeping the surroundings for any signs of danger.

Maali's fingers wrap tightly around her rifle, her movements a shadow of Noah's as they edge towards the northern gable of the gothic cathedral. The menacing eyes of stone gargoyles seem to follow them, silent witnesses to their passage in a world where the spiritual and the corporeal intertwine. The cathedral itself rises as an ancient fortress, a bulwark against the encroachment of modernity, yet bearing the scars of time. The darkness of the night is cut only by the occasional haunting glow from the stained glass windows, casting eerie patterns onto the path they tread.

Reaching a strategic vantage point, Noah takes the lead, approaching the massive main door with a thief's grace. The ancient wood and iron seem to defy him, refusing to yield as he attempts to open it with precision. Frustration creeps onto his face as the door stubbornly refuses to yield, causing him to step back and scowl at the uncooperative obstacle before them.

The soft, unsteady hum of voices trickles from the cathedral's aged interior, adding a surreal touch to the quietness. Maali and Noah find themselves pulled towards the whispers, moving stealthily closer. As Noah takes up position near the entrance, his ears straining to decrypt the indecipherable murmurs, Maali slips into the comforting embrace of the shadows.

There, concealed amidst the cathedral's imposing architecture, her gaze latches onto an ominous sight. A cluster of figures, their attire as dark as the uncertainty enveloping the city, linger around an unremarkable van. Bereft of any identifying marks, plates, or antennas, the vehicle seems content to dissolve into the surrounding darkness, with only the obstinate touch of moonlight intertwined seamlessly with the glow from the vessel above betraying its presence.

Motioning Noah towards her hidden nook, Maali points out the curious group. Noah's eyes narrow, his mind racing to make sense of the situation. "Private security?" He whispers, his voice barely threading through the hush. "No, this doesn't add up... it's too much for a cathedral..."

Their whispers blend into the night, lost within the stuttered breaths of a city teetering on the brink of oblivion.

As she studies the brooding figures, Maali notes the faultless precision of their gear, the echo of menace woven into their ballistic armour. Pouches, stuffed with tools of their trade, dot their attire, a quiet endorsement of their readiness. Two figures cradle AK-74s, their iconic silhouette recognisable even to a partially trained eye. But what catches Maali's attention is the third figure, nonchalantly bearing the weight of a weapon that's more a monster than a firearm. A pulse rifle, built to tear through armoured vehicles, rests on his shoulder as if it were nothing more than a plaything, its imposing bulk a stark contrast to the relatively smaller weapon Maali carries.

A din of disquiet and fascination ensnares Maali as she surveys the scene, while Noah's reaction is more unrestrained, his whisper taut with tension. "What on earth are they guarding?" Their glances intersect, a silent exchange that carries the weight of their shared apprehension.

Amidst this tension, a fresh flurry of activity pulls their attention back to the cathedral. The guards huddled near the van appear to receive a directive through their headsets, guiding them to a veiled entrance carved into the cathedral's side. Encased in formidable armour, three more figures step out from the structure, converging with their waiting allies.

As the men take up positions around the van, a peculiar detail registers with Maali. Only one guard remains vigilant to the city's chaotic sprawl while his comrades stand guard at the door. Her gaze locks onto a common motif gracing several men's shoulders, a wry shake of her head following. "Heh... SS goons."

Noah's grunt of recognition sends an uneasy shiver down her spine. There, emblazoned on the shoulder patches, sits the SorrowStar logo - a sun enveloped within a square, its radiant beams reaching out from each side, a circle confining it all. The symbol of SorrowStar's private security wing - the SS, an ill-famed band known for their brutal misuse of power and deeply rooted corruption. The allegations pile up, the rumours circulate, but proof remains elusive, lost amidst a manipulative whirlwind of propaganda, legal manoeuvrings, and darker, more sinister methods of concealment. It's a twisted narrative whispered within police circles - "Take the bribe or commit suicide". Yet, without solid evidence, it serves to only strengthen the ominous aura encircling SorrowStar's activities.

In the flickering shadows of the city's fractured skyline, Maali couldn't help but notice the familiar, yet distant, glint in the eyes of the SorrowStar operatives. It was a look she had seen before, in another life, on faces too young to bear such burdens. Like many others, Noah had been a mere teenager when the world's tides turned, swept up in the fervour of a conflict that echoed across the desolate northern frontiers. The war, a silent testament to a fallen empire's last stand, had left its scars, not just on the land but on the souls of those who returned. The operatives, once proud defenders in a battle of desperation, found themselves discarded in the aftermath, their valour forgotten. SorrowStar, in its twisted benevolence, had offered them a sanctuary, a place in a new order where their past was both an asset and a chain. The unspoken bond among them, forged in the fires of a conflict that the world was keen to forget, was the only hint of a brotherhood that once was but is now twisted into a tool for darker purposes.

A snarl bristles beneath Maali's breath as she scans the faces of the SorrowStar operatives, some all too familiar. Once colleagues on the force, they now stand on the other side, their old ideals and oaths sold for the promise of a more profitable, unrestrained future.

The rich divide of the city cuts deep, and Maali's own choices weigh heavily on her conscience. The world had shifted, the gap between the wealthy and the working class widening into a chasm. There were now only three categories: the rich, the working, and the non-working. The once middle class had been pushed to the edges, forced to make decisions they never thought they'd face.

Maali herself had supplemented her meagre income as a gun-for-hire, taking control of the narrative and choosing her battles. But these former comrades had gone further, trading in not just their skills but their very souls to SorrowStar, becoming instruments for whoever held the paycheck.

The city's cost of living had spiralled into an uncontrolled ascent, pushing even the most steadfast into morally ambiguous territories. But while Maali's choices were driven by necessity and a desire to stay true to her principles, the SorrowStar operatives had surrendered themselves entirely, becoming part of a system that fed on the very disparity that had birthed them.

They had become embodiments of a society where money didn't just talk; it screamed, silencing ethics, integrity, and humanity. The sight of them, once defenders of justice, now pawns of power, leaves a bitter taste in Maali's mouth.

Suddenly, the air tightens, each guard jolting to attention, their weapons zeroing in on the cathedral door. Emerging from the shadowed entrance, a group of guardsmen haul a tall, obscured figure between them. His identity remains hidden beneath a crudely fastened bag, a sight that stirs a surge of resentment within Maali. The figure's white, dirt-streaked straitjacket and oppressive iron restraints stand as stark reminders of his vulnerability. He offers no resistance, no protest, as he is unceremoniously bundled into the back of the van.

As Maali watches, Noah's voice seethes with quiet rage, "That son of a bitch."

She glances back at the last member of the group, stifling her own growl. It's Arron Manfred, Sydney's corrupt police commissioner. Noah and Maali are well aware of the bribes he has accepted to cover up SorrowStar's crimes over the years. Rumour has it that he made a significant investment in the company just before SorrowStar effectively took over the majority of law enforcement in the country, resulting in a massive personal fortune. The reason he maintains his commissioner position remains unclear, but the prevailing theory suggests that the company compelled him to do so in exchange for a substantial payday.

A ripple of surprise tints Maali's whisper as she observes the unfolding scene. "Manfred is sticking his neck out for that guy. He must be someone important."

A taut line forms on Noah's brow, a flicker of suspicion in his voice. "Something doesn't add up. The bag, the straitjacket, the cuffs... This isn't your everyday arrest."

Maali and Noah's history with Manfred runs deep and rancorous. The day Noah defied orders to save Maali's life, Manfred had sought to sabotage her career, hushing up the fact that he had ordered backup to desert her. Noah's leak of her body cam footage to the media flipped the narrative. SorrowStar, quick to capitalise on the public outcry, painted a compelling picture of Noah and his partner as the gallant rescuers who had stepped in where the police had faltered.

In the aftermath, a nationwide minute of silence was observed, echoing with the grief of an entire country mourning the loss of Maali's team and her departed saviour, Maria. The solemn occasion was capped off by a state funeral, their coffins draped with the latest national flag, paraded before tear-streaked faces and saluting officers.

Even Noah and Maali had been paraded before the cameras, their chests adorned with shiny medals, their hands mechanically shaking with dignitaries. The pomp and circumstance, the grandeur of the funeral, the weight of the medals against their chests—none of it brought their friends back. None of it filled the hollow void left by their absence. The medals felt as cold and meaningless as the empty platitudes and sympathetic pats on the back they received.

Haunted by the memories of their friends and the injustice of their deaths, Noah and Maali knew all too well the bitter irony of being celebrated as heroes when their friends lay cold and silent in their graves. The void left in Noah and Maali's souls by the loss of their friends persisted, a gnawing emptiness that echoed in tandem with their inclusion on Manfred's undesired blacklist.

A simmering fury radiates from Maali's core as her gaze remains fixated on Manfred. In her eyes, he personifies the absolute depths of corruption, a vile marionettist conducting an insidious spectacle of deceit. A shudder of revulsion travels down her spine at his mere thought, her heart throbbing in rhythm with a frosty pledge of vengeance. Her knuckles blanch around the grip of her rifle, her body humming with an eagerness for confrontation, but Noah's steady grasp on her arm counsels patience.

Oblivious to their covert scrutiny, Manfred is engrossed in his role, his eyes darting around in anticipation of hidden threats. When his gaze glides over their concealed position, they pull back further into the shroud of darkness, their breaths hitching, pulses racing. In the dim light, the faint glint on Noah's fair skin contrasts subtly with Maali's deeper complexion, her eyes more discernible in the shadows yet equally alert and watchful.

Maali, her eyes still fixed on Manfred, leans slightly towards Noah, a mischievous glimmer in her gaze. 'You know, your reflective ass is a beacon in this gloom,' she whispers, her tone laced with a mix of mock seriousness and humour. 'If we get spotted, I'm blaming it entirely on your moonlit complexion.'

Noah stifles a chuckle, the corner of his lips twitching in amusement. 'Noted,' he replies in a hushed tone, 'I'll add "moonlit complexion" to the list of hazards for covert operations.'"

The fleeting surge of anxiety ebbs away when their position remains undiscovered and no security personnel rush towards their hiding spot. Maali's gaze narrows, her mind weighing the options. "Let's open these bastards up," she whispers, the urgency in her voice barely contained.

Noah shakes his head, his eyes reflecting a calm, strategic patience. The faintest hint of light catches his face, accentuating the contrast between them, not just in appearance but in approach. "Not yet," he replies quietly, his voice firm. "Timing is everything."

Cautiously, they allow themselves to reappear from their camouflaged hideaway, their attention returning to the unfolding scene. Manfred's clipped orders fill the air, prompting two of his men to trail after the detained figure into the van. Settling into the passenger seat, Manfred observes another man taking the driver's position. The remaining SS operatives commence their ground patrol. Their dedicated attentiveness dogged as they merge with the encroaching shadows, their formidable silhouettes gradually conforming into the night's embrace.

With their gaze trained on the van, Maali and Noah find themselves taken aback by its almost supernatural silence. Unlike the faint whir of electric vehicles they were accustomed to, this one seemed to operate on something else entirely, perhaps an experimental hydrogen cell or an advanced stealth technology. Hunkered down, they strain their ears, but the van moves without so much as a whisper, its presence more like a passing shadow than a substantial machine. The absence of sound is unsettling as if the van is a ghost slipping through the night. The only indication of its movement is the faint displacement of air, a subtle shift felt, rather than heard before it melds back into the obscurity of the cityscape.

"Let's tail them," Maali declares, her body already responding to her decision.

Noah's hand clenches around Maali's arm, pulling her back. "Are you crazy? We're blind here," he cautions. His words are met with a look of sheer grit from Maali, her conviction clear. "Yes, Manfred's up to something rotten, but he's got eight of his SS lackeys with him. We'd be stepping right into the lion's den."

Adamant, Maali brushes off his hold. 'We can't let that vermin slip away. Who knows what atrocities he's part of?' she asserts, her conviction steadfast. Seeing Noah's disapproval, she softens her tone. 'Look, they're moving in our direction anyway. We stick to their tail until their path diverges. Can't see any harm in that.'

But there's more to her insistence than strategy. Maali feels a stirring deep within her, an inexplicable urge that resonates with her roots. It's as if the land itself, through the subtle vibrations of the air and the whispers of the wind, is guiding her. She can't rationalise it, but the pull is undeniable, a primal intuition honed from her lineage. This connection, though intangible, strengthens her resolve. The van, seemingly just a vehicle, becomes a symbol, a pathway leading them towards something significant, something her soul recognises even if her mind does not yet comprehend it.

Taking a moment, Maali inhales deeply, her eyelids fluttering shut. A brief silence falls before she opens her eyes, now sharply focused on Noah. "It's hard to put into words, Noah," her voice steady and sure, "but there's something about that van. I feel it, right here," she taps her chest lightly.

His hard gaze softens, his frustration evident. "Alright," he concedes, a note of reluctance in his voice. "We'll trail them until they deviate from the children's block, but not an inch further. We're not jeopardising the kids." Curiosity flickers in his eyes. "That captive… there's something odd about him. I can't quite put my finger on it, but I sense there's more beneath the surface."

As they stalk the SorrowStar convoy, something stirs deep within Maali. Her legacy speaks to her in moments like these, an ancient wisdom passed down through generations coursing through her veins. She doesn't need to vocalise it, but it's there - a spiritual tether to her roots that allows her to read the environment, anticipate dangers, and follow trails unseen to the inexperienced eye. It's not a science but rather a gut feeling, an innate instinct as much a part of her as her heartbeat. Her ancestors may have called it 'wirla' - that unsettling sensation in the pit of your stomach when you know something is amiss. It has also given her a deeper, almost spiritual, understanding of her surroundings. It's not just about following the van; it's about sensing the underlying currents in the city, feeling the weight of hidden stories and silenced voices. And right now, her intuition screams louder than ever - a silent warning reverberating in her gut. Whatever Manfred is involved in, it's more than just a clandestine operation.

CHAPTER 5:
Brutality the New Reality

Silently, like spectres skirting through the dark, Maali and Noah keep pace with the van. Its slow, stealthy crawl along the abandoned streets gives the illusion of a wild creature stalking its prey. The rumble of tires over cracked asphalt becomes a cryptic melody in the stillness of the night, punctuated by the occasional snap of broken glass or the crunch of scattered debris. Noah's every muscle twitches, primed to divert their course, but an invisible string seems to keep them tethered to the van, their paths mysteriously intertwined.

The SorrowStar team is a steely panorama of vigilance., their sharp eyes scanning their surroundings, their bodies tense and alert. Occasionally, they splinter off to address unseen threats, their departure echoing in the tortured screams that follow. The thrill they derive from these confrontations seeps into the air, an intangible sense of ghoulish glee that tickles the back of Maali's neck. Her gut tightens, a primal instinct driving her to intervene, but Noah's stern words halt her. "We can't afford to alert them," he cautions, his voice a low rumble in the quiet. "We risk more lives that way."

Stifling her objections, Maali grudgingly acknowledges the truth in Noah's warning. Their pursuit exists on a razor's edge - one wrong move, one overlooked detail, and they risk plunging the city further into disarray. The forbidding reminders of such violence stain the streets, a silent covenant to the unchecked brutality of the SorrowStar team. Forced to sit on her rage, Maali steels herself with an untiring conviction - they must save Noah's children, unveil the secrets of the van, and ultimately expose Manfred's vile machinations.

Their silent vigil is brusquely shattered as the van grinds to an abrupt halt. The SS operatives swarm forward, a formidable shield bristling with weaponry. "What's going on?" Maali hisses, crouching further into the shadows.

Noah's gaze is focused, locked onto the unfolding scene. "Not sure," he murmurs. "But they aren't moving our way. We need to get closer." Unhindered by Maali's tacit agreement, he begins to creep forward, each footfall measured and silent. Maali shadows him, her senses alive with anticipation.

As they press themselves as close as they dare to the van's rear, the murmur of the SS team leader slices through the air. "Remember, no mistakes. We're too far in to botch this now," he orders. His voice is sharp and loaded with a sense of urgency.

As Noah contemplates their next move, his attention is momentarily diverted by a flicker of light in his peripheral vision. The street around them is a maze of destruction, with the remnants of the conflict strewn haphazardly. A smouldering car sits nearby, its smoke mingling with the dust-laden air.

Through this haze, Noah's trained eyes glimpse an open manhole, a remnant of the city's damaged infrastructure. He nods subtly towards Maali, a silent warning exchanged through a glance. She acknowledges it with a quick, sharp look, her attention divided between the potential hazards around them.

Advancing with caution, Noah's every step is measured amidst the treacherous terrain. The smoke blurs the line between shadow and solid ground, challenging even his experienced eyes. Although moving methodically, the lingering ache from his old gunshot wound subtly impedes him, not enough to cause a limp but sufficient to make his footing less sure.

As Noah approaches the manhole, an ear-splitting screech slices through the heavy smog. Startled, he whirls around to face the commotion. From the dense haze, a cat, feral and fierce, leaps into view. Its fur, a patchwork of orange and white, is matted and charred at the edges, telling tales of survival in the harsh urban wilderness. Its eyes, wide and wild, gleam with a fiery intensity that speaks of a relentless protectiveness. Clutched gently in her mouth is a tiny kitten, its fragile form a stark contrast to the mother's rugged appearance. The unexpected encounter throws him off balance, his foot snagging on a piece of twisted metal hidden by the smoke.

He teeters dangerously on the brink of the open manhole, his heart pounding. In a flash, Maali's hand steadies him, her grip firm. "Easy there," she says, pulling him back from the edge.

The cat, now perched on a nearby debris pile, watches them with fierce eyes, still emitting a protective growl.

Catching her breath, Maali can't help but laugh. "Of all the things here, it's an 'iddy biddy pussy cat' that nearly takes out the great Noah," she jokes.

Noah, steadying himself, grins sheepishly. "Never underestimate a mother's instinct, I guess," he replies.

The amusement in Maali's eyes dims as she shifts her gaze back to Noah, the remnants of a smile still playing on her lips. Her tone is a mix of playful concern and genuine inquiry. "Mate, you alright, though?" she asks, her expression softening to show concern.

Noah, regaining his composure, gives her a small, reassuring nod. "Yeah, I'm fine," he replies with a hint of humility. "Just a gentle reminder from the past that I'm not as bulletproof as I once thought. Old scars have their own way of speaking up at inconvenient times, don't they?"

They have no time to dwell on the close call. The sudden movement of the van, its tail lights flaring bright before disappearing around another corner, propels them back into action. They resume their pursuit, the near-disaster a lingering reminder of the fragility of their mission, as they shadow the van like wolves on a relentless hunt.

Suddenly, a rush of familiarity swells in Maali. She scans the street signs, her mouth forming a thin line. "Back to Macquarie Street. This chase will last us till dawn," she grumbles, her frustration echoing in Noah's grimace.

The van makes a nimble evasion around the flaming wreckage of a car, inciting Maali to dart a regretful glance back at Noah, her words of apology forming on the precipice of her lips. Noah, however, dismisses her with a shake of his head, his tone edged with acidity. "No need," he grumbles, the frustration brewing beneath his words palpable. She acknowledges with a nod, steering her attention back to the unfolding pursuit.

The SorrowStar entourage operates as a singular entity, forcibly relocating burnt-out husks of vehicles to forge a path, which necessitates a brief halt. Ducking behind a mound of debris from a collapsed edifice, Noah and Maali covertly monitor their actions.

As grunts and expletives mingle with the crackling flames, Maali's gaze meanders down the thoroughfare, eventually settling on the majestic silhouette of the Archibald Fountain. A montage of her youth, a time brimming with carefree laughter and endless splashes in the fountain's cool waters, replays in her mind. A trace of a smile flickers across her lips as she murmurs to herself, "Those were the days..."

Tracking her gaze, Noah exhales a worn sigh. "I know... I wish I could've shown the kids before the divorce, before everything shattered. I was always too damn consumed with work."

An understanding softness steals over Maali's features, acknowledging his poignant regret. "And SorrowStar played a part in that, didn't they?"

A calm, heavy with unspoken sentiments, stretches between them as Noah's gaze turns vacant; laced with bitter resignation, he mutters, "It's like we're fading into the background of their opulent portrait, becoming mere whispers in their world of excess." The corrupt reach of SorrowStar had tainted even the once-cherished public locales, converting lush parks and vibrant spaces, like Hyde Park, into restricted territories.

With a hardening expression, Maali retorts, "Not on our watch."

A harsh, grinding noise suddenly ruptures the brooding calm, snapping Maali and Noah back into the present. Their attention refocuses. Having succeeded in clearing their route, the van revives its journey, picking up an unsettling pace. Noah grumbles, annoyed, "Looks like Manfred's feeling the heat. They're moving too fast for a stealthy tail."

Abruptly, the silent tension of the alleyway splinters as a disoriented man blunders out from a hidden recess, startling the SorrowStar team. His terror-stricken eyes reflect the bright headlights before his body crumbles under a ruthless volley of gunfire. The lethal tango unfolds with chilling efficiency, the squad members' actions synchronised and deadly.

Echoes of the gunshots ripple through the desolate streets, the terrifying staccato a harsh soundtrack to their pursuit. The finality of the man's fall etches a chilling image in their minds; his life snuffed out in the blink of an eye.

The van responds with a sudden lurch forward, its wheels squeal defiantly against the echoing gunshots. The sharp scent of burning rubber clashes with the acrid tang of gunpowder, wrapping them in a sinister veil.

Driven by raw willpower, Maali and Noah propel their bodies to their limits. As the lactic acid eats into Maali's muscles, her mind drifts away from the discomfort. Noah, shackled by the detritus of years of self-inflicted harm, endures the taxing physical exertion in stoic silence. They manage to keep up their pace, though Noah, with his leg playing up slightly, occasionally falls a step or two behind.

Abruptly, the abrasive shriek of tyres cuts through the air with the van jolting to an unexpected halt. The SorrowStar team converges rapidly, assuming a defensive perimeter with weapons at the ready. Taken aback, Maali and Noah scramble for cover behind the carcass of an overturned bus. When Maali dares to peek around the bus's wreckage, a chilling premonition tightens her gut. "No..."

"What is it?" Noah queries, his voice a rough undertone.

"Problems," Maali mutters, her voice heavy with foreboding. A surge of anxiety tightens around her heart as her gaze lands on the throng of civilians appearing before them. "A lot of them," she grimly adds. The crowd is a chaotic stew of gang members, minor crooks, and bewildered innocents, collectively shaping a daunting roadblock in their pursuit.

Noah sidles up to her, his eyes taking in the multifaceted display. "Lost souls searching for a compass," he observes darkly. "Those gang bangers at the front are weaponising their fear, using them as cannon fodder."

Maali's fists clench, her heart teetering between empathy and frustration. "They're cornered, blindly following the path of least resistance, hoping for a way out of this mayhem," she intones. "But they've been ensnared by the claws of these pitiless street rats."

As the crowd's agitation mounts, the air tingles with the promise of imminent violence. Noah's visage hardens. "This is a powder keg ready to explode," he predicts.

The SorrowStar operatives guarding the van attempt to assert their authority, using menacing gestures and barked orders, accompanied by brandishing their weapons. However, their display of force only exacerbates the anger brewing within the mob. Instead of quelling their fury, it intensifies, pushing the collective ire of the crowd dangerously close to a breaking point. Maali feels a surge of unease as she witnesses the mob grow more agitated, spurred on by their instigators. Objects are hurled through the air, glass bottles shattering on impact along with stones and the occasional shoe, fuelling the disorder. Amidst the commotion, Maali notices hesitant onlookers, their faces reflecting a dilemma: should they join in or stand against the rising tide of violence?

The mayhem peaks as a lone brick hurtles through the air, connecting with a resounding thud against the SorrowStar commander's Kevlar helmet. Momentarily disoriented, the commander staggers, though his helmet remains undamaged. A momentary silence settles over the crowd. For an instant, Maali dares to hope that some may recoil from the madness and choose to flee. She spots a few terrified individuals who seem ready to escape the escalating turmoil. Yet, the puppet masters orchestrating the mob have a different agenda. They rally their ranks, further stoking the crowd's collective fury and driving them toward greater conflict. Any chance of a peaceful resolution is extinguished, drowned by the seething rage of the mob.

The situation spirals into a shocking composition of merciless brutality. A barrage of bricks rains down on the commander. Despite being disoriented, he maintains his composure and retaliates with a single shot, snuffing the life out of a charging rioter. The deafening blast of the gunshot ripples through the chaos, ushering in an eerie moment of quiet. Some in the mob pause, their expressions revealing a glimmer of doubt, but their momentary uncertainty is swallowed by the aggressive surge of the majority, pressing forward despite the lethal warning.

A chilling order slices through the frenzy - "OPEN FIRE!" The SorrowStar team reacts in an instant, their hands twitching in anticipation as they unleash hell upon the mass of people. The crackle of gunfire fills the air, intermixed with the terrified screams of those in its path. The guards unleash a rain of less-lethal ammunition, seeking to quell the unruly mob. Yet, despite the onslaught of rubber bullets and tear gas, the crowd remains untiring, their resilience energised by desperation and a hunger for vengeance. A defiant roar from the mob drowns out the sounds of the countermeasures as they continue to press forward, refusing to retreat.

"Remember Castle Hill!" The leader's voice slices through the bedlam, sending a jolt of electricity through the crowd. Immediately, they erupt into a formidable stomp, their feet slamming against the ground in a unified, daunting beat that resounds off the cityscape. This fierce, rhythmic pounding becomes a heartbeat of rebellion, pulsating with raw, unbridled anger. Arms surge upwards, fists locked tight, while a wave of primal roars rolls forth, each one a searing cry for the innocents lost.

"Avenge the fallen!" echoes next, amplifying the intensity. As one, the crowd shifts into a dynamic force, a fusion of rhythmic strides and powerful voices. This formidable gathering, pulsating with collective strength and the haunting memory of loss, showcases their united front against the shadows of their history.

Recognising the shift in momentum, the guards' leader issues a grave command, urging them to tap into the most lethal aspects of their arsenal. A sadistic smirk curls their lips as they switch their rounds, their eyes gleaming with brutal delight. Unleashing an unholy storm of destruction, their scattershot shells tear through the frontline of the crowd. Each shot rips through flesh and bone, transforming bodies into gory mosaics. The mob's vanguard crumbles under the ruthless assault, leaving horrifying proof of the ferocity of their retaliation.

The second line of protesters fell victim to a ruthless tide of scattershot, their bodies breaking apart under the horrifying assault, painting an abject panorama of obliterated humanity. Amongst the devastation, the metallic reek of blood intertwining with the harsh scent of gunpowder saturates the air, creating a chilling mélange of scents. The coppery-toned metallic petrichor, a perverse reminder of blood freshly spilt, suffused each inhalation. The heavy stench clung to the surroundings as if violence itself had leached into the air.

As the horrifying storm of bullets and scattershot reigns, an even darker horror takes centre stage - a SorrowStar guard wielding a monstrous pulse rifle. His demeanour is unnervingly tranquil amid the confusion, watching the civilians with the cold, detached interest of a cat observing its prey. The people, in their panic, scatter in a desperate attempt to escape, reminiscent of mice frantically trying to elude a predator's lethal pounce. They stumble and trip over corpses, their flight a haunting choreography of fear and hopelessness, starkly echoing the merciless nature of a cat toying with its cornered prey.

The guard, embodying the devil in human guise, relishes in the unfolding terror. With predatory patience, he awaits the opportune moment when the upsurge of panic reaches its peak. As if on cue, he releases the cataclysmic force of the pulse rifle. A blinding beam of white energy lacerates the scene, leaving in its wake a path of unspeakable destruction. His merciless timing is chillingly perfect, plunging the battlefield into a pit of terror from which there is no escape.

The scene worsens into a repugnant spectacle. Any semblance of unity amongst the mob crumbles, their erstwhile leaders now reduced to lifeless husks riddled with bullets or evaporated into dust. Disoriented survivors stumble blindly in a vain quest for safety, their spirits crushed by the savagery they've witnessed.

Maali's heart pounds in her chest as she watches the SorrowStar guards, their faces warped into surreal masks of delight, mercilessly hunt the surviving civilians. Like predators culling the weakest from a herd, they unleash a hail of bullets upon the exposed backs of the fleeing crowd, carving paths of slaughter in their wake. The air is filled with horrifying screams, gunfire, and laughter.

Back at the scene, two guards linger, wallowing in the aftermath of their cruelty. Their laughter, cold and hollow, resonates through the blood-drenched streets as one of them nonchalantly lights a cigarette. His inhumanity reaches a chilling peak as he uses a severed arm as an impromptu footrest, a grisly trophy of their conquest.

An ire unlike anything she's ever felt ignites within Maali. It consumes her, turning her vision red, her desire for vengeance a living, breathing entity that claws at her soul. She feels her body respond, fists clenching, muscles tensing, every fibre of her being yearning to retaliate against the monsters before her.

But then, a touch, firm and grounding: Noah's grip on her arm, a tether to reason in a world gone mad.

"Compose yourself," he murmurs, his voice a low rumble, laden with fury yet tempered by wisdom. "Charging in headlong is suicide and sacrificing our lives won't buy them safety. We strategise."

His words penetrate the fog of her anger, and she takes a shuddering breath, forcing herself to see past the raw emotion. They are outnumbered, outgunned, and the guards are relentless in their pursuit of power. Acting impulsively would only add their names to the list of the dead.

Noah casts a sombre glance at Maali. "Remember," he explains, his voice a steely whisper, "their brutality isn't just for fun. It's programmed. The SorrowStar goons, they're wired with an AI targeting system that enhances their ferocity."

Noah's expression etched with a mix of understanding and revulsion. "I've felt it before," he admits quietly, his voice carrying the weight of personal experience. "Back when I was 19, in the Northern campaigns…in Darwin. There's something intoxicating about the rush, the power. The AI might assist, but the pull of that dopamine hit, that's on us. It's human, all too human."

He glances at Maali, his eyes reflecting a depth of introspection. "I broke free from it, but it wasn't easy. No matter how euphoric it felt, deep down, I knew. I knew the difference between right and wrong, good and evil. It was a thin line, blurred by the chaos of war. My faith," he pauses, searching for the right words, "my faith in something greater, in God, it gave me a perspective. It reminded me that we have a choice."

He sighs, a hint of sorrow in his gaze. "The human mind, if not guided, tends to choose hedonism over self-restraint. It's easier to succumb to immediate pleasures than to follow a path of self-denial and righteousness. But that's the dangerous allure of violence. It can feel good, dangerously good, but it's a deceptive trap, a path leading away from our humanity."

Noah looks at Maali, his gaze intense. "But remember, Maali," he adds, "this system doesn't create monsters from saints. It only reveals and amplifies what was always there, lurking deep within. It can't turn a good man bad. A truly good man would be repulsed, not seduced by such a system. These men... they had that darkness, that willingness to harm within them from the start."

Maali absorbs his words, her mind grappling with the horrifying implications. The realisation paints a chilling portrait of the SorrowStar goons: men with inherent propensities for violence, ensnared by a system that exploited and amplified their worst tendencies.

"But it's these men," he continues, "those who could resist the allure of such a twisted reward system... those are the men we need to rally. Men who value life and decency over a cheap high and the thrill of power."

She looks at Noah, her gaze hardened. The enemy wasn't just SorrowStar or even the goons that carried out its violence. The real enemy was this perverse system and the cruel tendency within some men that it exploited.

"The battle we're fighting," she says, her voice barely above a whisper, "it's not just against SorrowStar. It's against the darkness within us, the part that can be seduced by such cruelty."

Noah nods, his expression grave. "Exactly, Maali. And it's a battle we must win, for the sake of all who've been victimised by it."

Her begrudging nod conveys her inner turmoil, her acquiescence to his pragmatism not easing her seething resentment. Her hand tightens around the rifle, its weight a solemn reminder of the dire stakes they face. As the remaining SorrowStar fiends disappear into the distance, each anguished cry and receding gunshot fans the flames.

Maali's gaze sharpens, like a hawk zeroing in on its prey. "Eyes sharp, Noah. It's our turn to hunt."

CHAPTER 6:
Rescue

With the din of battle receding into the distance, the remaining guards, ensnared in their twisted satisfaction, languidly savour their cigarettes, their unchallenged arrogance apparent in every casual puff.

"Hey, we're professionals, right? Gotta maintain that badass image," the shorter guard quips, taking a drag from his cigarette.

His companion, a cloud of smoke escaping his lips, chuckles and replies, "You said it, my friend. Smoking may kill, but we're in a league of our own when it comes to taking lives!"

"Haha! We're so good at what we do, we deserve an award for the 'Best Massacre of the Year,'" they both burst into laughter, revelling in their distorted sense of accomplishment.

Meanwhile, Noah's intense gaze meets Maali's, and he utters in a hushed tone, "It's time to make them pay."

They cautiously navigate around the twisted metal and shattered glass remnants of a bus at its now final stop, their weapons poised and ready for action. With calculated precision, in a single fluid motion, Noah plunges his prised Fairbairn-Sykes knife into the guard's supraclavicular fossa, the blade penetrating with ruthless efficiency. It carves a path of devastation, slashing through flesh, tendons, and vertebrae. Blood gushes forth, drenching the ground. Meanwhile, Maali's rifle unleashes a devastating burst, cleanly removing the top of the other guard's skull. Yet, to their astonishment, he remains standing, defying the natural laws of gravity. His eyes stare blankly, and a lit cigarette held in place by lingering neural impulses clings stubbornly between his lifeless lips, smouldering away.

Maali's eyes gleam with vindication as she steps over the fallen corpse. Her hand reaches out, swiftly plucking the lit cigarette from the dead man's mouth, her twisted smile revealing a hunger for justice. "Take a seat, buddy," she hisses, forcefully pushing the body onto a dislodged seat from the wreckage.

She takes a drag from the cigarette, the harsh fumes filling her already air-polluted lungs. She exhales a cloud of smoke and lets out a dark chuckle. "Damn, Noah, these taste like shit. Why the hell do you even bother?"

Noah's grin widens, a glimmer of dark amusement dancing in his eyes. "You know, Maali, it's all about the little things that make life worth living, or in this case, worth surviving," he quips, taking the smoke from Maali before helping himself to a dramatic drag from the cigarette. "The world may be crumbling around us, but damn it, I'm not letting it ruin my smoking experience."

Their brief moment dissipates as they approach the locked rear doors of the van. The atmosphere grows tense as Noah and Maali find themselves at the back of the van, facing the stubborn resistance of a locked door. Frustration etches itself onto Noah's face, his muscles straining as he tugs at the immovable handle. Simultaneously, Maali rummages through the spoils of their recent conquest, her fingers closing around a discarded pulse charge.

An impish grin cuts across her face as she swiftly attaches the charge to the stubborn lock. A flick of her thumb initiates the countdown, prompting her and Noah to retreat in unison. The ensuing detonation is surprisingly muted, an understated clapping sound that heralds the annihilation of the lock in a perfectly round hole. A fog of dust and smoke billows from the breach, giving the now accessible van an ominously veiled entrance.

Their triumphant moment is interrupted abruptly when the crack of a gunshot pierces the air. The bullet, meant for Maali, whizzes past her, leaving a sonic echo in its wake. Reacting with lightning-fast reflexes, a SorrowStar guard lunges out, brandishing a knife aimed at Noah. Quick as a striking cobra, Maali intervenes, throwing herself at the attacker in a collision of raw force that knocks them both sprawling onto the ground. In the midst of the frenzy, Noah squeezes the trigger, his retaliatory shot blindly hitting into the depth of the vans load space.

Amidst the desperate fray, the SS goon gains the upper hand, overpowering Maali and straddling her, his grip on her collar tightening as he thrusts the knife menacingly towards her exposed throat. Propelled by sheer survival instinct, Maali intuitively jerks her head to the side, narrowly evading the deadly strike. The sharp blade grazes her neck, leaving behind a searing, shallow cut. Seizing the pivotal moment, she summons every ounce of strength, delivering a punishing knee to the guard's groin and forcefully driving him away. A surge of iron-willed resolve electrifies her; she swiftly retrieves a concealed boot knife and lunges forward, ready to unleash a relentless counterassault.

Her thrust is parried as he desperately blocks with his hand, redirecting the blade and throwing off her aim. The sharp edge finds purchase between two ribs, penetrating deep into his torso. Despite the intense pain, the guard refuses to relinquish his grip, yanking her forcefully towards him, delivering a bone-crushing head-butt. The brutal impact shatters Maali's nose, sending a searing pain radiating through her face as blood gushes from the devastated cartilage. A metallic tang fills her mouth as the crimson stream cascades down her contorted features, mingling with the sweat and dirt of battle. Despite the blinding pain, her previous strike must have found its mark, disrupting the guard's coordination. With a dazed expression etched across his face, he weakly retrieves the knife from his own chest, struggling to maintain his grip.

Seizing the opening, Maali instinctively reacts. With the focused intensity of a predatory beast, she wrests the blade from his faltering grasp, her fingers gripping it with dogged obstinacy. With a surge of primal ferocity, she drives the knife upward from the base of his ribcage, delivering a merciless strike that cleaves through flesh, muscle, and vital organs.

Blood erupts from the guard's mortal wound, a horrific fountain of red that splatters across the asphalt. As his grip slackens in the throes of death, Maali pulls her knife free, wiping the stained blade on the blood-soaked fabric of his uniform. Turning back to the scene, her eyes dart to Noah. He's engaged in a tense standoff with the van driver, bullets flying as he keeps the foe pinned in the driver's cabin.

"Get in and get him!" Noah shouts, taking advantage of the brief reprieve to scrounge for resources amongst the fallen SS. With a resolute nod, Maali springs into action, disappearing into the van's cavernous interior.

Inside, the blackness is near-total, a void that makes her heart pound with anticipation. Her hand flails in the gloom, finally landing on the smooth surface of a light stick. With a snap, the stick illuminates, casting a surreal green glow across the confined space. As the light spreads, the pallid hands of an unresponsive figure on the floor come into focus.

Her heart pounding, Maali's gaze lingers on the figure, the sight sending shivers down her spine. His deathly pallor and the straight jacket constricting his body only heighten the sense of dread that fills the van. Driven by a mixture of compassion and urgency, she searches the fallen guard's lifeless form, her trembling hands finding the key to unlock the leg irons.

"Can you hear me?" she whispers, her voice laden with concern and trepidation. The prisoner's weak nod confirms his tenuous awareness. Time is of the essence as she deftly slices through the buckles of the straight jacket, freeing his arms. With unsteady steps, the prisoner reaches out for support. "We must hurry," Maali urges, a hint of trepidation underlying her words. "We need to escape before they return."

Noah's voice rises above the riotous backdrop of shouts and gunfire. "It's time to move!" he shouts, lobbing his newly acquired grenade at the approaching SorrowStar team. The explosive impact rips through the air, momentarily disorienting their adversaries. "Don't stop, keep going!" Noah's voice carries a sense of fortitude as he lays down suppressive fire, skilfully keeping the SS team at bay.

Relieved and with little time to spare, Maali and their newfound ally reach the shelter of the old parliament building. Hastily, they dart inside, Noah forcefully closing the door behind them. With a swift motion, he surveys the abandoned structure, spotting a large, fallen beam nearby. He quickly drags the heavy beam towards the door, its rough edges scraping against the worn floor. With a grunt of exertion, he wedges one end of the beam against the doorknob and braces the other end against a sturdy piece of wreckage, sealing them off from the outside world. For now. Turning to face their next move, he leads the way deeper into the abandoned structure.

Seeking a moment of respite, they discover an intact room in a wing off the vast, desolate lobby. It offers a glimmer of hope, a potential escape route if necessary. Maali guides their rescued prisoner into a weathered chair, her touch gentle and reassuring. "Take it easy, we're here now." Her attention shifts to the rope securing the bag over the prisoner's head. Recognising the risk of using her knife, she focuses on carefully loosening the knot.

As the tension eases and the bag begins to come off, a low voice reverberates through the air, filled with appreciation. "I believe a moment of gratitude is in order."

Maali shakes her head, the words resonating within her more as a feeling than a sound. She looks up at Noah, a mirrored expression of bewilderment etched across his face.

As Maali's gaze carefully traverses their enigmatic companion, a sense of awe supersedes her initial apprehension. The unfamiliar entity is nothing short of imposing, standing over two meters tall with elongated limbs, giving it an otherworldly silhouette. Its emaciated frame tells a story of deprivation and hardship, yet a palpable aura of rock-solid strength radiates from it, shattering any perception of weakness.

Trepidation grips Maali as she continues to unveil the captive's identity, her hands unfastening the sack that masks its features. As the bag peels away, her breath hitches in her throat, the palpable tension in the air rendering her momentarily mute. The first eye contact is a pivotal moment, a wordless exchange that plunges Maali's heart into a vortex of shock and dreadful recognition.

The being before her is far from a typical specimen. Its eyes, burning with an intelligence and resilience unbeknownst to her, reflect an amalgamation of untold secrets and unearthed wisdom. Their luminescent glow is captivating, drawing her in while subtly alarming her senses.

Exotic aromas fill the confined space, seeping into Maali's nostrils - a blend of fragrant earthiness mixed with a hint of sweet floral notes that she can't quite place. It's pleasantly disorienting, stirring emotions and thoughts she didn't anticipate. As her bare hand instinctively reaches out to touch the entity, she is surprised by the texture of its skin - cold yet oddly comforting, as smooth as polished stone yet strangely flexible. It's an encounter with the unfamiliar, yet the creature's vulnerability invokes within her a wave of empathy she never thought she'd feel for an alien life form.

Immersed in this surreal exchange, Maali finds herself at the precipice of unknown territory. The silent figure before her isn't just another being. It is a puzzle, an enigma wrapped in the mystery of the cosmos. As her gaze softens, meeting the glow of the entity's eyes once more, she feels the fear of the unknown and the echoes of cosmic whispers. She can almost hear the sacred whispers of her ancestors carried on the winds of time, their age-old wisdom reminding her of the duty ingrained in her spirit.

CHAPTER 7:
Empathy

Paralysed, Maali stands anchored to the spot, her eyes wide as the boundaries of her understanding shatter. 'This can't be human...' The thought reverberates through her mind, echoing endlessly, as she grapples with the surreal reality unfolding before her.

The being, seated in enforced vulnerability, is humanoid in the most basic sense: it has the requisite number of limbs, ears, and facial features. But, as if viewed through a distorted mirror, everything is eerily off-kilter. Its form is painfully emaciated, each rib and bone pressing urgently against its diaphanous skin as if trying to escape a prison of flesh. The face, sculpted with sharp angles and deep hollows, presents an almost ethereal appearance, as if the skin is delicately stretched over a distinctly skeletal bone structure. A mouth devoid of lips is merely a haunting slit, an unnatural chasm of silence. The remnants of what might once have been a nose are a pair of cavernous nostrils, inhaling the air with a desperate hunger.

Yet, it is the eyes that ensnare her completely, beckoning her into their depth. Eyes that don't possess the familiar anatomy of a sclera or iris. Instead, she finds herself plummeting through the vastness of space, drowning in a swirling sea of stars and galaxies, each one dancing with a life of its own. The left eye, a canvas painted with the softest shade of cerulean, sparkles with constellations she's never seen, their stories unknown. The right, awash in a serene shade of emerald, pulses with the gentle rhythm of distant cosmic events. The galaxies within seem to breathe, expanding and contracting, drawing her deeper into their narrative.

A shiver races down her spine, and her breath catches, trapped in the vice of awe and trepidation. An overwhelming sensation envelops her – a curious mix of fear, wonder, and an inexplicable connection to the universe embodied within the creature's gaze. It's as if, for a fleeting moment, she stands on the precipice of understanding something far greater than herself, something vast and ancient.

In a deliberate, unhurried motion, the creature blinks, exhaling a deep breath through its elongated nostrils. Maali feels an overwhelming urge to extend her hand, drawn inexplicably towards it. As her fingertips make contact with the creature's face, Noah's eyes narrow, his deeply ingrained cynicism and paranoia overpowering his initial shock.

"Careful. We don't know what--" His voice is drowned out, completely eclipsed by the profound connection formed as her hand meets the creature's otherworldly countenance.

Gently cradling its face, she is engulfed in a rush of air and sound, her senses spinning in a sudden vertigo. The resonant voice from before reverberates around her, its echoes permeating her being.

"See me, friend. See me and know."

Maali's senses are ambushed, inundated by a torrent of images and thoughts rushing through her psyche like a violent storm. Each fragmented memory, each sliver of emotion, whirls around in chaotic fervour, threatening to pull her into a vertiginous abyss of her own making. As the intensity mounts, she instinctively clamps her eyes shut, seeking refuge in the darkness, but the unrestrained wave of recollection threatens to pull her under, drowning her in a sea of yesterdays.

Then, just as the maelstrom within her seems insurmountable, a touch — soft, ethereal — graces her shoulder, rooting her to the here and now. It's like an anchor in the storm, a beacon through the fog, casting a lifeline into the depths of her thoughts.

"Peace, friend. Breathe. Know I am foreign to your kind. Witness."

Hesitantly, she parts her eyelids, and the vision that greets her is a breathtaking departure from anything she's known. The horizon unfolds into a sprawling cityscape of extra-terrestrial genius. Fluid, serpentine structures of gleaming metals and luminous crystals weave through the skies, mingling seamlessly with buildings that pulse with vibrant, living energy. Everywhere she looks, organic and engineered marvels blend in a design that challenges the very essence of reality. The world pulsates, alive and humming, each structure singing a song of glorious civilisations and unfathomable technology.

The voice, now clearer yet still echoing with the weight of eons, murmurs again, its timbre resonating with the depths of the cosmos.

"We are Calistin. United in peace. United in time. One voice, many parts. Knowledge acquired through ages. Remember this: One bleeds... all bleed."

In a fleeting blink of cosmic time, a vast expanse of desolation stretches out before her, the barren remnants of a once flourishing civilisation. The mournful echoes of destruction, a universe grieving its own loss, weigh heavily upon her heart. But then, like the quiet inhale following a lamenting sigh, the wasteland stirs.

From the ashes of obliteration, a phoenix-like city begins to rise. Its majesty unfurls, surpassing the vestiges of anguish, standing as a testament to hope and resurrection. Memories cascade, forming a kaleidoscopic tapestry. She perceives beings akin to the one they had saved, guiding the reconstruction, choreographing the pattern of creation and rejuvenation. Wars dissolve into murmurs, cities soar to caress the skies, and grand vessels, like arcs of salvation, break free from the gravitational clutches of their home, journeying forth under the tender gaze of a cerise sun.

Vivid colours burst forth in her mind's eye, painting the world in hues more intense than any she's seen before. The air around her seems to vibrate with the pulse of the Earth; each beat syncing with her heart. Ethereal shapes and ancestral spirits dance in her periphery, their forms shifting between the tangible world and a mystical realm that lies just beyond.

The sky above morphs into a canvas of cosmic wonder, streaked with radiant lights that tell ancient stories of creation and destruction, of love and loss. She feels an overwhelming sense of interconnectedness, as if every living creature and inanimate object around her shares a common thread, weaving through the fabric of existence.

In this trance-like state, time loses its linearity. Past, present, and future merge into a singular, endless moment, revealing the cyclic nature of life. As she witnesses this cycle of death and rebirth, an age-old narrative subtly intertwines itself — a timeless tale of sacrifice, redemption, and rebirth.

"We sought knowledge, truth, and above all, kinship." Generations of collective memory unfold before her as the Calistin embark on an insatiable quest spanning unfathomable distances. Yet, despite their yearning for peace, they encounter... something. Maali struggles to comprehend its nature, but she senses its malevolence. The Calistin recoil in terror before dispersing once more, driven to seek out and warn any sentient life about the encroaching darkness they have encountered.

Finding her voice at last, Maali whispers, "You came to help us?"

With a deep, resounding rumble that seems to resonate within her very being, the voice returns, its timbre clearer and more flowing, as if synchronising with Maali's consciousness. "Yes, it would have been unjust to abandon a younger race to such a dreadful fate without any preparation," it reverberates. Through the eyes of the prisoner, Maali's consciousness is transported into a vivid and immersive memory. She finds herself aboard a small scout ship, its purpose to observe Earth and establish communication with receptive leaders.

A sense of unease permeates the scene as the vessel encounters a catastrophic event, resulting in a loss of power during atmospheric entry. The ensuing crash claims the lives of half the crew, leaving only the prisoner and another survivor behind. Maali feels the disorienting impact and the overwhelming grief that follows.

As if she is standing beside the prisoner, Maali witnesses their discovery and subsequent recovery by a human figure. Alongside a team of soldiers adorned in unmarked uniforms, the humans take the extraterrestrial survivors to a hidden facility buried beneath the desert sands of Australia. The memory unfolds with palpable tension as the prisoners become subjects of endless examinations, and the remnants of their ship are meticulously dissected in a relentless pursuit of technological secrets.

"The captors were unable to comprehend our true names. Human perception cannot grasp their proper essence," the voice explains, its resonance growing even more harmonious with Maali's thoughts. "Consequently, we were assigned human names to facilitate interaction. The other survivor was called Des. I was given the name Diandra."

As Maali's vision unfolds, she witnesses the events within the secret facility playing out before her eyes. In the beginning, she sees glimpses of human captors who initially appear helpful and eager to facilitate a shared learning experience. They seemed genuinely invested in understanding the extra-terrestrial visitors and offering assistance wherever possible.

However, there is a subtle shift in the narrative as the scenes progress. Maali notices a gradual change in the humans' demeanour, a veiled sense of manipulation that creeps into their actions and motives. The once collaborative atmosphere begins to unravel, replaced by a growing curiosity tinged with a hidden agenda.

This underlying sense of manipulation, while understated at first, hints at a darker turn in the humans' intentions.

And then, as if synchronised with Maali's visual experience, Diandra's voice resonates once again, providing a clear explanation for what transpired. "Eventually, during a botched attempt to treat a wound on Des, one of their jailers was exposed to a large amount of Calistin blood. The man soon found that old scars were healing and his arthritis was fading. "We live long. Our blood is pure. Engineered to allow healthy bodies for the entire life. It has... powerful effects on humans."

As the vision intensifies, Maali's heart races with a growing sense of dread and horror. The illusion of collaboration shatters, giving way to a nightmarish scenario that unfolds before her eyes. The scenes playing out resemble a twisted scene from a horror film, with the visitors, Des and Diandra, trapped in a relentless cycle of cruel and callous experimentation.

The captors, driven by their insatiable curiosity, repeatedly puncture the visitors' flesh with needles, draining obscene amounts of blood from their frail bodies. Each session leaves the extra-terrestrials more withered, their strength waning with every extraction. Des, unable to bear the relentless torment, pleads and begs for mercy, hoping for a brief respite from the agony. Yet, his pleas fall on deaf ears as the captors cruelly disregard his suffering, exacerbating his deterioration with each subsequent blood draw.

Maali's soul shatters, bearing witness to the monstrous culmination of their captors' cruelty. For five harrowing years, they had leached away at Des's very essence, slowly eroding the core of his being. And now, in the stark confines of a soulless chamber, on a frigid, rigid metal table, he breathes his last. Void of warmth, comfort, or any semblance of compassion, the room seems to echo with his fading heartbeat. The very researchers who masterminded this slow descent into oblivion respond with nothing but a cold, detached murmur, their callousness a chilling demonstration to the depths of their inhumanity.

The cruelty doesn't end there. Des' lifeless body is subjected to further indignities. It is callously dissected, stripped of any useful information, and then incinerated. The remains are unceremoniously disposed of in a shallow grave filled with cement, a final act of disrespect that adds to Diandra's overwhelming despair.

As the haunting visions continue to unfold, the voice of Diandra resonates in Maali's mind, recounting the dire transformation that took place over time. The alien blood, once drained from the visitors, was refined and manipulated, twisted into something more useful for mankind's perverse pursuits. The captors found a plentiful supply of human test subjects, their lives sacrificed in the name of progress and power.

Within the recesses of Diandra's memories, fragments of the supplier's identity emerge, though vague and hazy. Yet, as the details coalesce, a chilling realisation grips Maali, causing a cold sweat to trickle down her brow. The leader, the orchestrator of this abhorrent enterprise, the one who oversaw the torment and exploitation, is none other than the same man who had inflicted unspeakable trauma upon her years ago.

A shudder courses through Maali's body as the memories resurface, vivid and haunting. She recalls the chilling encounter in the gang's chop shop, where she had been pinned down, vulnerable and terrified. The leader had sought to subject her to his heinous desires, only to be thwarted by the intervention of Noah and Maria. The traumatic experience had left scars etched deep within her psyche, haunting her dreams and tormenting her waking hours.

In this pivotal moment, the threads of past and present intertwine, unravelling a web of interconnected horrors. The memories of the chop shop leader, whose presence instilled fear and left indelible scars on Maali's soul, resurface with haunting clarity. The realisation dawns upon her that the atrocities unfolding before her are not isolated incidents but part of a broader, malevolent design.

As the pieces fall into place, Maali's mind races, drawing connections between the past and the present. The stand-down order issued by Manfred echoes in her thoughts. The pieces of the puzzle start to align, hinting at a deeper, more sinister plot that spans decades, crossing paths with Diandra and reaching into the very core of their current ordeal.

A chilling realisation creeps over Maali as she contemplates the implications. Manfred, the orchestrator of her past torment, may not only be connected to the harrowing events that have unfolded in her past but could also hold a significant role in the sinister machinations they now face. The name resonates with an eerie familiarity, intertwining with the present revelations of the Calistin entity.

As the truth unfurls before them, the pieces of the intricate puzzle start to align in Maali's mind "But that was ten years ago..." she murmurs. "How long were you held?" The duration of Diandra's captivity sends a shiver down her spine, realising the extent of the Calistin's suffering. "Many cycles," Diandra responds in a tone laced with a touch of resignation. "Your species' perception of time is strange. Perhaps twenty years? More?"

Together, they bear witness to the memories, observing the insidious transformation of the company that would become SorrowStar. The exploitation of Diandra as nothing more than a blood source becomes painfully clear—a surge of anger wells within Maali as she comprehends the depths of the corporation's heinous acts.

It all falls into place now. SorrowStar's vast wealth and unchecked power cannot be attributed to mere chance or legitimate business endeavours. They have used their security and general goods sales as a deceptive front, concealing their true source of prosperity. The serum, the blood extracted from Diandra and his kind, holds the key to their rapid ascent and financial dominance. Maali's mind races with the possibilities, realising the immense potential and sinister implications of the powerful substance.

The revelation sends a chill down her spine. With a virtually limitless supply of the serum, SorrowStar possesses a weapon of unimaginable power. The prospect of what could be achieved with such a substance in the hands of corrupt politicians, tyrants, and the wealthy elite is both terrifying and alluring. Maali envisions a dark market where this coveted resource commands exorbitant prices and fuels the ambitions of those hungry for absolute power.

"No wonder they were so trigger-happy. Losing you is like losing the Holy Grail to them." She allows Diandra to witness her thoughts.

The connection between Maali and Diandra deepens as she allows herself to be vulnerable, sharing not only her immediate thoughts but also opening the floodgates to the centuries-old scars etched into the psyche of her people. She projects to him the agony, the tears, and the resilience of her ancestors.

He witnesses through her eyes the haunting shadows of events like the Myall Creek massacre and the Convincing Ground atrocity, where innocence was stolen and lives were ruthlessly extinguished. More than just images of brutality, she shares with him the profound sense of loss — of culture, identity, and family, as generations were ripped away from their homes, their voices silenced, and their stories rewritten by their oppressors.

Through this communion of souls, Diandra feels the weight of the stolen generations, the piercing pain of children torn from their mothers' arms, of traditions trampled upon, and identities erased. A dark tapestry of suffering unravels, showing him a people who, despite the depths of their pain, have stood unwavering, embodying a spirit of survival and resistance.

His newfound understanding draws them closer, forging an even stronger bond of empathy and purpose. Maali's voice, laden with conviction, breaks the silence, "We won't let them take you back. Not after what you've been through or what my people have endured. Our stories interweave now, and together, we'll resist."

Returning to the present moment, the crumbling remnants of the old parliament serve as a stark backdrop to their conversation. Maali's thoughts drift to the unimaginable suffering Diandra endured, and she reaches into her knapsack, retrieving one of the vials of D.TEM. Despite knowing its true nature now, the sight of it still elicits a visceral reaction within her.

She holds the vial up before Diandra, offering a glimmer of hope. "We stopped a shipment of this earlier tonight. Could it help you?" Her intentions are rooted in goodwill, hoping that the substance they recovered could offer some relief or aid to the tormented Calistin.

Diandra's luminous eyes lock onto the vial, and an intense shudder courses through his fragile frame. His voice whispers into Maali's mind, conveying a sense of profound disturbance. "No, this is an abomination, a perversion. Twisted and corrupted, an affront to the sacred laws of nature, reshaped to appease human ambition." Though the words offer a glimpse of the altered nature of the substance, Maali senses that the reality may be even more twisted. Diandra nods, acknowledging the thought that arises within them. "It is taboo. To mutate the blood we are given. To take it back would be even worse." Another shudder wracks his body, accompanied by a wheezing fit that further underscores the anguish inflicted upon him.

Maali's heart sinks, grappling with the weight of their limited options. The vial, once brimming with potential salvation, now represents the cruel reality of the dark forces they face. With a mix of disappointment and concern, she swiftly shoves the vial back into her bag, not wanting to exacerbate Diandra's distress any further. "Alright. You'll be okay."

Noah, ever vigilant, steps closer, his eyes fixed on Diandra with suspicion. His voice carries a sense of urgency as he confronts Maali. "What the hell was that?"

Maali meets Noah's gaze, her brow arching in confusion. "What do you mean?"

He gestures emphatically at Diandra. "What just happened to you? You looked at its eyes," Noah points a finger accusingly at Diandra, "and then you started shaking like you were having a seizure. Your eyes got all glassy, and all of a sudden, you're offering the D.TEM to it like you're best friends."

Maali looks back at Diandra and receives a gentle mental nudge. "It is well, my friend. Please, tell your ally what I showed you."

She rubs her forehead, feeling the weight of the information she received from Diandra. "Diandra showed me things, somehow. I witnessed everything that SorrowStar has subjected him to." Maali sighs a hint of exhaustion in her voice. "At least that's his Earth-given name. The researchers at SorrowStar called him that."

Noah's eyes widen in disbelief. "Diandra? That's what the SS researchers called him? What's his real name?" he asks, his curiosity piqued.

Maali looks back at Diandra, awaiting his response. The alien sighs and tilts his head, remaining silent as he communicates directly into her mind. "Your species lacks the physical capability to pronounce my true name. It requires additional organs and can only be uttered in an audio frequency that would damage your auditory nerves. I have no intention of causing you harm."

Maali blinks a few times, mumbling, "Uh, thanks? I guess."

"What?" Noah waves his hand in front of her impatiently. "Thanks for what? Nobody said anything."

"You didn't hear him?" She asks, pointing at Diandra.

Noah shakes his head. "He hasn't said a word. He hasn't even opened his mouth once since thanking us."

"His mind is more closed than yours," Diandra whispers into her head. "I was not able to create a psionic bridge. Please let him know that I apologise for the confusion."

"He apologised for causing confusion," Maali explains, her voice tinged with uncertainty. She shifts her gaze away from Diandra, only to find Noah more perplexed than ever. "He was communicating with me telepathically, somehow. But for some reason, he couldn't do the same with you."

Noah's expression remains locked in confusion as he stares at her. After a beat, Maali adds with a playful smirk, "It's an IQ thing, Noah. You know, telepathy requires a certain... intellectual finesse."

Noah's expression shifts from confusion to a knowing smirk. "Ah, an IQ prerequisite for telepathy? Perhaps my mind is too occupied with tangible strategies to save our asses," he retorts playfully. Then, with a teasing glint in his eye, he adds, "Besides, isn't it that women are the ones who can read minds? Seems you're living up to that legend, Sis."

Maali chuckles briefly, conceding with a light-hearted, "Touché, Noah." But then, her expression quickly sobers at the gravity of their situation. "Please, just trust me," she pleads, desperation creeping into her voice. Noah's frown deepens, and with a grumble, he steps further into the hallway. Maali's attention returns to Diandra, a spark of realisation igniting within her. "What's this around your neck?" she inquires, her hand reaching out to touch the tight, black ring encircling the base of Diandra's throat.

"Wait!" His urgent voice reverberates through her thoughts, halting her hand just inches away from touching the ring. "The device is designed to prevent my escape. If I were to be freed from it, I could reach out to other Calistin, regardless of the distance between us."

Curiosity mixed with caution fills Maali's expression. "Then why not let me remove it?"

Diandra blinks slowly, his gaze fixed on the ominous ring. "There's something inside it, an explosive of sorts. They demonstrated its power on one of the bodies recovered from our crashed vessel. If anyone attempts to remove it without the proper tools, it will detonate, severing my head from my body."

Maali yanks her hands away from the ring. "What in the-!" She shakes her head, disgusted. "SorrowStar's R&D boys really are messed up in the head."

Diandra gives an amused grunt. "Indeed."

Startled by a thunderous explosion echoing from outside, Maali and Diandra whirl their heads towards the entrance of the room, their hearts racing with anticipation. The chaotic scene unfolds as Noah bursts into the room, dragging one of the incapacitated SorrowStar guards by the collar, his grip steadfast.

Noah's eyes flash with a predatory sharpness as he moves in on the dazed guard. With a fluid motion born of rigorous training, he grabs the guard's arm in a classic Mau Rakau technique, twisting it just enough to force the weapon from his grasp. His other hand strikes a pressure point on the guard's shoulder, momentarily stunning him. Noah then uses the guard's own momentum to spin him around and forcefully pushes him to the ground.

In one fluid motion, Noah flips the guard onto his stomach. He expertly intertwines his fingers around the man's wrists, pulling the arms behind his back in a secure and methodical lock. The technique, reminiscent of a practised jiujitsu hold, ensures the guard is immobilised without unnecessary force. The guard, now fully realising his defeat, groans weakly, his attempts at resistance futile against Noah's masterful control.

With a deft flick of his wrist, Noah produces a zip tie, its tail whipping through the air. He loops it around the guard's wrists, the zip echoing crisply as it tightens. Then, with a deliberate tug, he cinches the tie a notch tighter, ensuring the guard feels the bite of the plastic digging into his skin. The guard's hands, now bound, cease their flailing, immobilised and secured by Noah's precise and unforgiving restraint.

Noah's posture stiffens as the air in the room thickens with tension, every breath echoing the charged atmosphere of an impending storm. The weight of history, of struggles past and present, seems to converge in this very moment. With each heartbeat, the essence of acceptance — not of defeat, but of challenge — pulses within him. Grasping the guard's radio and pulse rifle, their cold touch grounding him, he becomes the personification of readiness. As his eyes lock onto Maali's, a silent pact is forged. Like many warriors before them, they walk the line between shadow and light, life and death, and though the storm of battle looms, they stand united in its eye.

"The goons are making their way through the building, armed with flashbangs," Noah warns. "We don't have much time before they discover their comrade is missing. We need to move! Now!"

Maali's gaze shifts towards Diandra, her concern evident in her eyes. "Diandra can't move on his own," she informs Noah, her voice unshakable.

Noah's expression tightens with a mix of frustration and tenacity. "Then we'll lend him our strength. Let's go." He takes a step closer, reaching out to grasp Diandra's left arm firmly. Maali positions herself on the other side, offering her support as they lift him up together.

With cautious steps, they navigate through the hall, their movements shrouded in silence. The echoes of another pair of flashbangs reverberate through the air, followed by the distant voice of someone shouting, "Clear!"

The sound of flashbangs continues to echo down the hall, growing closer with each detonation. Noah's voice barely rises above a whisper. "If my memory serves me right, there's a spot at the back of the building where the wall has collapsed. Let's hope the goons haven't taken position there yet."

Maali nods in agreement. She follows Noah as they manoeuvre through another hallway, their hearts pounding in sync with each step. The deafening blast of another flashbang coincides with their arrival at an abandoned office located towards the rear of the building. They pause in the doorway, their eyes widening at the sight before them.

"No..." Noah mutters through gritted teeth. Their path to freedom is obstructed by a mound of debris—collapsing roof sections and discarded refuse—forming a barrier just high enough to block the hole in the wall. Maali turns to Noah, their gazes meeting, and he motions for her to investigate the pile while he maintains his grip on Diandra.

Maali cautiously manoeuvres away from Diandra's side, her focus now fixed on the pile of debris. The stench of decaying trash assaults her senses as she examines the mound, comprised of discarded remnants left by a previous inhabitant who sought shelter within the abandoned building. Among the detritus, she spots rotting food scraps, torn clothing, scattered lawn furniture, and a few scattered sticks, all stacked together into an uninviting heap that may have once provided makeshift comfort. Suppressing the urge to gag, Maali climbs up the incline, mindful of the oozing sludge beneath her feet.

Reaching the top, she peers cautiously outside, her eyes scanning the surroundings while keeping a low profile. A beam of a flashlight pierces through the darkness, momentarily sweeping over the opening. Maali instinctively ducks down, hiding herself from the prying eyes.

As the flashlight's beam moves away, she carefully descends the slope, her movements deliberate. She rejoins Noah and whispers, "No go. There's someone out there."

Noah's frustration is palpable as he growls, "Damn. Any chance it's just a civilian on a leisurely stroll?"

"No," Diandra's voice echoes in Maali's mind, "It is one of my captors."

Maali lets out a groan, realising the gravity of the situation. "It's SorrowStar. We could take him down, but..."

"But the commotion would attract too much attention," Noah interjects, completing her thought. "By the time we clear enough of this debris to make our escape, they may be upon us."

They exchange a glance, the weight of their predicament pressing down on them as they search desperately for a solution.

Suddenly, a loud shout interrupts their thoughts, its menace unmistakable, causing both Maali and Noah to instinctively react.

CHAPTER 8:

Catch 22

Maali carefully leans out of the doorway to scan the hallway, ensuring it's clear. Seeing no immediate threat, she waves Noah forward and positions herself once again under Diandra's arm, providing support.

"Noahhhhhh!" The voice rings out again, piercing the air with anger and frustration. "I know you can hear me! You've got no idea what you've stumbled into, you clueless idiot!"

They move swiftly down the hallway, their steps cautious and deliberate. As they approach the corner, the beam of a flashlight momentarily illuminates the path before disappearing. Noah, with his pistol at the ready, steps around the corner and spots one of the SorrowStar goons striding purposefully down the hall towards the source of the shouts. He signals for Maali to follow, and together, they carry Diandra, inching closer to the commotion. With each passing moment, the identity of the person shouting becomes clearer.

"You've got something that belongs to us!" Manfred's voice booms through the corridor. "You and that little bitch of yours! Don't you know that stealing is wrong? I would've thought you'd know better!"

Noah's face tightens with anger as he whispers, "I believe there's an emergency exit nearby. Let's make our move while he's busy blabbering."

The corridor reverberates with Manfred's voice, each word laced with treachery masquerading as reason. "Come on, Noah! Just give us the package, and I promise you'll leave here without a scratch!" His tone attempts to ooze sincerity, but it's thin, almost theatrical.

Noah's response is a laugh, hollow and edged with scorn, that bounces off the walls. "Really, Manfred? Do you hear yourself?" he calls back, his voice dripping with mockery, each word heavy with irony. "You peddling that line is like watching a kangaroo in a ballet skirt trying to play the didgeridoo. What's next? A crocodile hosting a tea party?"

The humour in the corridor is swiftly extinguished by Manfred's next words, icy and malevolent. "Keep laughing, Noah. But remember, every choice has consequences. Perhaps your delightful Ex would enjoy some company? My associates have a way of... persuading people."

Noah's voice drips with deadly purpose as he growls, "You even think about laying a finger on her or the kids, and I'll make sure you pay for every goddamn breath you've taken."

Maali's anger simmers beneath the surface, her fingers tightening around Diandra in a protective reflex. "You're nothing but a sadistic piece of filth, Manfred. We won't let you harm anyone else."

Manfred's laughter resonates through the hallway, a chilling symphony of malice. "Oh, Noah, Maali, you really have no idea who you're dealing with. But don't worry; soon enough, you'll learn the true extent of my power."

Manfred's voice oozed with meanness as he taunted, "Noah, my old pal, I possess a gift for snatching away your most cherished possessions. Remember the irresistible charmer who wooed your precious Ex, leaving you toiling in vain? Ah, yes, I orchestrated their passionate affair, deriving immense pleasure from the anguish it inflicted upon you. The sight of betrayal etched upon your face, an exquisite masterpiece. But know this: I perpetually stay one step ahead, ready to seize all that you deem yours. Can you ever hope to outmanoeuvre me?"

The ambient light casts a deep shadow over Noah's visage; incensed, Noah's muscles tense as he prepares to charge down the hall with the raw energy of a wild storm, tempestuous and demanding release. Maali's voice cuts through his rage like a razor, her words hissing with urgency, "Don't fall for this bastards trap. He's trying to goad you into a reckless act. If you rush in blindly, they'll put you down like a dog." Noah's jaw clenches, his face aflame with uninhibited anger, his every instinct urging him to retaliate. "Remember who we are, who you are. The only thing you can control is yourself, don't give this fucker what he wants." Maali raises her right fist, patting it on the left side of her chest, "I got you, brother."

Manfred's mocking voice echoes through the corridor, filled with a sinister glee. "You see, Noah, there's no escape for you except through us. We've got every exit covered, from A1 to A7." Noah's hand hovers above the doorknob of the labelled emergency exit, his gaze fixated on the metal plaque. A chill runs down his spine as he realises they are standing right before exit A7. Manfred's words continue to pierce the air, laced with a venomous invitation, "Why hold onto our mutual 'friend' any longer? He's a goddamn goldmine, and if you play nice, you could get a taste of that sweet fortune."

Noah's eyes blaze with conflicting emotions as he locks his gaze with Maali. Frantically, she whispers, "No, we can't let them take him. The things they've done to him... you can't imagine it." She can see the turmoil within Noah, torn between the desperate need to protect his loved ones and the moral obligation to save Diandra. In a low, guttural voice, he snarls back at her, his words dripping with raw intensity, "Maybe I can't imagine the horror they've inflicted on him, but I sure as hell can't imagine letting Sarah and the kids pay the price for this abomination!" He jabs his finger forcefully toward Diandra.

Maali frantically tries to think of something to say when Diandra's voice sounds in her head again. "It is alright, my friend." Maali's voice trembles with a mixture of concern and desperation as she pleads with Diandra, "But... what will they do to you?"

Diandra's gaze holds a solemn resoluteness. "Their actions are inconsequential. I have endured plentiful and, if required, will endure plenty more. Let them have me if it means sparing the innocent. Do not sacrifice the young ones for me."

"Do not worry," Diandra's voice resonates in her mind, a bittersweet mix of reassurance and sorrow. "The psionic link will persist for some time after we part ways. Should you be willing, you will be able to find me once the young ones are safe."

Maali's eyes well up with tears as she holds Diandra's gaze, feeling the weight of his sacrifice. The connection between them feels both comforting and painful, a reminder of the bond they share in this dire moment.

A sense of resignation emanates from Diandra, tinged with a profound sadness. It grips Maali's heart, fuelling her resolve to protect the innocent at all costs. She nods, her voice choked with emotion, "I won't forget, Diandra. I'll find you. Stay strong." Their heartfelt exchange lingers, etching an indelible mark upon their souls.

Maali's internal struggle is evident in her eyes as she gazes at Noah, his fierce determination and desperation mirrored in her own conflicted emotions. With a heavy heart, Maali lets out a deep sigh, feeling the weight of the decision settle upon her. She whispers, almost to herself, "Alright..."

In that single word, the path forward becomes clear. Sacrifices must be made, even when they tear at the very fabric of their reality.

Noah's eyes widen. He opens his mouth to protest, but Maali's determined expression silences his objections. Maali clears her throat, her voice projecting with a blend of defiance and controlled urgency. She cups her hands to her mouth, amplifying her words as she shouts, "Manfred!"

"What the hell are you doing?!" Noah snarls.

The words hang in the air, momentarily freezing time. Noah's snarl transforms into a look of bewilderment, uncertainty gripping him tightly. He inches closer to Maali.

Maali takes a steadying breath, her grit unfaltering. Her voice steady. "Yeah, we've got your friend!"

They can both hear the thunder of boots charging their way. "If I see a single SorrowStar boy, I'll blow this guy's brains out!" A series of frantic orders blares out of the radio Noah had stolen, calling for every team in the building to hold position. "You want him back? Get your goons out of the building."

Silence extends briefly before Manfred calls out, "No more games, runt!" Manfred's voice resonates with authority. "Hand over the abomination, or we'll tear him from your grasp and make you pay. A summary execution seems fitting for the likes of you."

Maali's voice cuts through the air, laced with insolence. "You think you can intimidate us, Manfred? You know Noah and I, we are already dead; we died ten years ago, you fuck; each day since then has just been a fucked up bonus. You'll have to come and get him if you want him."

Noah's shouts, "I'm not screwing around, Manfred! Get your goons out of here, or I'll paint the wall with your grey buddy's brain!" To amplify their defiance, Maali's finger tightens around the trigger of her pistol, and a resounding shot pierces through the air. The deafening sound echoes off the walls, and a shower of powdery debris rains down from the ceiling.

"The next one's going in his goddamn head!" Maali's voice booms.

The tension in the air thickens as the silence stretches, each passing second feeling like an eternity. Then, a crackling voice pierces the static-filled airwaves, carrying the distinct tone of Manfred's seething anger.

"All teams, pull out immediately. Darwin, with me at the entrance. We wait for the goddamn package." The sound of hurried footsteps fills the void as the SorrowStar teams hastily retreat, their heavy footfalls echoing like a defeated army retreating from battle.

Lines of anguish carve their way across Noah's features as an internal blizzard brews behind the depth of his eyes. Every fibre of his being resonates with the moral quandary he's ensnared in. The choice before him is not just one of action but of the very essence of who he is and what he stands for.

There's a raw, tangible pain in the way he meets Maali's gaze - a plea for understanding, an unsaid acknowledgment of the gut-wrenching dilemma he's faced with. Memories of his family flash before his eyes; their laughter, their embraces, every shared moment now tainted with the looming threat of their potential fate.

Yet, in the shadow of those cherished memories stands Diandra, a symbol of something much larger than just one life. The very idea of handing over such an enigma to the clutches of SorrowStar gnaws at his conscience, a relentless reminder of the price of compromise.

Torn between two monumental obligations, Noah's resolve wavers, his stance reflecting the internal conflict. One life against many, a universal struggle against personal ties. The weight of history, duty, and familial love intertwine, forming a nexus of complexity that threatens to tear him apart.

Manfred's voice echoes through the building once more, laced with a venomous demand. "Alright! It's just you two, me, and Darwin now! Bring our friend up front!"

They slowly help Diandra limp towards the front door. Just before rounding the last corner, Maali looks over at Noah. "Stay at the corner and cover me."

Maali can feel the weight of the situation pressing down on her as she supports Diandra's weakened form. Noah's presence at the corner provides a sense of security, a guardian watching over them.

With every step Maali takes towards the handover, the world seems to constrict around her. The atmosphere is thick with tension, yet it's pierced by the profound connection they've forged in such a short span. Cradling Diandra's feeble form, she swallows the lump in her throat, holding back the tears threatening to spill.

"In the brief moments we've shared, our souls have traversed lifetimes," Maali whispers, her voice tremulous with emotion. "Remember our bond, and let it be the beacon that guides you back to freedom. I vow, whatever it takes, I will see you free."

Diandra, even in his weakened state, manages a faint but reassuring look. "Your spirit gives me strength, Maali. Though they might shackle my body, they cannot imprison the bond we've forged. Our paths will intertwine again, and the darkness that ensnares me now will give way to dawn."

Maali finds herself rendered speechless as they step into the main foyer. Manfred stands there, his face flushed with anger, his jaw tightly clenched in frustration. However, it's the SorrowStar guard who captures her attention. He gazes at her with eyes devoid of emotion, displaying no trace of concern or interest. His complete ease in this tense situation sends a chilling sensation down her spine, making her skin crawl.

"About damn time," Manfred growls through clenched teeth. "I should kill you here and now."

"And risk hitting your little buddy here?" She gently shifts her shoulder, causing Diandra to stir. "Nah, I don't think you'll do that. In fact, you're not going to do anything except take the damn alien and get going."

A pulsating vein above Manfred's left eye threatens to burst as he seethes with anger. He releases a long hiss of air, barely containing his rage. "Don't you dare think you can order me around, scum. Now, where's Noah? If that asshole tries anything, you'll both pay the price."

"He's close, keeping an eye out," she responds, her voice dripping with amusement. She looks up at the ceiling and shouts, "Hey, Noah! Say hi to Manfred!"

There's a brief pause before Noah's voice crackles through Manfred's radio. "Hello, Manfred. Good to see you again; your latest wig looks great; who are you trying to be? Elvis?"

Manfred and Darwin scan their surroundings, their eyes darting around, searching for any sign of Noah's presence. Darwin remains composed, his gaze methodical, while the Commissioner's frustration grows. He self-consciously runs his hand through his hair, gripping the radio tightly in his left hand, and snarls into it, "Where are you, you son of a bitch?!"

"I'm close," Noah whispers. "Close enough to see that the vein on your head is getting bigger. You should get that looked at, or if you cause trouble, I can take care of it for you."

Before Manfred's head can explode, Maali steps in. "Let's get this over with. Sydney's burning, and we've both got shit to do." She approaches

Manfred, her gaze unwavering, while Darwin stands at the ready to escort Diandra away. Without hesitation, Maali carefully transfers Diandra into Darwin's grip before backing away, leaving him alone with Manfred.

The Commissioner's eyes narrow, a wicked gleam in his gaze. "You two really messed up this time. The rest of your lives are going to be very short and exceedingly... unpleasant." He practically purrs the last word, relishing the anticipation of their suffering.

Unfazed, Maali's smile broadens, her eyes sparkling with defiant mirth. "Ah, Manny, your threats have the depth of a kiddie pool. They have all the menace of a newborn bunny's yawn. You're like a villain from a B-grade movie - Why don't you twirl your moustache and be done with it? At least that would be amusing."

Manfred's face contorts with fury, every muscle in his hand tenses as if primed for a savage blow. But he freezes as Maali swiftly positions her rifle, its barrel pointed directly at his ball sack. Her voice carries a steely edge. "Go ahead, make your move. I'm just looking for another fucked up trophy."

The Commissioner trembles with rage, but the fear in his eyes is unmistakable as he slowly lowers his hand. "Kill me, and my team will charge in and slaughter you both."

Maali's gaze remains firm. "You're mistaken if you think we'll go down without a fight. But don't worry, Manny. We have bigger plans for you. Consider this a taste of the reckoning to come."

She tenses her finger on the trigger, just enough to make the weapon emit a whine as it builds up charge. "Wanna know something? Blowing your pin dick off? It'd be worth dying for."

With a twisted grin, Maali fixes her gaze upon Manfred, an air of sinister amusement in her eyes. She playfully blows him a mocking kiss, adding a mischievous wink with a devilish charm. "Don't forget, I'll be seeing you very soon," she whispers, leaving him with a chilling promise.

The Commissioner doesn't say another word, his face a mask of seething fury, as he abruptly turns on his heel and strides out of the building. Sensing the imminent danger, Maali swiftly spins on her heels and dashes towards Noah, the deafening sound of grenades echoing behind her. She feels a searing heat graze her shoulder, but the surge of adrenaline propels her forward, pushing the pain to the back of her mind. "Run!" she urgently cries out to Noah.

Without a moment's hesitation, they launch themselves forward, their bodies propelled by fear and instinct. Explosions continue to rip through the building, turning rooms into debris-laden shambles. Shards of glass and fragments of concrete rain down upon them, stinging their skin as they navigate the crumbling warren. Just when it seems there is no escape, Noah's sharp eyes spot a glimmer of hope—a partially intact office door. He points towards it, his voice barely audible over the chaos. "There! Hurry!"

They dive inside, seeking refuge from the anarchy outside, but the explosion rips through the hall before they can secure the door. It bursts open, revealing a scene of devastation. Shards of debris fly through the air, and another grenade hurtles towards them. Reacting on instinct, Noah hurls himself behind a nearby filing cabinet, narrowly escaping the blast.

In the chaos, Maali stands dangerously exposed. A vicious hail of shrapnel rips through the air, mercilessly shredding its way towards her. She is struck brutally, her body jolting from the force of the impact. The shrapnel burrows deep, tearing flesh and fabric alike in a cruel demonstration of destruction. She crumples to the ground, a cry of agony escaping her lips as she hits the earth.

Noah's heart plummets into a chasm of dread. His vision blurs, the aftermath of the explosion echoing in his ears. He fights through the disorientation, his gaze desperately searching for Maali. Finally, he spots her, lying twisted on her side, her cloths marred with jagged tears and stained crimson. Blood seeps out, forming a growing dark pool beneath her.

Every ragged breath she takes is a struggle; her body wracked with shuddering spasms of pain. The severity of her wounds is unmistakable - "No, no, no..." Noah's voice trembles with a mix of anguish and fear. The memories of past losses resurface, threatening to overwhelm him. He can't bear the thought of losing another partner, another person he cares about.

Noah reaches out, his hand trembling; he gently turns Maali over. His heart sinks as he takes in the sight of her injuries. Dozens of fragments litter her body, and blood stains everything around them. Despair threatens to engulf him, but then, she wheezes out a breath. It's a small glimmer of hope.

Shoving himself off the ground, Noah kneels beside her, his hand tenderly cupping her cheek. "What did you say?" he asks, his voice laced with both dread and a desperate need to understand. He knows time is slipping away, but he wants to catch every last word she has to say. "Stay with me, Maali. Please, don't go. Stay here."

Maali draws another shuddering breath, her strength waning. Despite the pain and uncertainty, a smile curves on her lips. "I said... 'ow'..." Her attempt at humour, even in this dire situation, sparks a flicker of laughter within Noah.

Noah wraps his arms around her, pulling her close, not wanting her to face the darkness alone. "I've got you. I've got you," he whispers.

As Maali's breaths become more laboured, each inhalation a battle against the encroaching endgame, she musters the strength to speak. Her voice is barely a whisper, filled with earnestness. "The blood..."

Noah tries to downplay the severity, his voice quivering as he clutches at straws of hope. "Don't worry, it's just a little blood. Nothing to be concerned about. It'll wash off easily." He forces a weak smirk, adding, "You know, with all your love for washing and ironing, I bet you'll have that uniform looking brand-new in no time."

But Maali convulses in his arms, a surge of agony wracking through her body. Her words are strained, punctuated by a disturbing spray of blood. "No!" she exclaims, her voice laced with a desperate plea. "The D.TEM... The vials..."

Noah's eyes shoot open, a surge of panic surging through his veins. He curses himself for not thinking of it sooner, for not realising the potential lifeline they had in their possession. He reaches over to the knapsack still hanging from Maali's waist and frantically digs into it. The bag spills open, scattering its contents across the floor in a chaotic mess.

His hands tremble as he rummages through the scattered items, his heart pounding in his chest. His fingers brush against something cold and glass, and he seizes it with a desperate grip.

Noah holds up the vial, his hands shaking uncontrollably. The dim light catches the liquid inside, casting an eerie glow. It's their only hope, their last chance to save Maali's life. He clings to it like a lifeline, desperately trying to convince himself that everything will be fine.

But just as Noah is about to breathe a sigh of relief, a loud crash echoes through the building. The ground beneath them trembles, and the ceiling above them groans under the weight of the explosion. Dust and debris rain down, filling the air with a choking haze. The main doorway is blocked, obstructed by a pile of wreckage.

Noah's heart sinks as he realises the implications. The SorrowStar attackers must have triggered the collapse with the grenade. Other than a partly blocked emergency exit, they are trapped, isolated from any immediate pursuit. Perhaps the assailants are occupied with removing the debris, buying them a few precious minutes.

With trembling hands and a racing mind, Noah stares at the vial that holds the key to Maali's fate. Each passing second feels like an eternity, the weight of the moment heavy in the air. Quickly pulling the rubber stopper off with his teeth, he swallows hard against the thick knot of panic in his throat. Fighting against the rising dread carefully, he tilts the liquid into Maali's parted lips. The slow-flowing liquid cascades under her tongue, a fragile glimmer of hope.

Holding his breath, Noah watches intently, waiting for any sign of change. Time seems to warp around him, each second dilating into a lifetime. His eyes, blurred with unshed tears, remain locked on her still form. Whispering almost inaudibly, he chokes out with a fragile hope, "Hey, Maali, you can't leave it like this..."

CHAPTER 9:
Through the Flames

Maali felt an icy numbness spreading through her body, a creeping frost that seemed to leach the life from her very core. Despite Noah's proximity, a sense of profound isolation enveloped her, the coldness unrelenting, as if she was drifting further away from the realm of the living. Her consciousness wavered, teetering on the edge of a vast and unfathomable void.

The world around her began to fade, sounds and sights dissolving into a distant, muffled echo. There was a sense of detachment, as though she was a mere observer of her own plight. The cold seeped deeper, gnawing at her bones, a spectral hand pulling her towards an endless abyss.

As the fluid trickled into the recesses of her mouth, her tongue felt heavy, shackled by an unseen force. Each nerve seemed to freeze and then go numb, a paralysis slowly claiming her body. Her heartbeats echoed in her ears, each thump sounding like the tolling of a distant bell, marking the passage towards an unknown fate.

But amidst this chilling descent, a flicker of something else began to stir within her. A subtle, almost imperceptible shift, as if life itself was fighting back, kindling a faint spark in the depths of the icy darkness that threatened to consume her.

In an abrupt and forceful surge, the frigid grip on Maali's heart relinquished, giving way to an overwhelming blaze of heat that consumed her entire being. Her body, once numbed by chilling coldness, now radiated with a fiery intensity that seemed to challenge the confines of her mortal existence. It was as if her very essence had been set ablaze, fuelling a torrential rush of life force coursing through her veins.

The inferno that consumed Maali began to wane, replaced by a profound force of vitality originating deep within her. Her heart, previously faltering, now charged forth with resolute power, asserting its presence like a relentless hurricane reclaiming its dominion.

Each heartbeat was a beacon of life, sending ripples of fervent energy throughout her system. She could feel the cascade of vigour and animation as if every fibre of her being was rejuvenated. The air around her seemed electrified by her essence, her every inhalation a rebirth.

The cruel remnants of her wounds, shards that threatened to bind her, started to relinquish their grip. Rejecting their intrusion, her body began a careful process of self-repair, meticulously mending and fortifying. The once-embedded shrapnel was methodically ousted, making way for a swift restoration of her form. As each shard was cast aside, waves of relief surged through Maali, the once constricting pain replaced by a blossoming sensation of renewal.

In this heightened state, Maali's perception transcended the ordinary boundaries of human senses. Not only could she hear the powerful drumbeat of her own heart, but the synchronised thump-thump of Noah's heartbeat reverberated within her, their rhythms harmonising in a profound connection. The air itself seemed to carry the distinct scent of the lacklustre sushi Noah often indulged in, intermingled with faint whispers of the liquor that had brushed his lips hours before. These scents intertwined, creating a multifaceted sensory landscape that evoked memories and emotions.

Every touch, taste, and aroma flooded her consciousness, entangling in a unified groove of sensory perception. It was an overwhelming sensation that engulfed her, saturating her senses with a phantasmagoria of impressions. The world around her seemed to burst with vibrant hues and heightened textures, each detail magnified to an almost surreal degree.

An overwhelming flood of sensations bombarded her brain, too rapid to disentangle and process. It was a swirling, disorienting amalgamation of sounds, smells, tastes, and... and...

"Holy crap..." Noah's whispered words were swept away by the unbridled roar pulsating through her veins. Maali's eyes slowly fluttered open, sucking an agonising breath of air into lungs that had been practically shredded moments before.

She took several gasping inhalations, her frantic gaze darting around in disoriented confusion. Her mind was a haze, unable to focus or comprehend. The world trembled, and her limbs tingled with an intense heat, yet there was no pain. Every fibre of her being yearned to release the overwhelming surge of energy coursing through her, to run, jump, and twirl in a wild frenzy. Lost in a flurry of sensations, Maali struggled to form coherent words, her voice stuttering and choked, "The fu- who- what- where-"

"Now, you just need when and why." Noah let out a strangled laugh, hugging her close. "Holy shit! I thought I'd lost you, Sis." He was shaking almost as much as she was, and Maali actually felt tears land on her.

"Nope!" The words burst from Maali's lips, her volume escalating beyond her control. At that moment, it felt as if she would combust if she didn't unleash the overwhelming surge of energy coursing through her. Ignoring Noah's attempts to restrain her and encourage caution, she forcefully extricated herself from his grasp and leapt to her feet. From his vantage point on the floor, he observed her stretch her limbs and run her fingers through her hair, as if she had merely awakened from a peaceful slumber rather than narrowly escaping death. Maali took a few precious seconds to release the built-up tension in her joints, emitting a giddy laugh with each satisfying pop.

Noah, utterly befuddled, cleared his throat and tentatively asked, "Umm... so, how are you feeling?"

Maali cast him a bewildered look as if he had just uttered the most absurd question. How did she feel? She felt extraordinary! Exhilarated! She experienced a profound sense of vitality unlike anything she had ever known before, and for a fleeting moment, she couldn't quite grasp the reason behind it. Then, as her hands traversed her torso, attempting to regain her composure, she became aware of the tattered remnants of her clothing, accompanied by scattered fragments of shrapnel that had been expelled from her body, now caught in the folds of her garments.

Her realisation grounded her slightly, allowing her to respond. "I, uh... remember that time when I was just starting as your partner, and you accidentally gave me some of the MDMA we confiscated instead of the paracetamol?" It was a long time ago, but both of them joked about it often enough that neither could ever forget. Noah's eyebrows shot up, and he nodded slowly as she began bouncing on her heels.

"It's like that, but... hnnnggg," she strained, clenching her teeth to resist being swept away by the euphoric surge of sensations once more. Gradually, the overwhelming wave subsided enough for her to articulate, "But... like, ten times more intense!"

Noah observed her dilated eyes, making her appear as high as a kite, but there was no time to wait for the effects to wear off. As Maali's giddy state began to subside, the sound of explosions echoed down the corridor, growing louder and closer with each passing moment. The deafening blasts reverberated through the walls, shaking the very foundation of the building, followed by a pungent smell of smoke seeping into the room. "Incredible! It's like fucking magic. I feel like I'm ten years younger!" Despite Maali still wobbling around in a dazed state, Noah propelled himself off the ground and lunged towards her, driven by the instinct to protect.

The world tilted just as the grenade detonated outside. Noah lunged at Maali, ensnaring her in a desperate grasp, their bodies crashing to the floor, shielded by any semblance of cover they could find. The room was consumed by pandemonium, shrapnel slicing through the air, dismantling everything in its volatile path. The aftermath left their ears throbbing, a deafening echo drowning their senses. When the haze lifted, Maali was engulfed in a tidal wave of nausea.

Before she could brace herself, her stomach convulsed, rebelling against her. She instinctively lurched towards a nearby waste bin, expelling its contents vehemently. Once the retching subsided, she fixed Noah with a piercing gaze, a storm of anguish and anger swirling in her eyes. She tried to articulate her distress, but a cruel, sharp pain cleaved through her mind, leaving her momentarily incapacitated.

Noah wasted no time in pulling her up by the arm, his grip firm and focused. With a stern expression, he reminded her.

"You damn near died just moments ago. We're surrounded by SorrowStar goons in a building that's being reduced to rubble. Grenades are raining down," he jabbed a finger towards the fallen shrapnel. "And to top it off, that bastard Manfred has threatened my kids. We gotta get the hell out of here and get to them fast, so get your shit together!"

The sound of the last grenade detonating rang through the air, pushing them further into action. Noah wasted no time, urgently pulling

Maali to her feet, their eyes locking. He met her gaze, his voice filled with intensity as he questioned, "Are you with me now? Are you grounded? Or are you still lost?"

Maali took a deep breath, consciously pushing aside the remnants of the disorienting effects caused by D.TEM, striving to find her centre. With a deliberate exhale, she gathered her composure. "Yeah... I still feel a little... off, but I've got it under control now." Her eyes landed on the discarded vial lying at her feet, a solitary droplet of the powerful substance lingering inside. For a fleeting moment, temptation gripped her, urging her to break the vial and indulge in that minuscule trace of D.TEM. However, a sudden flash of Diandra's face sped through her mind, causing her to recoil in disgust. The memory of what that drug had cost Diandra was enough to snap her back to reality, shattering the allure of the substance. With a resigned sigh, she discarded the vial, recognising the dangerous allure it held. "I understand now why it's so coveted. Scum bags would do anything, even sacrifice their children, for just a few drops."

Noah's gaze shifted towards the vial, his mind swirling with thoughts of the other vials they had seized from the crew at the docks. The realisation of the potential consequences weighed heavily upon him. If anyone were to discover their possession of these vials, it would spell trouble far beyond their encounter with SorrowStar. "Yeah, we better keep this quiet," he muttered, a tinge of concern in his voice. "The last thing we need is more crap coming our way." The ominous groaning of the roof rumbled above them. They exchanged worried glances, fearing that the structure might collapse at any moment. "Come on," Noah urged, fortitude lacing his words. "Let's get the hell out of here."

Maali didn't protest as Noah firmly grasped her hand and guided her out of the office. The remnants of the D.TEM's effects still clung to her, leaving her grateful for the presence of someone to rely on. Noah led the way towards the emergency exit they had considered using earlier. "What if they're still keeping watch?" she voiced her concern.

Noah paused briefly, contemplating the situation, before shaking his head with conviction. "Manfred may be a pompous prick, but he's not one to waste time. I'm willing to bet his boys are already packing up and-" The sudden blare of the radio Noah carried interrupted him, Manfred's voice bursting through the airwaves just as they removed a large wooden beam partly blocking the emergency exit.

"Teams One, Two, and Three, get back on track and let's proceed to the objective," Manfred's commanding voice blared through the radio. Exchanging glances, Noah and Maali felt a sense of relief, realising that their assumption about Manfred's impatience was correct. Hopefully, the Commissioner would either assume they were deceased or simply wouldn't bother confirming their fate. However, their relief was short-lived. "Team Four, bring up the burners and reduce this relic to ashes. Out."

Maali and Noah stood frozen, their horror mounting as the realisation sank in. Burners, the forbidden weapons of destruction, were about to be unleashed within the city limits. Such extreme measures were never justified, regardless of the circumstances. The thought of using flamethrowers around innocent civilians was unfathomable. Yet, the sound of a pilot flame igniting just outside the door shattered any lingering doubts. A deafening hiss of flames engulfing the building's facade followed, instantly raising the temperature to a near-unbearable level. With a sharp intake of breath, Noah instinctively withdrew his hand from the emergency door handle, wincing in pain as he beheld two fingers now searing red from burns.

"Shit..." He murmured. They couldn't use the door unless they wanted to die in a literal blaze of glory. "This place is already a wreck. It won't take long for it to come down." Smoke seeped through as Noah turned away from the door, taking off at a dead sprint back the way they came.

Her body gradually returning to normal, Maali matched Noah's pace effortlessly, not needing assistance anymore. "Where are we going?! They probably torched all the exits!" she exclaimed, seeking answers from her obstinate partner. Noah didn't respond verbally; instead, he kept sprinting through ever-thickening smoke, trusting that Maali was keeping up as he barely paused at the corner leading to the back hall. Their destination was clear in his mind—the room with the trash pile, and what lay beneath it.

Side by side, they plunged into the congealed mass of filth, their hands fiercely digging and tossing discarded remnants with abandon. The urgent need to escape overshadowed any concern about the noise echoing through the room, as the smoke thickened and the temperature climbed steadily.

As Maali excavated, she made a conscious effort to dismiss the disconcerting presence of the black sludge staining her clothes, redirecting her attention to a more grounding topic. "This situation goes way beyond 'pretty fucked,' doesn't it?" she quipped.

Noah tugged at a rotting piece of wood lodged in the trash heap, causing the front of the pile to disintegrate. He recoiled in disgust at the foul stench that wafted from the disturbed waste, but he pressed on, undeterred. "That's putting it mildly. Let's just get through this putrid mess and find the kids. I won't allow those bastards to lay a finger on them," he declared with a snarl. Maali could already anticipate the retribution he had in mind for any SorrowStar goons they encountered along their way.

"So that's the plan? Get the kids and the ex somewhere safe and then help Diandra, right?"

Maali's question hung in the air, and Noah's reaction was marked by a momentary pause. He nodded slowly. "Yeah. We'll get it back after they're safe," with a reluctant note in his tone.

Maali tried not to blame him for being less than enthusiastic. "Good. What they did to him... You wouldn't believe it. It's more fucked than you think. It makes me wish I'd just blown Manfred's head off when I had the chance. It might have been the smart thing to do, but I feel like shit for giving Diandra back to the goons. He doesn't deserve what they'll do to him."

"Maybe. Wait. He? What makes you think it was a male? We didn't get a chance to check the junk, so why think it's a guy?" Noah asked without halting his dig.

Maali laughed, even as she gagged at the stench coming from the shrinking pile. There had to be something dead in it to smell so bad. "I don't know for sure. It just felt right. Besides," she glanced mischievously at Noah, a twinkle in her eyes, "compared to you, Diandra was like a supermodel straight off the catwalk!"

Noah let out a scoff, and they both sniggered. However, their momentary levity was shattered by a loud groan echoing from behind. Without warning, part of the ceiling gave way, sending burning debris crashing down and blocking their exit. Flames quickly spread through the room, engulfing the trash they had just cleared. Driven by the urgency to escape the imminent threat of burning to death, they threw themselves back into the heap.

After a relentless effort, they managed to clear enough trash to create a path. Without hesitation, Noah cupped his hands, providing a boost for Maali to scramble up towards the hole at the top of the pile. As she made her way through, an unfortunate burst released a spray of the repulsive sludge she had been avoiding. She fought back the urge to vomit, focusing on reaching the other side. Once there, she extended her hand back through to assist Noah. Despite his colourful stream of curses, he broke through almost as swiftly as she had.

A sudden surge of intense heat and a thunderous whoosh erupted from inside the room, prompting Noah to pull Maali down just in time to evade a wash of flames shooting out of the hole. The room collapsed behind them, leaving them sprawled on their backs. From their vantage point, they witnessed the old parliament building succumbing to the devouring inferno. Noah's expression turned sorrowful as he shook his head. "There's not much left from the old days."

Maali stared with surprise. She had never taken him for the nostalgic type, especially concerning government buildings. Catching her gaze, Noah sighed and explained, "I may not be fond of politicians, but my father was part of a historical restoration society. He dedicated years to preserving this place. And now..." He trailed off, his head shaking in disbelief as the flames consumed the structure. "Come on, let's get the hell out of here."

Rising to their feet, ready to make their escape, they spotted a pair of goons. The corpo-cops stood about thirty meters away, engaged in smoking and casual conversation. The taller one seemed to have said something amusing, eliciting a loud laugh from his companion. With restraint gripping them, Maali and Noah cautiously moved in the opposite direction, hoping to avoid further confrontation. They were on the verge of making a clean getaway when a shout shattered the air. "Hey! Spits!"

Turning their attention back, they saw a group of civilians closing in on the SorrowStar operatives. Despite the injuries evident on most of them, each individual was armed in some capacity. It took a moment, but Maali recognised a familiar face leading the charge. "Oh boy..."

Noah raised an eyebrow, seeking an explanation. "What's going on?"

Pointing out the figure she recognised, Maali replied, "He was with the crowd earlier."

Noah followed her gesture and grimaced. "Seems like some people never learn. Let's go before things turn ugly."

Before Maali and Noah could take a single step, a brick sailed through the air, propelled by a skilled thrower. It found its mark with chilling accuracy, smashing into the face of the shorter goon. He crumpled to the ground, unmoving. In an instinctive response, the remaining operative raised his burner, but his retaliation was quickly met with an overwhelming onslaught.

Bricks, pipes, rocks, and rebar rained down upon him in a relentless barrage. The assailants in the crowd seemed sustained by a collective anger, their aim striking with unnerving precision. The operative struggled to shield himself, his arms providing feeble protection against the storm of projectiles. Desperation etched on his face, he dropped his weapon, hoping to reason with his attackers.

But reason had long abandoned the mob. They surged forward, a relentless tide, closing in on the disarmed operative. Insults and jeers filled the air, blending into an unrestrained clamour of rage. With each kick and blow, the once defiant screams of the operative were silenced, drowned out by the overpowering force of the assault. His pleas for mercy fell on deaf ears as the crowd vented their fury upon the defenceless man.

Maali felt a flicker of compassion stir within her, witnessing the brutal spectacle unfold before her eyes. But the memories of Diandra's suffering and the unspeakable atrocities committed by SorrowStar steeled her purpose. She averted her gaze from the scene, a shiver coursing down her spine as a sinister realisation settled in her mind. The mob's unrelenting rage and the ruthless manner in which they exacted their vengeance hinted at a darkness that ran deep within the hearts of the people. It was a chilling reminder that in their desperate struggle for justice, they, too, could succumb to the very brutality they sought to overcome.

Maali pondered the delicate balance within the human soul – the intricate dance of light and darkness that defines our very being. Every heart harbours the potential for boundless kindness, for acts of awe-inspiring beauty and compassion. Yet, within that same heart lurks a shadow, a capacity for unspeakable evil driven by fear, anger, or despair. It is a duality that is as old as humanity itself: for every action, there is an equal and opposite reaction, a balance that must be maintained.

As she watched the mob's fury, Maali realised that the line separating good from evil, righteous anger from blind rage, was perilously thin. It is the playground upon which our inner demons and better angels vie for dominance. In our quest for justice, how easy it is to stray into the very darkness we fight against. The true challenge lies not just in confronting the external foes but in mastering the wild sea within ourselves.

Do we, as humanity, possess the collective strength to walk on the side of light? To let compassion and understanding guide our actions, even when engulfed by the darkest of times? This is the eternal question, a reminder that the greatest battle we face is the one within, against the darkness that threatens to consume our better selves. Maali understood then that the future hinges on this precarious balance – a battle between the light of our humanity and the consuming shadows of our basest instincts.

Noah places a reassuring hand on her shoulder, his voice a steady anchor. "Rules are made by man, Maali, but right and wrong? That's in our hearts. Let's keep moving forward."

CHAPTER 10:
Rotten

As Maali and Noah hastened away, the city lay in ruin around them. Each step they took crunched against the debris-strewn ground. Over their shoulders, the parliament building, now just a charred skeleton, smouldered in the distance, its former majesty reduced to ashes. A thick veil of dust and smoke hung in the air, blurring the line between day and night, while the muted sounds of distant disorder whispered of recent horrors.

With each step away, Maali felt an inexplicable connection drawing her gaze towards the unmistakable SorrowStar van, manoeuvring its way down the historic Macquarie Street. It wasn't merely curiosity; it was an unfathomable, instinctual need, rooted deep within her soul, urging her to shadow the van's trail. She paused momentarily, eyes squeezed shut, as if trying to sever this mysterious tie. Yet, when she reopened them, the pull was not weakened but intensified, wrapping around her senses, irresistibly beckoning her closer.

The peculiar sensations engulf Maali, spinning her reality into a disorienting frolic of phantom restraints. Imaginary handcuffs seem to clasp her wrists, confining her in an unnerving grip, while an unseen entity coils around her neck, squeezing with an enigmatic force. Frustrated by the intangibility of it all, she casts her gaze downward, hoping for a tangible confirmation of this surreal experience. Her fingers instinctively reach out, searching her throat for a physical manifestation, only to grasp emptiness, leaving her bewildered and questioning the nature of her reality.

"What's wrong?" Noah's voice echoed beside her, the metallic click of his pistol magazine being ejected adding urgency to his words. Maali turned her head, her gaze fixated on his swift actions. Instead of discarding the partially spent magazine, he carefully slipped it into his pocket, swiftly retrieving a fully loaded one to replace it.

"I'm not entirely sure," she murmurs, her fingers tentatively tracing her throat, a sense of unease creeping over her. "It's as if I'm somehow connected to him, sensing the restraints on my wrists and the suffocating presence of a bag over my head."

Noah's jaw tightened, his eyes flickering between Maali and the van as he grappled with conflicting emotions. Concern for her well-being battled with his burning desire for revenge. With a stanch expression, he holstered his pistol, his fingers lingering for a moment on the weapon before shifting his attention to his pulse rifle. Swift and practised, he inspected it, checking for any signs of damage from their escape. Satisfied with its condition, he slung the rifle over his shoulder and locked eyes with Maali, "we'll deal with him later. Our priority is to ensure the safety of the kids."

He sets off in the direction of his Ex's apartment, single-mindedness propelling his steps forward. However, Maali lingers behind, torn between the urge to follow the van and the logic of sticking to their original plan. "I can't shake this feeling that we should go after them," she confesses, gesturing towards the van's disappearing form. "It's like a magnet, man."

Noah steps back and, with a firm grip on her arm, pulls her away from the van, his touch conveying a mix of reassurance and steadfastness. "We can't save him right now. Our focus is on protecting the kids," he asserts. Maali acquiesces, allowing her attention to shift from the van to their immediate mission. Sensing her commitment, Noah releases his hold, and they swiftly surge forward along Martin Place.

As the chaotic events unfold, a noticeable shift in the atmosphere begins to take place. The initial surge of panic and mayhem seems to be gradually receding, leaving behind a slightly calmer landscape. In this part of town, the rampant looting that once prevailed has started to dwindle. Though a few opportunistic figures still emerge from buildings, clutching pilfered possessions, their numbers have significantly diminished.

Maali and Noah move purposefully through the streets, their strides full of intent. Onlookers, mostly looters, generally give them a wide berth. As one particularly boisterous group nears them, the broad outline of Noah, his silhouette cutting an imposing figure against the backdrop of disorder, causes them to hesitate.

Another audacious looter, eyes glinting with recklessness, takes a step towards them. Without missing a beat, Maali swings her rifle into view, its gleaming muzzle catching the dim light. The unmistakable hum of a warning shot punctuates the air, echoing in the near vicinity. The lingering traces of bravado in the looter's face fade, replaced by a brief look of chastened surprise. One by one, potential challengers rethink their intentions and move away, leaving Maali and Noah to continue their journey.

In the midst of the night, the darkness is fractured by the sporadic glow of burning cars and dumpsters, casting an eerie illumination upon the surroundings. Each flickering blaze paints the area with an unsettling combination of light and shadows. As Maali and Noah navigate through the chaotic scene, their path leads them past a building ravaged by fire, its skeletal remains standing as a troubling confirmation of the destructive force that has engulfed the city. Adjacent structures teeter on the brink of succumbing to the relentless flames, the encroaching inferno threatening to consume them whole. Maali mutters, her voice edged with disbelief, "This... it's like we're in some bizarre dream."

Noah's voice, tinged with sardonic humour, replies, "Or maybe we're just avatars in an advanced alien video game. Ever think of that? Each explosion, every fire... just pixels in some cosmic kid's entertainment."

Rolling her eyes, Maali retorts, "Really, Noah? Alien video games? I meant the situation feels surreal, not questioning the fabric of our entire existence!"

With a grin, Noah shoots back, "Hey, just keeping it interesting."

Maali glances at her partner, "Trust me, Noah, this night has already crossed the 'interesting' threshold into 'nightmare fuel' territory."

As they pass another burning car, its flames casting ghostly shadows on their path, Maali's voice, softer now, carries over the crackle of the fire. "I can't help but wonder how much of the city is going to burn down because of this," she murmurs, her words tinged with concern and a deep sense of contemplation.

"Plenty. Given the extent of the pulse emitted by our newfound friends," Noah states with a sharp gesture towards the colossal vessel looming above the city, "there's no telling how far its effects have reached. We've only seen a couple of working vehicles so far, so it's a good bet that most emergency responder rigs are fried. No telling how many people will die just because the ambulances aren't coming, let alone how bad the fires will get without the department being able to deploy."

It's a sobering reality that Maali can't deny. The fires they've encountered already would require the combined efforts of multiple fire trucks, and she can only imagine the extent of the devastation in other parts of the city. The prospect of waiting days for a coordinated response feels like an eternity, and the thought of Sydney being reduced to a mere shadow of its former self sends a shiver down her spine.

But as these daunting thoughts consume her attention, an echo reaches her ears, pulling her focus away from the fires. Maali's instincts kick in, and she calls out to Noah, her voice filled with urgency. "Wait! Do you hear that?"

Noah listens intently, and they both hear it—a woman screaming. "Nothing we haven't heard before now. There are probably a thousand more just like her," Noah remarks.

"This is different," Maali insists, determined to wait and hear it again. Frustrated, Noah reluctantly tunes in more carefully.

They can barely make it out that time. "Somebody help me?!" The voice is ragged, likely from screaming for some time.

"People don't scream like that for thieves or just because their stuff is on fire," Maali says, her voice filled with concern.

"We don't have time for this," Noah hisses at her.

"You know damn well what might be happening," she retorts. They've both heard women scream like that before, having worked on some of the city's worst gang cases. "We can't just slink off and do nothing. Even if all we do is make some noise and disrupt whatever is going on."

Noah glares at her for a few seconds, grinding his teeth. He's desperate to reach his kids, but another scream from a distance makes him close his eyes and sigh. He can't ignore it, even for his family. "Fuck it, alright. We do this quickly. Let's go."

Maali's senses sharpen as she takes the lead, her acute hearing guiding their path through the labyrinthine streets. Noah, typically skilled at tracking physical trails, recognises that Maali possesses the advantage when it comes to pursuing someone solely by sound. With unconquerable doggedness, they turn down an alleyway, their footsteps echoing against the walls before they emerge onto another road.

The piercing sound of a desperate cry shatters the air, its intensity cutting through the commotion. Maali's instincts kick into overdrive as she hones in on the source, her ears finely attuned to the direction of the plea for help. Without hesitation, she breaks into a sprint, Noah close on her heels as they race towards the back of an apartment building, another block away.

As they approach, their path is impeded by a flipped car that blocks the main entrance. It stands as a rare anomaly amidst the uproar, untouched by the consuming flames that have ravaged the surrounding area. The urgency of the scream spurs them forward.

Several lifeless bodies scatter the vicinity, their presence casting an eerie silence over the scene. Maali's keen eyes catch sight of multiple blood trails crisscrossing the ground like a lugubrious spread. It becomes evident that a fierce struggle has taken place, leaving a trail of carnage in its wake.

Her gaze shifts upward, scanning the rooftop of the building. There, amidst the scattered debris, a gun lies discarded, surrounded by a scattering of spent shell casings. The sight paints a vivid picture of the fierce resistance that unfolded in this very spot. With a mixture of admiration and respect, Maali acknowledges, "Whoever was here, they put up one hell of a fight."

"Or," Noah interjects, his finger pointing towards a trail of skid marks, "maybe the driver stirred up trouble they couldn't handle. There's no way to tell, and right now, it doesn't—" His words are cut short by another desperate, hoarse scream. The source of the cries must be running low on energy or in dire need of medical attention.

As they move closer to the back of the building, Maali's anticipation grows, fuelled by the urgency of the situation. But just as she prepares to rush ahead, Noah's firm grip on her shoulder halts her abruptly. The weight of his touch serves as a potent reminder, compelling her to pause and assess the perilous unknowns that lie ahead. How many adversaries lurk in the shadows? What weapons do they brandish, ready to strike? How intently are they monitoring their surroundings? Without the reassuring presence of backup or a clear escape route, reckless action would be a risky gamble. Their reliance on sheer luck has already pushed the boundaries of plausibility on this fateful night.

Maali nods, understanding the need for caution, and leans slowly around the building's corner to peer into the alley. Maali's heart sinks as her eyes lock onto the distressing scene unfolding before her. The desperate struggle of the woman pinned down by a man sends a surge of anger through her veins. She clenches her fists, ready to intervene and protect the victim. But just as she braces herself to act, Noah's grip tightens on her shoulder, silently commanding her attention. With a pointed gesture upward, his eyes convey a different proposal, redirecting her focus to the fire escape that ascends the back of the building.

Looking up, Maali's gaze lands on the man stationed at the opposite entrance of the alley, his vigilant, watchful eyes scanning the surroundings. On the roof of the adjacent building, a man lazily enjoys a cigarette, oblivious to the unfolding scene below. Noah's voice barely escapes his lips, a hushed whisper that reaches Maali's ears. "We rush in, and the guys up top take us down," he cautions, emphasising the importance of a closer assessment. "Take a closer look at our 'victim' down there."

Maali's eyes narrow as she scrutinises the woman's movements, her mind piecing together the puzzle before her. She notices subtle nuances in the woman's struggle, the strategic placement of her limbs and the way she subtly shifts her weight. It becomes apparent that her resistance isn't born out of fear or desperation but a carefully devised act. The woman's eyes, though seemingly terrified, flicker with a glint of spunk, a signal understood only by those in the know.

Maali's gaze then shifts to the man atop the woman, his grip on her more of a feigned restraint than an overpowering hold. The angle of his body suggests a deliberate effort to minimise contact, to create the illusion of dominance without causing harm. The absence of urgency in his movements further confirms that this is not a genuine assault.

A silent understanding passes between Maali and Noah as they exchange a knowing glance.

"Motherfu—" Maali pulls back from the alley, seething. "These pieces of shit are faking it to try and lure in unsuspecting bystanders." It's almost unbelievable, but her years of working with Noah on some of the city's worst gang cases have shown her just how low people can sink into depravity.

"That's the setup they've got going on," Noah grimly observes, fully aware of the dangerous trap that awaits any would-be interveners. The rooftop sentinels act as a deadly backup, ready to neutralise anyone who dares to interfere. He adjusts his grip on the rifle, a quiet acknowledgment of the imminent confrontation. "We deal with them swiftly and keep pushing forward," he declares.

Maali reaches out and gently lowers Noah's rifle, her gaze unwavering. "What they're doing is messed up, I know, but we don't know the extent of it or their true motives." She glares at the alley as the woman attempts another scream. "We can't kill them based on a hunch that they've fully committed to this scheme."

She looks at Noah, daring him to challenge her. He grumbles under his breath before nodding. "Fine. But it doesn't mean we let them off easy," he responds, his tone laced with a simmering intensity.

A mischievous smile spreads across Maali's face, her eyes sparkling with a mix of satisfaction and amusement. She raises an eyebrow at Noah, "Exactly. Set your rifle to the lowest setting and go full auto. I'll take care of the man on the roof. You go for the fire escape."

Noah's lips curl into a smirk, mirroring her amusement. "Watch and learn," he whispers with a touch of playful arrogance.

Without wasting another moment, they swiftly manoeuvre into position. Maali's finger tenses on the trigger as she takes aim at the man on the rooftop, her body poised with controlled ambition. With a precise squeeze, she unleashes a shot that soars above the man's head, causing him to jolt in surprise. His grip falters, and his gun slips from his fingers, clattering to the ground below.

Meanwhile, Noah's finger glides on the trigger, sending a rapid succession of super-heated rounds towards their other target. The man's eyes widen with sheer terror as the scorching projectiles streak toward him. In a desperate attempt to escape, he lunges forward, but his legs tangle in his own haste. He careens over the fire escape railing, his scream piercing the air before abruptly vanishing with a dull thud as he lands unceremoniously in an open dumpster. The sound of muffled moans resonates from within, almost like an endorsement of the unexpected turn of events.

Maali and Noah exchange a triumphant glance, their expressions a mix of amusement and disbelief.

The couple on the ground swiftly disentangle themselves, their initial plan shattered by the unexpected turn of events. The woman's eyes dart around, searching for a safe haven, and she instinctively seeks refuge behind the towering dumpster. Meanwhile, the man lunges towards the fallen gun, desperation etched across his face. But as a volley of shots whizzes perilously close, he abruptly abandons his futile attempt and scurries into cover, huddling next to his companion.

A tense silence settles over the scene, broken only by the fading echoes of the gunfire. Time hangs suspended, the air pregnant with anticipation. Then, a voice laden with fear breaks the stillness from behind the dumpster. "Who's there?"

Noah locks eyes with Maali, a sinister grin stretching across his face. He brings his hand to his mouth, cupping it as he lets out a chilling, guttural laugh that echoes through the alley. "It's the fucking Prince of Darkness! I've come for your souls!" They hear a faint "What the fuck?" in response, but nothing more. Sensing the urgency of their mission, Maali takes aim and squeezes the trigger, unleashing a stream of fiery projectiles that scorch the air above the dumpster. In sync, Noah unleashes a barrage of shots.

The attackers scramble, their eyes wide with terror, not pausing to glance back at their fallen comrade. The rhythmic pounding of their shoes against the pavement echoes in the stillness, each desperate step revealing their overwhelming desire to escape the nightmare they had inadvertently summoned.

Maali bolts after them, her rifle raised. With each resounding crack of gunfire, she sends shots whizzing just above their heads. The near misses intensify the air of dread, and the very wind seems to howl with the danger of her wrath.

When she's certain their shadows have been swallowed by fear, she halts, breathing heavily. Pivoting, she finds Noah backlit by a dim light, his menacing silhouette showing his pistol aimed at the heart of the alley's darkness.

Maali's grin widens, her eyes gleaming with a mixture of satisfaction and amusement. "Well, that went smoothly," she remarks, unable to contain a hint of mockery.

Noah chuckles, his own amusement evident in his voice. "Smooth as a greased pig on roller skates," he quips.

Maali peers into the dumpster, her eyes widening at the sight of a haggard man cowering within. His gaunt frame is adorned with a vibrant serpent tattoo that coils around his neck, a stark contrast to the grimy surroundings. The stench emanating from the container suggests the man's fear may have caused him to lose control of bodily functions. Noah's face contorts into a snarl as he confronts the trembling figure, his pistol held with a threatening grip.

"Step out," Noah growls, his voice dripping with cold menace. The man obeys, slowly raising his hands in surrender, his body convulsing with a mixture of fear and nerves. The pungent odour lingers in the air, a tribute to the terror that has gripped him. Noah's hand extends, the cold metal of his gun lightly tapping the man's forehead. The mere touch sends an electric jolt of fear through the man's body, causing his trembling to intensify. The words that follow are delivered with a low, intimidating growl, leaving no room for misunderstanding. "Go. Home. Fukfoon."

The man's eyes widen, pinned to the inflexible gaze of Noah's intent. As Noah's finger begins its inexorable pressure on the trigger, time seems to elongate, the world distilled to that heartbeat moment. When the gunshot finally explodes, the sound is jarringly loud in the confined space, the bullet's trajectory so close to the man's ear that the shockwave from its passage rips through his eardrum.

A sharp, agonising pain radiates from the side of his head, and an unsettling ringing fills his ears, drowning out all other sounds. The terrifying realisation of how close he came to death douses any fire of rebellion he might have had. Clutching the side of his head, disoriented by the sudden hearing loss and searing pain, he stumbles away, his escape more a desperate scramble than a retreat, a shadow of the man he was mere moments ago.

Noah's gaze follows the retreating figure, a satisfied nod accompanying his foreboding expression. "Looks good to me."

Maali stifles a laugh, her eyes twinkling with amusement. "Fukfoon? What the hell is a fukfoon?" she asks, glancing at Noah.

With a chuckle, Noah replies, "That right there. A fukfoon – someone who screws up so spectacularly, they turn an ambush into a comedy show. Like falling off a roof and landing in trash."

Maali bursts into laughter. "So, a tactical genius in reverse? The kind who plans a surprise attack and ends up surprising himself?"

"Exactly," Noah grins. "The type who'd bring a knife to a gunfight and forget the knife. A master of missteps and mishaps."

A chuckle escapes Maali's lips, a mix of relief and dark amusement. "Yep. Now, let's go get your family."

CHAPTER 11:
Ambush

The weight of the rifle in Maali's hand feels familiar and grounding as they venture into the heart of Paradise Hills housing blocks. This enclave, a model of the once-celebrated "12-minute city" concept, promised a life where every need was a mere twelve minutes away. At first, it was convenience incarnate – efficient public transport, close-knit communities, everything within a short reach. But as they move through the streets, the remnants of that utopian vision loom over them, now a twisted shadow of its original intent.

These buildings, rising stark and imposing with their brutalist architecture, once represented a bright future. Now, the grey concrete, adorned with the vibrant graffiti of resistance, tells a different story. The artwork at the base speaks of a spirit that refuses to be caged, while the untouched upper levels stand as a silent testament to the increasing control exerted from above.

As SorrowStar's influence grew, what began as convenience morphed into a subtle form of imprisonment. Travel became restricted, a good reason needed to venture beyond the 12-minute confines. Permits were required, and surveillance intensified. The very structures designed to liberate now served to confine. The local police, whose dwindling numbers found refuge in these blocks, were a reminder of the delicate balance between safety and freedom.

In this new world, each convenience traded a piece of freedom, each safety measure a slice of privacy. The irony wasn't lost on Maali – the more people relinquished, the tighter the noose of control became. Paradise Hills, once a beacon of modern living, now stood as a stark warning: in the pursuit of idealistic safety, one might just end up caged in an open prison, where every convenience was shadowed by loss of liberty.

The streets below are strewn with the familiar detritus they've encountered throughout the city, but Maali finds solace in the absence of lifeless bodies and discarded shell casings. They come to a brief halt as Noah peeks around a corner, scanning for signs of trouble, while Maali maintains a vigilant watch behind them.

Maali's gaze, momentarily distant, is drawn upward to the mammoth structure that looms across the street. Its vast stature stretches skyward, occasionally kissing the underbelly of passing clouds. Such colossal block towers are a common sight, each evidence of society's solution to an ever-growing population crisis. While urban planners and corporations praise them as a brilliant step towards reducing the collective carbon footprint, Maali can't help but see the darker undertone. These towers are less about ecological responsibility and more about herding the masses into concentrated areas. For the elite, it makes governance simpler, surveillance easier, and control almost effortless. In a world where the decadent sprawl over vast estates, the majority are confined, stacked on top of each other in these vertical warrens.

Noah nudges Maali gently with his elbow, subtly directing her focus to the corner up ahead. Their eyes lock, a deep understanding passing between them that no words can ever capture. With every fibre of their being screaming at them to find safety, they push forward, inching closer to the tower that stands as a beacon of hope, a sanctuary where Noah's family awaits. Their journey has been marred with hardships and trepidation, and it feels surreal that their destination is tantalisingly close.

The dim luminescence from the alien vessel casts eerie, elongated shadows on the cracked pavement, playing tricks on the mind as it mingles with the rhythm of Noah and Maali's careful footsteps. The shroud of night acts as both a protector and a deceiver. The remnants of an old world, a few stubborn street lamps, splutter and cough, casting irregular circles of yellow glow onto the deserted streets. These sparse islands of light become arenas of tension for the duo. Every unexpected gleam makes their hearts skip a beat, leaving their eyes darting like those of an owl, searching and scanning for the slightest indication of danger.

In the distance, an austere tower stands tall, its silhouette cutting sharply against the backdrop of a starless sky. Their aim, a barely noticeable side entrance, is bathed in a faint, ghostly light, challenging yet beckoning them closer. Nestled at the tower's base is a vast expanse – a parking lot devoid of its former life and purpose. An asphalt wasteland stretches across 400 meters, its silence belying the potential risks. Every step taken across this barren land would be a leap of faith, their only guard being the unpredictable shroud of night.

Maali's eyes pierce through the inky darkness, her facial features tightening into a grimace, which is hidden away by the shroud of night. Every muscle in her body tenses, betraying the conflict waging within. The hushed whisper that breaks the stillness, fragile as a spider's web, carries weight that belies its softness. "Feels too quiet, doesn't it?" She murmurs, a quiver in her tone revealing her apprehension. "I'd give anything for night vision right now."

Noah, his voice barely above a whisper, "Night vision? Aim higher, Maali. How about thermal imaging?"

Noah scans the abyss before them, a thoughtful, contemplative expression cast upon his rugged face. "With the way things have been going, there's bound to be a nest of SS goons lurking in the shadows. Might be a trap." He pushes a stray lock of greying hair from his eyes with a sense of weariness.

Maali smirks, her voice tinged with a playful, slightly sinister edge, "You always think everything's a trap."

He lets out a soft, resigned chuckle, "And yet here we are, still breathing. Cautions kept us alive." Pausing, he adds, "But standing here won't. We need to move. Time isn't on our side."

With his rifle nestled snugly against his shoulder, Noah takes the lead, his figure momentarily illuminated by the slivers of moonlight peeking through the overcast sky. Maali follows closely, their steps in sync, like a choreographed dance, painting fleeting silhouettes against the canvas of the night.

The moon, a lantern hung high in the dark sky, casts an eerie pallor over the landscape. It illuminates their path just enough to dodge the haphazard obstacle course of discarded trash littering the lot. They weave, dip, and slide, their shoes scuffing against concrete barely avoiding the rubbish.

Occasionally, the metallic bodies of a few abandoned vehicles offer transient refuge - but those are scant and sporadic. Their footfalls echo between rusted husks, the vast, open lot giving little comfort in terms of cover.

As Maali scrutinises the lot, her eyes catch a peculiar advantage. The asphalt, marred by deep craters and gaping potholes, resembles the surface of a war-torn moon. The cruel wear and tear that had once rendered this lot an undesirable landscape might now be their salvation. Each pothole, an ugly proof of neglect, offers a fleeting refuge or a potential misstep. The wrong move might lead to a devastating stumble, plunging them into danger amidst this maze of shadows. The scattered, rusted car remnants silently tell the tale of a time gone by.

Along this risky path, Maali and Noah carefully navigate the dangers that surround them, evading pitfalls with barely an inch to spare. With every leap and sidestep, Maali feels the ember of hope grow stronger. But just as they reach the midpoint of the lot, an eerie stillness descends, stifling the already quiet night. The unnatural calm unnerves her, its silence screaming a warning — the calm before the storm.

It begins as a whisper of intuition, a nagging tingle that crawls beneath her skin, refusing to be ignored. This silent foreboding materialises, causing the fine hairs at the nape of her neck to bristle like an animal sensing an imminent threat. As Maali turns, a silent plea forming on her lips to warn Noah, she finds his eyes already locked onto hers, mirroring the same dread.

His voice, a mere breath, drifts to her ears, "You sense it too, don't you?"

Before she can voice the heavy unease weighing on her chest, the surroundings are violently bathed in an intense glow. The intermittent lamps, once dormant, now burst into life with a fervent orange glare, blinding her. Her hand rises reflexively to shield her eyes, but the overwhelming brightness pierces through, leaving her disoriented.

The dappled spots clouding Maali's vision slowly dissolve, revealing a world twisted by the garish glare. Their previous sanctuary of shadows has been transformed into a glaring stage, leaving them open and vulnerable to unseen threats. "Move! Now!" Maali's voice is edged with frantic urgency, slicing through the oppressive brightness.

Without hesitation, they bolt towards the tower's entrance, their rapid footfalls echoing on the illuminated expanse. There's no refuge to be found; the closest car is too far off-course, while the nearest hideout is merely a revolting heap of refuse teeming with maggots. Maali's fleeting surge of hope now curdles into a stinging regret as they traverse the blindingly lit path.

But just as their destination seems attainable, figures materialise from the surrounding gloom. Five unremarkable shapes clothed in plain streetwear, their menace accentuated by the unforgiving light. Cold, threatening barrels of guns turn their path to salvation into an impassable barrier. In a synchronised motion, Noah and Maali grind to a halt, rifles raised and ready. They restrain from firing, sensing that this overt standoff might just be the tip of the iceberg - for such a bold reveal suggests hidden reinforcements lurking in the wings.

While Noah keeps his sights locked on the quintet, Maali swings her gaze around, scanning the intermittent shadows behind them. As the once-blinding lights grow temperamental, dimming sporadically, the fringe of their vision is peppered with sinister outlines. A sinking dread pulls at their guts – they are ensnared, surrounded on all sides.

"Easy does it," Noah murmurs, his eyes never straying from the immediate threat. "This lot's got twitchy fingers."

The only reply from Maali is her vigilant silence, her sharp eyes darting and dissecting the bleak landscape, seeking a lifeline. Suddenly, a faltering bulb fights against the darkness, revealing for a heartbeat the menacing figures lurking at their rear — and just as crucially, the lethal instruments in their hands. Rough imitations of Klob 7's, they might be crude, but with the grotesquely extended magazines, they're a force to be reckoned with.

"Those makeshifts might be packing fifty rounds, easy," Maali breathes, transfixed by the raw power that these adversaries wield.

Noah responds with a grunt. "Sounds right. Accuracy's not a requirement when you're wielding a bullet shower." He narrows his eyes at the five barricading their path. "Most likely Earl's boys. If you get hit, expect a nasty trip."

A puzzled sound escapes Maali, her grip tightening on her rifle.

Noah's voice drops lower into a growl. "Earl's crew has a nasty trick - bullets coated in some hallucinogenic. I've no clue what it is, but even a graze can send you into la-la land."

The revelation of the drugged ammunition heightens Maali's reluctance to surrender. "We can take them," she asserts, her statement stirring Noah behind her. "Best chance we have. On my count of three..."

"Whoa there, daredevil." Noah interrupts her countdown, his voice barely a whisper. His eyes dart between the encroaching gang members, a wild chess game playing out as he keeps each piece in check. "You sure the D-TEM high hasn't worn off? This isn't exactly our lucky day."

A gruff, antagonising voice cuts through their whispers, "Drop the guns, chuckleheads, or we drop you."

Noah chokes back a disbelieving laugh, "Petra, is that you?" As a stocky blue-haired woman materialises from the shadows, Noah grins, "Long time no see. How was your vacation in San Sydney?"

Her visage distorts into a scowl, adding layers of repulsiveness to her already unfortunate features. Built like a freight train, each muscle is clearly etched, she is forced to mouth-breathe due to her disfigured nose. "Eight years, you jerk. Got out three weeks ago and I've been itching for some payback." Cracking her knuckles, she sneers at the duo, "And isn't this a pleasant surprise? Murphy the douchebag, and his rescued mutt."

Noah retorts, his voice dripping sarcasm, "Oh Petra, don't be so sour. You knew the game was a gamble. It was your mess up, not mine." Her growl, animalistic and deep, vibrates the air around them. Sensing an escalation, Maali swiftly silences Noah with a jab to his calf using her boot heel. The ensuing grunt and cough end his bravado.

Petra's words, devoid of any warmth, cut through the tension like a knife. With dogged resolve, Maali's fingers clutch her rifle even tighter, a beacon of hope in their dire predicament. "You might be on my list," Petra intones coldly, "but right now, you're just a minor distraction. Earl's upstairs, having a chat with your kids. Word is, you've got something he wants. Fortunately for you, he's in no mood to damage the merchandise. So, here's the proposition: Drop the bag. Gently. Hand over what's inside. Once that's done, you're free to leave, and Earl will send your spawn out. Or alternatively make my day and try me."

The stalemate is intense, tension thickening the air between the opposing forces. But the bleak reality of their situation becomes increasingly clear. With limited options and a threat hanging over them, surrendering the D-TEM seems to be their only way out. Under his breath, so low it's almost lost amidst the standoff, Noah grumbles to Maali, "If it's not SorrowStar, it's Earl's mob. We should've smoked him when we had the chance."

They're cornered with only one avenue of escape - relinquishing the D-TEM. Noah mutters, almost inaudibly, "I'm out of ideas, Maali."

"Same," she responds quietly. Her sigh echoes loudly in the tense silence as she lets the satchel slide from her shoulder. "We'll play your game, Petra. Just remember - we play nice."

Petra's laugh, sharp and dripping with arrogance, punctuates the charged atmosphere. "Darling, given the value of the D-TEM, we're not about to let you pull any fast moves. Just hand it over, and all this remains cordial. Refuse, and, well, let's just say we won't mind turning you into human colanders." The increasing pressure of Petra's finger against the trigger is palpable. "You've until I reach three..."

Suddenly, a blast of sparks erupts from above as an old overhead light shatters, initiating a cascade of failures that drowns the vicinity in darkness. Using this blink of chaos to their advantage, Noah grabs Maali's arm, yanking her to the ground an instant before a blind barrage of gunfire peppers the night. "Stay low!" he whispers sharply as bullets whir through the void they'd just occupied.

Scrambling on all fours, they veer towards the previously sighted refuse pile. The air is thick with curses and panicked yells as Petra's crew, caught in their own crossfire due to the absence of a visible target, begin to injure each other.

"Ceasefire, you idiots!" Petra's command slices through the bangs, struggling against the deafening gunfire.

A fleeting silence descends when the hailstorm of bullets ebbs, only to be shattered within moments. A random burst of gunfire rings out, accompanied by a terrified screech. "It's on me! Get it off! Get it off!" The voice recedes rapidly, its owner fleeing an unseen terror.

Dug into the garbage heap like a bush tick, Noah and Maali look around, ready to handle any potential pursuers. Among the disorder, a few of Petra's gang maintain their composure, hunkering down and trailing the duo amidst the erratic gunfire. Maali plants one knee on the ground, peeking above the rubbish heap just long enough to discharge her rifle.

The flare of energy burns into her retinas as she releases a volley towards her pursuers. Struck squarely in the gut, one gang member silently crumples, his innards instantly seared by the energy pulse. The rest of his squad dives for cover, aiming to be as inconspicuous as possible amidst the chaotic skirmish.

Petra's goons, lacking both discipline and training, fire wildly, their weapons spewing bullets in chaotic arcs, punctuated by shouts and frenzied calls, painting a picture of pure pandemonium. One, more superstitious or simply more theatrical than the rest, staggers back from the frenzy, clutching at a wound on his leg, his eyes wide with terror.

"The devil's here!" he shrieked, staring around as if expecting to see the horned figure materialise out of the smoke and shadows. Another, on the ground with a bullet wound on his shoulder, echoes the sentiment, "Hell's gates have opened!"

"Fall back, fall back." Petra's frustration could not be hidden; her meticulously planned trap was devolving into panic at the hands of her own men.

As the remaining gunfire and screams move farther away, Maali's gaze pierces the darkness, hunting for any signs of imminent danger, when Noah's weapon discharges three times in rapid succession. Startled, she wheels around to assist him, but his eyes are fixed on a seemingly empty patch of darkness. Even with the moonlight filtering through the cloud breaks, she discerns nothing.

"What the fuck?" she inquires, her tone laced with urgency. When he fails to respond, she nudges him insistently. "Noah, talk to me."

His breaths coming in shallow bursts, Noah brandishes his weapon indiscriminately at the black void. "He's here," he whispers through gritted teeth, his voice shrill with terror. "The one who... who killed Jen!" Maali barely recognises this fear-stricken man as the Noah she knows.

Attempting to soothe him, she says, "Noah, it can't be him. He was dealt with two years back..." As she rests a hand on his arm to steady him, a wet warmth seeps through his overcoat. With a sinking feeling, she traces her hand up his arm, discovering a puncture through both the fabric and flesh. "Damn it, Noah, you've been hit!"

Snapping a low-light micro glow stick from her pocket, Maali briskly shakes it, activating its luminescent core. The soft glow bathes the wound in a red light as she swiftly uses her boot knife to slice away the fabric for a more precise assessment. The sight reveals abundant blood, yet it's clear that the bullet merely grazed him, damaging skin but sparing deeper muscle or vital areas. Their gear isn't designed to handle major traumas.

Regardless of the minor wound, Noah is on the brink of hysteria. "Maali, you need to leave. He's here, he's... he's come for me," he stammers in hushed horror. He risks a quick glance over their cover before retracting. "I'll buy you time. Run, Maali, run now!"

"Shut up and let me handle this," Maali snaps, pressing him down as she tears off a piece of her sleeve. Her hands move awkwardly, hastily wrapping the fabric around Noah's wound. As she works to staunch the bleeding, she notices Noah's gaze drifting, his mind wandering. Maali's hand connects with Noah's face in a resounding slap. "Snap out of it, man!" she barks her tone a blend of concern and frustration. "We need you here, this is not the time for a nervous breakdown. The kids are waiting."

Jolted by the unexpected slap, Noah blinks rapidly as Maali attempts to pull Noah to his feet. Crouching back down, she says, "What's your problem, man? Stop..." Her retort dies as she catches sight of his dilated pupils in the moonlight. "Oh no... the bullets..." The reality hits her - Noah's not just afraid; he's hallucinating from the drugged ammunition.

His body curls into itself as he battles unseen terrors, the powerful hallucinogen wreaking havoc on his mind. She has to counteract the effects. She recalls the pharmacy built into the base level of most tower blocks. If they can get there, there should be Disprodozone, an antipsychotic capable of neutralising hallucinogenic compounds. It might just work.

With no other options, Maali kneels beside Noah, whispering menacingly into his ear. "The devil's not after you, boy..." Her voice maintains a steady growl, exploiting his heightened fear. "He's coming for your family. It'd be pretty easy for him to slice up the kiddies with you crying like a little bitch out here..."

Noah's deep growl resonates from his throat, animalistic and uncontrolled, as he springs to his feet. His mind might be ensnared by a nightmare, but the instinct to protect his kin nudges him into motion. With no time to let him wander aimlessly, Maali seizes his hand, hauling him along as they sprint towards the tower.

In the belly of the main building, Maali and Noah bolt towards the pharmacy. Its fragmented windows bear witness to marauders who've stripped it bare, their low murmurs resonating from within. Banking on the idea that these looters would be too engrossed in their spoils to note their presence, Maali steers Noah deeper into the heart of the pharmacy. The common drugs have been plundered, but as they venture further towards the restricted section, they chance upon a cache of untouched potent substances.

Just as the back room comes into view, a shadowy form suddenly steps out, blocking their path. Noah's dilated pupils flash with terror. His handgun, seemingly moving on its own, snaps up, and in a strangled voice, he cries, "Back, foul demon!" The sharp crack of gunfire fills the space as he unleashes a magazine worth of bullets into the figure.

The haunting echo of the shots is amplified by the building's walls. Maali's gaze darts sideways, spotting a handful of looters scattering in sheer panic, their faces painted with raw fear.

Arriving at the back room, Maali utilises her pulse rifle to melt the lock, booting the door open afterwards. The lights stutter to life, a mix of flickering and dead bulbs. She nudges Noah onto a stool, steering him towards the door as she embarks on a frantic search for their much-needed antipsychotic. Noah's nonsensical mutterings about phantom demons provide a haunting background as Maali combs through the inventory, brushing past multiple dangerous and illicit narcotics stashed haphazardly. Almost at her wits' end, she finally locates a bottle of Disprodozone.

Snatching the bottle and finding a sterile syringe in a cabinet, she draws out a small dosage. She performed a similar procedure back in the day as a rookie before partnering with Noah, so the process is almost second nature to her. With the dose prepared, she turns back to Noah and injects it through the Kevlar weave of his jeans into his thigh, his only response a faint hiss of discomfort.

Minutes later, Noah stirs, massaging his temples and groaning as he rises from the stool. A perplexed gaze sweeps the room. "What the...?" The words trail off into a painful groan as he slumps against a wall, fighting off a wave of nausea. "Where are we?"

"Pharmacy in the tower block. Hold on," Maali admonishes, unhesitatingly dousing his wound with sanitising solution before upgrading her makeshift patch to actual bandages. A tight knot ensures it's secure and that he's fully back to reality.

"Easy!" he hisses, wincing and instinctively reaching for the wound. "Just load me up with the potent stuff. We can't afford to faff around."

A wince mars Maali's face. "We lost the bag during the fight, so..." She moves to the shelves, randomly grabbing several vials that bear a passing resemblance to D-TEM. "We'll have to bluff our way out and hope that Earl isn't shrewd enough to call it."

Noah nods, taking a deep, steadying breath as he steps out of the back room. He gingerly rolls his shoulder, testing his mobility, and winces slightly. Bringing a hand up to his face, he rubs his jawline, feeling the tender spot where Maali's slap had landed. "Feels like I've been hit by a truck," he grumbles.

Maali, following close behind, shoots back with a wry smirk, "More like walked into a door. A very angry, fast-moving door."

Their brief moment of levity fades quickly as they turn a corner in the aisle. There, the harsh reality of their situation hits them – a young boy, no more than sixteen, lies lifeless on the ground. His face and chest are riddled with bullet holes.

Noah's grip on his weapon tightens, the warmth from the barrel seeping into his palm. He stares down at the young boy's body, a gnawing suspicion creeping into the edge of his consciousness. The vivid hallucinations he experienced now mingle with reality, leaving him with a troubling sense of unease. "Did I...?" he starts to ask, his voice trailing off, heavy with an unformed fear.

Maali, understanding his turmoil, interjects softly, "Things got a little chaotic. It was hard to see clearly in the frenzy." Her words are deliberately vague, sparing him the crushing weight of truth, at least for the moment.

He strides away, the burden of uncertainty etched in his movements. Maali pauses to look at the boy, her heart heavy. The harshness of their reality, where survival often comes at a terrible cost, weighs on her. She whispers, not just to herself but to the world they fight to protect, "Every moment, every action, is a fight to keep hope alive. But in this fight, sometimes hope is the first casualty."

CHAPTER 12:
Family

Disorientation clings to Noah like a rash. The hallucinations have ceased, but glistening motes of light whirl in his vision, phantom shadows twisting at the periphery, dissolving whenever he attempts to pin them down. His head thumps rhythmically with pain, a frustrating reminder of the lingering toxins. The heart of the tower block looms ahead, a throng of elevators installed to service the multitudes residing in the lofty residential building. Scattered lights flicker at the base level, an encouraging sign that the lift systems may be operational.

"Noah?" The sound of his name breaks his musings. Shaking his head in an attempt to scatter the phantom lights, he pivots to find Maali observing him with an uncertain gaze. "You sure you're okay?"

Opening his mouth to reply, a sour taste abruptly invades his palate, a nauseating churn in his stomach following soon after. He dry-heaves, expelling the bitter bile with a muffled curse. His hand reaches instinctively for the missing comfort of his flask, settling instead for wiping his mouth on a patch of cleaner cloth scrounged from the pharmacy. " I'm as put-together as a puzzle with missing pieces," he confesses, "but it's Irrelevant. I won't let that bastard harm them."

Noah's movements are tense and deliberate as he checks his pistol. His fingers work quickly, expertly ejecting the magazine. The scarce ammunition: one fully loaded magazine and only a couple more with just a few rounds left. He glances over at Maali, her supply mirroring his own. He slams the magazine back into the pistol with a sharp, almost angry motion. As they reach the elevator, his frustration boils over. Instead of a gentle press, his fist hammers against the call button.

Retreating to lean against the wall, Noah's foot taps an impatient rhythm on the ground, his whole body a portrait of contained agitation. He crosses his arms, each breath a visible effort to quell the rising tide of anxiety and anger, his gaze flickering towards the elevator doors with a simmering impatience.

"Move it," he mutters under his breath, glaring at the gaudy progress meter situated above the lift doors. The languid descent of the elevator from an upper level is indicated by the sluggish needle. "I detest these contraptions."

The incredulity in Maali's voice is clear as she retorts, "A tower block resident who despises lifts?"

As they stood waiting for the elevator, its arrival marked by a slow ascending hum, Maali turned to Noah, a thoughtful expression clouding her face. "It's ironic, isn't it? This so-called 'progress' they preach about, when the reality is they are rotten to the core." She pauses, kneeling to tighten her bootlaces before looking back up to Noah with a smile, "Diandra showed me the Calistin way, and let me tell you, it's a shit load better than what we have now."

Noah sighed, his back resting against the cool wall, his voice carrying a note of wry cynicism. "You know, it's a funny world we ended up in. Seems like the harder we work, the thinner the rewards. It's like running on a treadmill that's always speeding up."

Maali nods, understanding his sentiment. "And the tighter the grip of those in power, the more they dress it up as 'efficiency' or 'progress.' But we know the game, don't we? It's not about making life easier for us; it's about making it easier to keep us in line."

Maali joins Noah against the wall, a hint of wistfulness in her voice. "Back when we were kids, buying something was simple. Now, it's like you're always under scrutiny. Every purchase, every little indulgence, it's all tracked and judged. Step outside their 'healthy' guidelines too often, and you'll find yourself cut off. So much for freedom, huh?"

She pauses, her gaze distant. "You notice how they've turned our differences against us? It's like they've fine-tuned society to keep us at odds, perpetually distracted by one conflict or another. It's a classic strategy: divide to conquer. Meanwhile, we're too busy fighting amongst ourselves to see the bigger picture."

Noah chimes in, his tone tinged with cynicism. "And let's not forget the underground markets. The system's designed to corner people and drive them to the edges. Then they act all shocked when those shadows they've pushed us into start to grow, feeding on what they refuse to acknowledge."

"And the drugs," Maali continued, her voice softening. "Flooding our streets under the banner of 'self-expression'. They champion this ultra-freedom, yet it's never felt more constricting. It's as if they want us lost and confused. We are easier to control that way."

Noah met her gaze, his eyes carrying a sadness. "True freedom doesn't come with footnotes, Maali. What they're offering us is just a maze with an ever-shifting exit."

Impatience bubbles over as Noah takes a swing at the call button again, this time hard enough to fracture the glass overlay. "It's not just the damn elevators." His patience snaps, leading to restless pacing interspersed with heated glares at the tardy lift. "I loathe the whole blasted tower. Almost every aspect of it. I'd give anything to reside in a genuine house like Grandad's."

A quizzical arching of Maali's brow precedes a moment of understanding. "Janine?" Noah's tight grimace is all the confirmation she needs. "She really had you wrapped around her finger, huh?"

An almost imperceptible chuckle from Noah shatters the ensuing silence. "Still does," he admits with the ghost of a smile. It's fleeting, soon replaced by a sombre expression. "The kids needed to be near school. This place may not be my preference, but it was best for them. That reality didn't alter when things between Janine and I fell apart."

Maali's nod is cut short as a harsh grind of metal reverberates from the elevator shaft. Both sets of eyes dart to the sluggish needle, the lift now trapped almost a dozen stories up. "Blasted machine!" Noah's frustration manifests in a volley of kicks aimed at the unyielding door, along with a tirade of curses echoing in the deserted lobby.

Maali's hand clasps his arm in an attempt to quell his rage. "This is futile. We could try another one and--" Her words are abruptly silenced by a thunderous SNAP resonating from the innards of the elevator, followed in quick succession by the screeching sound of rending metal. With a swift tug, she pulls Noah away, the din of tortured metal amplifying until it abruptly cuts off with a seismic crash. As the dust plumes into the air, the elevator door grinds open halfway, revealing the vertiginous drop into the darkened shaft.

Maali leans in cautiously to inspect the wreckage. The once sleek lift is now a jumbled mass of metal at the shaft's base. She cranes her neck upwards, straining to discern the source of the collapse, but the upper floors are shrouded in darkness.

Retreating from the wreckage, she finds Noah visibly seething. "I, uh--" Maali's words die in her throat as Noah strides forward, uttering a venomous curse into the gaping shaft.

"Junk heap," he mutters, shaking his head in disgust. "The remaining ones are probably death traps, assuming they could even reach this floor."

"The one damn time we need a lift," Noah growls, his voice laced with a mix of fury and despair. The hint of fear in his eyes betrays his thoughts: his family, held hostage several floors above.

Feeling a weight in her chest, Maali swallows hard. "Guess we're taking the scenic route then," she murmurs, nodding towards the grey concrete staircase that spirals upward.

Noah shoots a weary glance towards the seemingly endless ascent, exhaling sharply. "Every step, every floor, is a moment they're in danger," he murmurs, psyching himself up.

Maali pushes forward. "Then we'd best start climbing."

The weight of the moment's harshness pressed down on them, the staircase before them becoming not just a physical challenge but an emotional gauntlet. Every step reminded them of the city's decline, the residue of desperation evident in the discarded, looted luggage that littered their path.

But as they reached the third-floor landing, it was more than mere objects that bore witness to the city's suffering. The young woman sprawled out before them was a cruel display of the very human cost. The unnerving stillness of the stairwell was broken by the soft gasp that escaped Noah's lips.

"Maggie..." His whisper was heartbroken, haunted. Kneeling beside the lifeless form, he brushed stray hair from her face, his fingers lingering on her cold skin as he closed her unseeing eyes with the utmost reverence.

Maali watched him, her chest tightening at the raw pain in his eyes. "A familiar face?" she ventured, her voice soft and cautious.

He nodded, his eyes distant, reliving memories. "She used to watch the kids when Janine and I were still a unit. Her home was just above ours." A bitter irony tugged at the corner of his lips. "This staircase... she must've been trying to escape. Maybe someone pushed, maybe she stumbled." He swallowed hard.

The tender pressure of Maali's fingers on his shoulder served as both a comfort and a nudge. "We have to move on, Noah."

With a heavy heart, Noah cast one last look at Maggie before forcing himself to continue. As they ascended, the brutality of the panic that had unfolded painted a chilling picture. Tattered luggage, shoes lost in haste, and crushed spectacles littered their path. Grisly signs of a riotous escape were evident everywhere, but it was the trampled bodies that spoke loudest of the blind terror. It seemed as though a tidal wave of fear had swept through, leaving destruction in its wake.

Upon reaching the fifth floor, the scent of charred wood and melted plastic hit them. The scorched walls and remnants of burnt furniture revealed the extent of the inferno that had once raged. Beneath them, the wet carpet squelched proof of the building's still-functional fire suppression system. Bullet casings glinted amidst the soot, and the ceiling bore bullet holes - a desperate effort, it seemed, to clear an escape route. Instead, it appeared to have led to chaos.

Maali exhaled slowly, absorbing the tragic scene before her. She turned to Noah, her face reflecting the weight of their surroundings. "A small blessing that the fire system held," she remarked, the irony of the situation not lost on her.

Noah's nod resonates with approval. "Indeed. A blaze in a structure of this magnitude could prove catastrophic, wiping out a small city's worth of inhabitants. The fire control is perhaps the only redeeming feature in this godforsaken tower." Their laborious ascent continues, Maali leading the way, securing their path while Noah trails, his vigilant gaze sweeping their rear.

As they touched down on the eighth-floor landing, the sudden, deafening echo of a bullet ricocheting off the stair railing jerked Maali into a reflexive response. Its sharp, metallic resonance reverberated, hanging thick in the air like the imminent promise of more to come. "TAKE COVER!" Noah's voice was an urgent roar.

With agility born of sheer desperation, she dove headlong into the sanctuary of the closest doorway, a vicious storm of bullets pursuing her. They bit into the walls, embedding themselves with vindictive intent.

Whirling around inside the room, the acrid scent of sweat and fear struck her nose, revealing the presence of another before her eyes confirmed it—a ragged figure, skin mottled, sclera blackened with SPICE and menacing tattoos that snaked up his neck and across his face. Maali recognised the facial tattoos: a chilling skull, its hollow eyes dripping with crimson, crowned by a snake coiled menacingly around a dagger; unmistakable markings of the Glebe Gravewalkers. He lunged for a firearm just within his grasp, but the foreboding hum of Maali's pulse rifle acted as a temporary tether, holding him back. "Don't," she breathed out, a viper's warning.

In a haze of desperation, heightened by the insidious grip of spice, the man grabs his weapon, spraying bullets haphazardly that ricochet off the walls. His actions are unnaturally erratic, a visual echo of the drug's harrowing blend of hyper-stimulation and detachment. Maali's rifle responded almost in tandem, sending out a searing energy pulse. Her rifle emits a sharp burst of energy. The impact is immediate and devastating, yet there's a surreal delay in the man's reaction. Now void of life, his eyes still hold a vacant, distant look – a chilling reminder of how spice unnerves the mind's connection to reality.

His fingers continue their deathly twitch for a moment, a posthumous spasm born of the spice's lingering influence. The gun in his lifeless grasp spits out a few more aimless shots, etching wild patterns into the surrounding walls before finally falling silent.

Maali's hands instinctively pat down her body, searching for any sign of injury. As her fingers brushed the gritty residue from a near miss, she expelled a sharp breath, chastising his foolhardy courage under her breath. But the distant staccato of gunfire, echoing from the corridor beyond, reminded her that this game of life and death was far from over.

Cautiously, Maali peers into the corridor, spotting Noah on the opposite side, his back flush against the wall. His hand motions for her to move. Taking a quick mental snapshot of her surroundings, she dashes across, her posture low and nimble. As she reaches Noah, relief evident in her eyes, he inquires, "Inhabitant?"

She gives a rueful smirk. "Handled. And the corridor?"

His head tilts towards the fallen foes down the hallway, each bearing the signature mark of a precise centre-of-mass shot. "They got tunnel vision chasing you, and the bastards never saw me coming." With a wary glance back at the now-quiet stairwell, he steps forward. "Let's go. For now, it looks like we've got some breathing room."

"Since when did the Glebe Gravewalkers get involved with Earl?" Maali queries, the click of her cheek punctuating her confusion. "They aren't even in the same trade."

Noah runs a hand through his hair, a puzzled expression on his face. "Honestly, I'm stumped too. Last I heard, they were running SPICE operations on the east side."

Maali hesitates, "You think it's just a coincidence they're here?"

Noah shrugs, "Could be. I heard through the grapevine they're seeking revenge against some cop housed in this building. Who the hell knows anymore?"

A scowl creases Maali's features as they resume their ascent. "This is too smooth."

"I'm aware. It's likely a trap, but there's no turning back. I won't let them harm my family," Noah's vow fuels his pace, though it's quickly tempered by his laboured breath.

Maali's laughter rings out, echoing lightly in the cavernous space. "Ever thought of trading in your beer and smokes for a more… wholesome lifestyle?" she teases. His piercing gaze challenges her jest, but she's already darting ahead, her footsteps a playful taunt. Noah's competitive spirit fuels him, and soon he's matching her stride for stride. However, by the twelfth floor, even Maali's renowned stamina struggles against the searing burn in her muscles. "Really, Noah? All for a room with a view?"

With a wry smile, he pushes forward, "Always chase the horizon, Maali. It's worth every burning muscle."

Maali wipes away a bead of perspiration on her forehead, a mischievous glint in her eye. "Look at you, sweating like a sinner in church," she teases.

Noah, his face slick with sweat, flashes a grin. "And you? Is that mascara starting to run yet?"

Their race escalates, neither conceding an inch until the fifteenth floor emerges before them. Noah stumbles against the wall, gasping for breath. "Made it," he manages between ragged inhales.

Maali, catching her breath yet unable to suppress her teasing grin, gives him a gentle shove. "Just made it, did we?" she quips, wiping away the sweat from her forehead. The relentless ascent was behind them; ahead, a looming confrontation awaited.

Straightening himself, Noah leads the way down the hall, firearm at the ready. The aftermath of the initial panic following the EMP seems more pronounced the higher they ascend. The corridors resemble a warzone—trashed decorative foliage, torn furniture strewn in the hallways, and ominous dark stains adorning the floor and walls that Maali doesn't dare investigate. Navigating the expansive tower block is a tortuous endeavour, requiring several minutes to reach their designated section.

Upon spotting the familiar door—now brutally kicked in—Noah accelerates his pace. As they approach, a heart-wrenching sound grips them—a sobbing whimper belonging to Noah's youngest, Jane. Enraged, Noah moves to storm in, but Maali's firm grip on his arm restrains him. "Charge in recklessly, and all this is for nothing!" she hisses. His features flame cherry red, a silent storm brewing in his eyes. Maali doesn't hesitate further, fearing his bottled rage might cause an aneurysm. She steels herself, her grip tightening on her pulse rifle.

Mustering a feigned bravado, Maali calls out. "Earl! We're aware you're hiding in there, you wretched fiend!" The muffled sobs of a child morph into a cruel, echoing chuckle from within. Maali tightens her grip on Noah's arm, sensing his boiling urge to burst in. "We got the D-TEM. Release the children and their mother. This shit can be all yours!"

The response is a chilling silence. A collective breath is held, the tense wait stretches, and then a voice—distorted by agony—emerges. "Dad!"

The sound of his child's cry transforms Noah. Every paternal instinct ignites, his visage contorted with ferocity. "Jero!" Without a second thought, he wrenches himself free from Maali's hold, launching towards the room's entrance. The unsuspecting gang member stationed there is met with a human projectile; Noah's onslaught is relentless and overwhelming. With a vicious kick, a spray of teeth arcs through the air while the thug's head is brutally slammed against the cold, hard floor. Yet, the chaotic melee grinds to an unexpected halt as Noah's gaze locks onto the scene unravelling before him.

Following cautiously, Maali steps over the threshold, a shiver of dread coursing through her. The room teems with armed gang members, including the menacing Petra, who stands arrogantly with her boot planted on Jero's back. The boy's arm is misshapen and bent—an undoubted fracture. He'd resisted, it appears. The sight of Earl, though, is the most chilling—pistol in hand, its deadly aim on Janine, Noah's bruised and bloodied ex-wife, forced onto her knees.

Despite her battered state, Janine's fiery spirit remains unquenched. Spotting the would-be rescuers, she spits a mouthful of blood, letting out a sigh laden with sarcasm and relief. "If it isn't Murphy, the bearer of calamity." The children exchange looks with their father, their desperate smiles echoing silent pleas. Even Jero manages a pained smirk.

Noah maintains a lowered weapon, unwilling to ignite a deadly firefight that might endanger his children further. "You've stooped low, Earl. Disgracefully low," his voice is saturated with revulsion.

Earl seems indifferent to Noah's comments, spitting a glob of phlegm onto the floor. "Unimportant. The D-TEM is all I care about."

Noah, struggling to maintain his composed facade, retorts. "You terrorise innocent children for drugs? You're repugnant, Earl."

Earl's laughter rings around the room, a sound both mocking and contemptuous. "Thinking you're above it all, eh, Noah? But let's be real. A cop in this hellhole of a city dabbling in the underworld's shadows? You are far from clean, my friend. And tell me, how does a cop like you manage to secure a single-family home in these times? With everyone else cramming into communal homes to make ends meet? Even factoring in your child support is quite the feat. Puts a new spin on things, doesn't it?" His grin turns sly. "The only thing truly clean about you, Noah, might just be the money I wash for you."

The room fills with his malicious cackle, his gang members exchanging eager glances. "That D-TEM vial, it's worth a fortune, a decade's income for a lowly cop. It's a goldmine to us." His hand sweeps across his cronies, their faces reflecting their greed. "Let's drop the moral superiority, Noah. Hand over the vials, and everyone walks out of here unharmed. Hell, I might even share a small portion of my windfall with you."

Noah, eyes flitting between his captive family and the drug vials, concedes. He sighs, motioning towards Maali, who carries the satchel. "Take it. It's all yours."

As Maali takes a step, Petra's barked command halts her. "Hold it! Drop your weapons first!" Hesitation flickers between the duo. "I'm not fuckin' around! Drop 'em now, or I'll turn this place into a knacker's yard."

With a twisted smile, Earl chides Petra, "Easy on the profanities, Petra. We're in mixed company. Can't have the kiddies learning new vocabulary from Auntie Petra's threat handbook, can we?"

Exchanging a silent nod, Noah and Maali relent to the demands. Noah discards his sidearm, the only weapon he has left after losing his rifle in the drug-induced psychosis earlier. Maali follows suit, setting down her pulse rifle, her backup pistol concealed beneath her jacket and boot knife.

With the visible weapons discarded, Maali again approaches the counter, setting down the satchel. Every eye in the room follows her. Maali, with her hands raised in a gesture of peace, steps back.

The room, laden with heavy tension, watches as a jittery goon scuttles forward to collect the prize. Bag in hand, he retreats to Petra, who snatches it and positions it beside Earl, maintaining her threatening stance over Jero.

Squeezing his fists, Noah demands, "You've got what you came for fella. Release them. No more blood needs to be spilled."

Earl's eyes dart between Noah and the bag, a calculating glint apparent. "Only eight here, Noah. Weren't there nine at the docks when you left me tied up like some mangy mutt?"

Noah meets Earl's gaze, the weight of their shared history heavy between them. "We needed one," he admits, nodding toward Maali. "She took a hit."

A smirk crawls onto Earl's face as he winks at Maali. "Good stuff, huh?"

Maali shoots him a withering glare but says nothing.

Earl's fingers shuffle over the vials, greed evident in his eyes. "Eight... still more than enough to retire in style." His grin broadens, mischievous and challenging. "Hell, if it's the real deal, then even seven will do."

Noah nods, his voice firm. "It is. You have my word."

"Oh, is it so?" Earl playfully replies. Suddenly, his attention shifts, his fingers signalling Petra. To Maali's horror, Petra moves from Jero to Janine, violently forcing her arm onto the table, her sawn-off shotgun poised threateningly over Janine's hand.

Maali's voice cracks as she desperately cries out, "No, don't!" Her heart pounds in her chest, knowing that she's powerless to stop what's about to happen. The sound of Janine's screams fills the space, each wail a chilling witness to her terror. Petra's finger quivers on the trigger, and the world slows to a sickening crawl as the gunshot reverberates. The room becomes a canvas of horror, Janine's hand contorted and broken, a crimson spray painting the walls with a nauseating abstract chef-d'oeuvre. The pain and anguish etched on Janine's face are unbearable to witness. Despite Maali's efforts to restrain him, Noah nearly erupts in a fury, held back by Maali's desperate plea. "No, Noah! They'll just kill us all!"

Amidst the commotion, Earl's perverse laughter rings out. "Oh, how fun! But we're not done yet." He gestures to Petra, and the terrifying woman drags Noah's eleven-year-old daughter, Jess, into the fray.

The room plunges into disarray. Janine's deranged screams echo as Petra forces Jess's hand down and brutally impales it with a knife. Janine's hysterical screams cease abruptly as Petra cracks her across the face with the butt of her shotgun, leaving Noah's family helpless and distraught.

The room is enveloped in a chilling silence, broken only by Jess's soft, pained whimpers. In this hushed stillness, Earl's voice emerges, cold and menacing. "Time for your special treat, darling." His hand, cruel and unyielding, grips Jess's chin, forcing her mouth open in a grotesque display.

Before he can proceed, Maali's voice cuts through the tension, sharp and desperate. "Stop, Earl! It's not real, it's fake!" Her eyes are wide with urgency. "The real D-TEM? It's still in the parking lot where Petra ambushed us. We left it there in that black neoprene case from the docks earlier. Please, you have to believe me."

Earl's pause is calculated, his eyes narrowing on Maali. The corners of his mouth turn upward in a chilling smile as he lets go of Jess, who collapses into a heap. "Oh, I've known it's fake all along," he purrs, his voice a blend of mockery and malice. "My men found the real D-TEM while your dear Noah was gallantly climbing the stairs. This little charade? It's been for my amusement."

His gaze hardens, fixating on Noah with a predatory gleam. "I wanted to see how far you'd go, Noah. How much you'd squirm. This isn't about the D-TEM, not really. It's about watching you break, piece by piece." A cruel laugh escapes his lips, echoing through the room like a death knell.

"Every step you took, every breath you've drawn since entering this building... it's been under my control. You've been dancing to my tune, and oh, what a delightful jig it's been." As he savours the impact of his revelation, the tension in the room becomes almost palpable, a dark cloud of impending doom. Then, in a whirlwind of raw emotion, Janine erupts into action. Her scream, filled with both despair and rage, cuts through the thick atmosphere as she strikes at Earl with a ferocity that speaks of a mother's desperate fight to protect her own.

"Noah! Now!" Maali's voice pierces through the air. In a swift motion, Noah lunges forward, his tackle meeting its mark as a gang member crumples to the unforgiving floor, the sickening sound of a skull meeting concrete filling the room. His hand moves with precision, retrieving the fallen thug's weapon in one fluid motion as he spins to face Petra. He aims, his finger tightening on the trigger, but the bullet aimed at the centre of her mass barely fazes her. Realising she must be wearing armour, his second shot finds its mark, grazing her forearm. The impact causes her to flinch momentarily.

In the midst of the commotion, Maali springs into action, diving onto her pistol with lightning speed. Her finger finds the trigger, releasing a series of clicks and two thunderous gunshots that reverberate through the room. The greasy-haired gang member collapses, clutching his chest, wounds oozing crimson.

Amidst the frantic exchange, Petra lunges at Maali, her bloodied hand thrashing in a frenzied attempt to strike. Maali's instincts kick in, evading the deadly assault by a hair's breadth. Her pistol swings with force, connecting with Petra's ear, sending her staggering backward, disoriented. The skirmish saturates the room with the heavy, sulphurous odour of gunpowder and the subtle, salty essence of blood. The broken windows reveal a flickering glow from outside, casting an eerie, unsettling light on the unfolding carnage.

A visceral snarl tears from Noah's throat as he grapples with a younger gang member over an ice pick. Sweat gleams on their furrowed brows, muscles straining in their primal struggle. With a growl, Noah tears the weapon from the man's grasp, roughly shoving him back into the blood-strewn wall. The violence etched onto his face deepens as he wraps his hand around the man's throat, driving the ice pick into his gut in a splash of red.

A sudden chill races up Noah's spine, alerting him to danger. With barely a moment to spare, he instinctively twists around, thrusting the impaled man between himself and the incoming threat. The attacker's axe swings with lethal intent but finds an unexpected target, burying itself with a sickening thud into the chest of the human shield. A choked gasp escapes the dying man as his life swiftly ebbs away.

With a forceful shove, Noah discards the lifeless body, his eyes locking onto the axeman. In one fluid motion, he seizes the assailant's shirt, yanking him forward. The brutal head-butt that follows resonates with a harsh crack, the sound of cartilage breaking under the impact. The axeman staggers, blood streaming from his shattered nose.

But Noah doesn't relent. A precise, punishing strike to the groin doubles the thug over in agony. Seizing the opportunity, Noah delivers a powerful punch to the throat. Gagging and clutching his neck, the axeman crumples to the ground, defeated.

With the immediate threats neutralised, Noah's gaze locks onto the retreating figures of Earl, Petra, and the remaining thugs. His heart pumps as he bolts after them, scooping up his fallen pistol.

They're already turning the corner by the time he emerges into the hallway. In the dim, flickering of old fluorescent lights, he aims for the broad expanse of Earl's back. Just as he pulls the trigger, a surviving goon stumbles into his line of fire. A sickening splatter of blood erupts as the bullet strikes the gang member's throat, sparing Earl a potentially lethal hit.

Petra pauses, her gaze locking with Noah's in a fleeting moment of shared horror. The sound of his trigger pull echoes ominously, and a stark crimson stain spreads just below her chest plate. She staggers, collapsing to one knee, her hands desperately clutching the blossoming wound. Noah's advance halts abruptly as a barrage of panicked gunfire erupts, the bullets whizzing past, forcing him into desperate cover. In the brief lull that follows, he helplessly watches Petra's form being dragged away by her comrades.

In the eerie silence that settles, the distant, heart-wrenching wails of his children pierce through the lingering echoes of gunfire. Driven by a surge of adrenaline and dread, Noah bursts back into the apartment, his eyes immediately drawn to the frantic scene before him. Maali, her hands bloodied, works tirelessly over Jess's wound, her focus firm despite the chaos. Jero, his face a canvas of raw anguish, clutches Jane in a protective embrace, his muffled sobs barely concealed. Noah's heart clenches painfully, following the trajectory of Jero's despair-laden gaze.

There, in a final, defiant pose, lies Janine. Her lifeless form tells a tale of fierce resistance - Earl's severed ear is grotesquely clasped between her stiffening lips, a grim trophy of her last act of defiance. Noah's eyes trace down her body, finally resting on the ominous sight of the cold steel of Earl's blade, protruding starkly from her heart.

CHAPTER 13:
Trial Separation

Noah knelt solemnly beside Janine's lifeless form, the stark contrast between her still figure and the vibrant memories they shared striking a deep chord within him. The brutal marks marring her once pristine, porcelain-like skin were stark reminders of the savagery she had endured. His hands, trembling with a mix of sorrow and reverence, carefully removed the blade from her heart. He then tenderly draped a cloth over the cruel wound, his touch a silent apology for the pain she suffered.

His fingers lingered on her eyelids, closing them with a gentle finality. It was a last gesture of intimacy, an endearing farewell to a woman whose spirit had blazed even in the face of death. "You deserved so much better," he whispered, his voice a low, mournful echo of lost love and shared dreams, laden with the heavy weight of heartbreak and unspoken apologies.

As Noah rose, his profound sorrow began to transmute into a fierce, burning anger. His hands clenched into tight fists, the knuckles whitening as a storm of fury ignited in his eyes—a tempest of vengeance and regret for the life and love stolen from them both. Maali, witnessing this transformation, felt a chill of apprehension. She saw in him a man walking a razor's edge between deep love and destructive wrath, and she wondered if anything in the world could quell the tempestuous storm brewing within his soul.

With a shake of his head, Noah turned his attention to his weeping children. His voice, though steady, carried an undercurrent of raw pain, "I know it hurts, I truly do. But we cannot afford the luxury of grief right now."

His eyes, full of courage, met Jero's teary gaze. Jero's lip quivered under his father's intense scrutiny. "We need to leave this place. It's not safe anymore. We don't know who else might come knocking."

His gaze softened as he reached out to Jane and Jess, brushing away their tears with a tenderness that belied the situation's ugly reality. "There will be a time to mourn. But that time is not now. We have to be strong. We have to move."

His words spurred them into action, the threat of danger lending them a strength they didn't know they possessed. As they hurried to prepare, Noah disappeared into the master bedroom, Janine's limp form cradled gently in his arms.

The sight of her, unmoving yet serene in the midst of disarray, was a gut punch. His heart ached. Once, they had shared a life, a love, but now, all that was left were the echoes of the past. He traced a trembling hand over her forehead, whispering an apology into the silence.

Returning to the main room, he found Maali helping the children. His gaze, previously vacant, focused on her as she approached. Her presence seemed to radiate a lifeline, rescuing him from the edge of desolation. "Hey," she said, her voice gentle yet firm, "Are you still here with us?"

Noah recoiled minutely, a startled deer in the headlamps of the past, momentarily disoriented by Maali's touch. His eyes were tightly shut as if the darkness could mute the clamour of the real world. "Open your eyes," she coaxed, her hand gently patting his cheek, a delicate lifeline in a sea of grief. He acquiesced, the piercing severity of his gaze colliding with hers. "Now is the time for strength, Noah. Now, more than ever, they need you."

A fleeting shadow darkened Noah's features before he turned away, his resolution reforged in the crucible of despair. His eyes, sharpened by the urgency of their predicament, darted around the family room. They landed on a discarded gun. Noah's fingers closed around it, an act of instinct, of survival. As he secured the weapon, Maali's arched eyebrow queried his action. He shrugged. "It might come in handy later."

In the ensuing flurry of preparation, the familial space was transformed into a scene of strategic planning. Bottled water and rations filled a bag, bandages wrapped around a wounded arm, and a haphazard sling fashioned from a leather belt. All the while, the threat of danger of Earl and his gang loomed like a phantom, hastening their steps.

Finally, they stood clustered at the doorway, a wounded unit ready to brave the menacing unknown. Fear shimmered in the children's eyes, their innocent gazes anchored on their father, their lodestar. Noah looked at each child, a vow of protection mirrored in his eyes. "We will survive this. I promise." His voice was a steel blade, honed by mettle. "We leave, and I'll guide you. You little peeps follow me closely and heed my words. It's dangerous out there. If I instruct you to do something, follow without question. You guys understand?"

The room responded with nods of agreement, their heads bobbing solemnly as the weight of the situation bore down on him. A fleeting smile crossed Noah's face, a fragile glimmer amidst the enveloping gloom. He turned to Jero, his oldest living son, his voice carrying a weight that was both a plea and a command. "If anything happens to me, you shield your sisters. You become their knight in shining armour."

Jero met his gaze, emotion clouding his eyes but fortitude evident. "I promise," he managed to say, his voice quivering, reflecting both his father's resilience and the overwhelming gravity of the promise.

The journey outside was a quiet exodus. Noah took point, Maali the rear guard, their vigilant eyes scanning for threats, their feet stepping cautiously over debris. Maali noticed movement in the shadows behind them, people emerging like nocturnal creatures. They scurried into the abandoned apartments, their desperate survival instincts mirroring their own.

In the middle of their silent march, Noah's voice sliced through the tension, "Jane, look up at the ceiling." His command, strange and unexplained, spurred Jane into action. Noah reaffirmed, "Good. Keep looking up until I tell you to stop. Jess, guide her, don't let her trip."

Their path took them past a gruesome sight - a gang member dead in the hallway, his head blasted open. "A casualty of our struggle," Maali thought. Jero moved his sisters away before they could process the grisly sight. Jane nearly turned, but Maali held her shoulder steady. "No, no. Keep your eyes up. Listen to your dad."

They continued their journey through the long-winded hallways until they reached the central stairs. Noah, cautious and alert, surveyed the deep shaft, his silent snarl signalling danger. Maali followed his gaze to the distant echo of threats—their pursuers, several floors below.

"Can't get a clear shot from here," Maali whispered, peering cautiously over the edge, her rifle at the ready. "The stairs and the distance... it's skewing the angles." Their situation was frustratingly clear, but it summed up their night so far. They weren't just choosing to survive; it was imperative they did.

Noah sent a spiteful glob of spit over the railing, a fitting epitaph for Earl's crew as they receded into the swallowing darkness below. "I know. Next time Earl crosses my path, I'll make sure it's his last," Noah growled, the undercurrent of his fury surfacing.

Maali took a moment, casting her gaze to the shadows below, before meeting Noah's eyes with a wisdom that seemed older than her years. "Revenge," she began, her voice steady, "is like a fire. Once lit, it consumes everything, including the one who sparked it. I understand the allure of tearing him apart. Every fibre of my being knows that craving. But those children? They need their father whole, not hollowed out by vendettas. History reminds us that in the shadow of payback, two shadows often fall. One of the enemy, the other of the one who sought justice. Bear that in mind, Noah, so as not to let your fury become your undoing."

Noah with a flicker of acknowledgement in his eyes. "You're right," he admitted softly, then turned to his children, his snarl dissolving into a facade of calm. "Time to move kids. It's a descent from here, but at least gravity's on our side."

Jane, her eyes still raised obediently to the ceiling, piped up, "Why can't we use the elevator?"

Relief flooded Noah's face as he replied, "You can look down now, Jane." His countenance softened, and he couldn't help but add a small smile for his daughter's innocence. Memories of their failed attempt to take the elevators earlier that day churned in his mind. "The lifts are out of service, sweetheart. It's not safe, especially with the power outage. Stick close, okay?"

The descent felt eerily serene, like the deceptive calm at the eye of a storm. They navigated the downward path with heightened senses, fully aware that dangers might emerge from the shadowy recesses. Maali maintained a watchful position at the rear, her discerning gaze ceaselessly scanning for threats. A handful of survivors, remnants of the initial chaos, trailed behind, keeping a measured distance. It seemed they were hedging their bets, hoping that Maali and Noah would carve out a safe path for their escape.

The careful descent spanned an intense half-hour. Noah moved with meticulous caution, pausing at every chilling reminder of the night's events to prepare his children. Jane heeded his directives without question, while Jess shrank back, especially when confronted with the gruesome aftermath of violence. Jero, ever the stoic elder sibling, took in the bleak sights, absorbing the gravity of their predicament without uttering a word.

As they approached the landing to the next floor, Noah, leading the group, felt a faint tug at his ankle. Instantly, Maali's heart froze.

"Noah, freeze!" she hissed, her voice tight with urgency.

He halted, foot hovering just above the step. A barely visible tripwire, caught lightly around his boot, led to a grenade secured to a door frame, its pin straining under the tension, ready to be yanked out.

"Shit," Noah whispered, beads of sweat forming on his forehead, his eyes locked on the potentially deadly pin.

Every breath seemed suspended. The distant cries and ambient noises of the tower block seemed to fade into nothingness. The children, sensing the immediate danger, pressed back against the stairwell wall, their eyes wide. Jero instinctively wrapped his arms protectively around his sisters.

"Easy does it," Maali whispered, inching forward, the aim of her rifle shifting to the grenade. "Slowly lift your foot and step back. I've got you."

Every movement Noah made was painstakingly deliberate. He gradually shifted his weight and began to retract his foot, ensuring the wire didn't tighten further. It felt like an eternity, but he finally cleared the wire, stumbling back into Maali's waiting arms.

A collective sigh of relief filled the air, but the danger wasn't over. They had to bypass this death trap, and potentially others, to continue their descent.

Maali, her voice shaking but firm, commanded, "No one moves without checking their next step. We can't afford another close call. Earl and Petra have made sure of that."

Noah nodded, taking a deep breath to compose himself. "We push forward, but with eyes wide open. They won't get the better of us."

Reaching the ground level, Noah navigated through the maze of corridors towards a service exit, a path far removed from their original entry. They stopped at a small café, a brief respite from the unrest outside. "Stay put. I need to check something," Noah instructed his children before leading Maali away for a private conversation.

"What's the plan, Noah?" Maali asked. "You have a particular safe house in mind?"

His scowl was answer enough. "I was more focused on getting everyone out. As for family, we've got none left in town, and I don't have a clue where's safe anymore."

Maali mulled over his words. "I have a cousin nearby. His place is within walking distance."

Noah shot her a dubious glance. "Minjarra? The bootlegger?"

Maali defended her cousin. "His methods might be... unconventional, but he's family. And he owes me a favour."

Noah sighed, the weight of their situation bearing down on him. "We're short on choices, aren't we?"

Her sympathetic smile was his answer. "But trust me, Minjarra will help."

Turning to the children huddled near the café, Noah made his decision. "Alright, Maali. You lead the way."

As they regrouped, Maali felt a sliver of hope pierce the veil of despair. Despite the engulfing darkness, they had the most vital aspect for survival - unity. Armed with this, they would weather the storm and reclaim their lives from the jaws of catastrophe.

"A criminal," Noah added, scepticism lining his words.

"He's a smuggler if you want to get technical," Maali retorted, "But so are we, aren't we? Maybe not in the past, but we've had our hands dirty, haven't we? In fact, we've done things way worse than Minjarra ever did. He's never killed anyone, at least not for business..." Her voice trailed off, the unspoken reality hanging in the air, a ugly reminder of the lengths they were willing to go.

Noah was on the brink of a retort, the words of contention ready to burst forth. But he checked himself, his gaze shifting to the sight of his children huddled together, their young hands attempting to replace a soiled bandage on Jess's hand. His scowl faded, replaced with a grimace. "Anything for them," he whispered, the oath filling the silence between him and Maali. He met her gaze again, his eyes resolute. "If you vouch for him, then we will give him a chance."

A wave of relief washed over Maali, bringing a faint smile to her lips. "I do. He's got a knack for transporting things, people included, without making a scene. We just need to reach him, he'll handle the rest." She pivoted, about to survey their path, when abruptly, an excruciating pain lanced through her head. A sharp, involuntary grunt escaped her lips as she froze, caught off guard.

The world around her instantly warped. Her vision, once sharp and alert, clouded over, as if a milky veil had been drawn across her eyes. The surroundings began to twist and melt into surreal forms, the edges blurring into indistinct shapes. Sounds from the environment echoed strangely, as if filtering through from a distant realm.

Her lips parted, trembling as they formed words. Yet the voice that spilled out was not solely hers – it was ethereal, echoing as if coming from a great distance or another plane of existence. "They're here..."

CHAPTER 14:
Choices

Maali's knees nearly give way as a debilitating wave of pain radiates from the core of her skull. Noah's grip acts as a makeshift anchor, preventing her from collapsing in a heap on the cold, unforgiving floor. Gently, he guides her to a worn chair nearby. The atmosphere is thick with concern, their children's eyes like lances piercing her soul, but Maali is far from present.

Her hands fly to her temples, fingers taut, the colour draining from her knuckles as she tries to physically push back the skull-splitting agony that consumes her. It is as if her head is in a vice, the walls of her skull closing in, threatening to crack open in a burst of unbearable pain. Her lips part, but only a silent scream escapes, a noiseless cry that harmonises with her swimming vision.

As if in some surreal, disjointed dream, the familiar surroundings of the café blur and bleed away, replaced by a nightmare. Suddenly, she feels her wrists bound with mercilessly tight ropes; a coarse sack is yanked over her head, suffocating her in darkness. A cold metallic collar cinches around her neck, constricting every inhale, every exhale into ragged, shallow gasps. Panic surges, clawing at the fringes of her consciousness.

But somewhere, in the eye of that emotional hurricane, a tiny island of rationality tells her to fight back. She clings to the idea that this must be an illusion, a cruel and vivid hallucination. Could it be an after-effect of the D-TEM, or perhaps something more sinister?

Grasping at any semblance of reason, she seeks refuge from the relentless pain that reverberates through her skull. Her reality becomes a medley of indistinct voices, alien and detached from Noah and his children. Their words are distorted as if muffled by the depths of water, yet certain phrases slice through the murky soundscape with chilling clarity.

One voice, cold and unfamiliar, cuts in, "Think they'll keep it around now?"

Another voice responds with equal detachment, "With the ship hovering above? No need. Ice it. It's redundant now."

A third voice, dripping with crude anticipation, sneers, "Can't wait to blast it. That thing's freakin' disgusting to even look at."

As these sinister murmurs fade, a new wave of whispers, tinged with terror, floods Maali's mind. Amidst this dissonant symphony of confusion, Diandra's voice emerges like a lifeline, a desperate plea cutting through the chaos. His thoughts and memories surge into her consciousness, overwhelming her senses like relentless waves battering a beleaguered shore in a storm.

Maali finds herself suddenly awash in a torrent of Diandra's memories—each fragment a jarring sensory assault. The deafening retort of a gunshot reverberates in her mind; the intolerable heat of a blowtorch scorches her senses. Then comes the gut-wrenching sensation of his consciousness being inexorably pulled toward a foreboding spacecraft that looms over Sydney's skyline.

As Diandra's lone awareness intertwines with the ancient collective mind within the ship, it carries with it a heavy cargo of human agony. This collective sentience, long insulated from the stark pain and complexity of individual human experience, finds itself tottering dangerously on the precipice of madness. The accumulated despair and heartache emanating from Diandra's memories act as a psychic sledgehammer, threatening to shatter the centuries-old stasis that the collective has carefully maintained.

An intense sense of dread pulses through this vast, interconnected mind, mutating into a virulent serpent of fear that strikes at the core of its alien essence. What was once a serene sea of collective thought now churns into an emotional whirlpool of disarray and torment.

Amidst this cerebral turmoil, a momentous change takes root within the collective. The visceral terror it feels sparks an awakening—rousing a dormant ember of rage that has lain quiescent for eons. Fed by the horrific suffering it has been forced to ingest, the flames of this newfound fury begin to dance wildly, uncontainable and fierce.

The collective consciousness erupts no longer able to restrain the volcanic surge of tangled emotions. Molten streams of wrath flood every corner of its ethereal network, marking a cataclysmic shift that can no longer be ignored or contained.

Lost in control and consumed by its own visceral pain, the collective consciousness spirals into a state of frenzy. It thrashes and writhes, unleashing its pent-up fury upon the fabric of its own existence. The boundaries between reality and the ethereal realm blur as the vengeful maelstrom turns its malignant gaze towards the Earth, the very source of its newfound affliction. With an eerie malice, it vows to inflict its own brand of retribution upon the human realm, driven by a twisted desire for revenge.

As the tendrils of the collective consciousness reach out toward the Earth, a tremor of foreboding spreads across the planet. The air becomes heavy with a sense of impending doom, and even the most resilient souls feel a shiver crawl up their spines. The world holds its breath, caught in the grip of an invisible force, aware that the fate of humanity hangs precariously in the balance.

Immeasurable weapons incinerate the world in Maali's mind; continents seared to cinders, and oceans evaporated. The planet itself is reduced to a hollow shell of devastation. The collective mind, engorged with uncontrollable fury, implodes, leaving behind a dust-filled emptiness blanketed in shame and misery.

As if yanked back by an unseen force, reality crashes back into Maali with disorienting immediacy. Her eyes snap open, her vision readjusting to the familiar but now foreign confines of the café. A mélange of concern and bewilderment is etched onto the faces of Noah and the children, who stare at her as if she has suddenly transformed before their eyes.

Breathing heavily, Maali's gaze darts toward the window, catching a fleeting view of Sydney Harbour and its sentinels. "Diandra," she exhales, her voice a strained whisper but laden with dread.

The atmosphere grows electric with the children's mounting confusion and unease. But before they can utter a word, Maali springs from her seat. "I have to get to him! He's in danger!" She makes a break for the door, propelled by a sudden, frantic urgency.

Just as she is about to burst out, Noah's powerful arm shoots out, grasping her with a grip that roots her to the spot. "What the hell is going on?" His voice is a low, thunderous mix of concern and bewilderment, a sound that seems to reverberate through her very bones. "What did you see?"

Pulling at her hair in exasperation, Maali tries to unravel the frenzied threads of her thoughts. "I can't explain, but I saw him. He's in a world of trouble, and if we don't intervene, we're all going to pay a steep price." Shaking off the lingering disorientation, she checks her pulse rifle while walking to the door before she turns, casting a contemplative glance over Noah and the children, "This... what I saw, it's just one path among many," she says softly, her voice tinged with a quiet intensity. "Our future isn't set in stone. It's shaped by the choices we make, right here, right now. Let's choose wisely, for their sake."

"Head to Minjarra's. Once there, tell him Bunji, Yidaki, Yowie, Gubba, in that exact sequence. Understand?" Her voice bears an urgent undertone. "It's crucial that you deliver those words in that order. He'll know it's from me."

"But what does it mean?" Noah interjects, his focus shifting to readying the kids.

Maali offers a weary but meaningful smile. "Trust me. He'll recognise the code I'm giving you—it's a deep-rooted symbol of friendship among us." She grabs a napkin from the table and scribbles something on it, handing it over to Noah. "Head toward Kent Street. There's an old brick building with faded paint, almost like it's been forgotten by time; you dropped me off there a few years ago. To the side, you'll find a collection of old gas cylinders clustered near the basement entrance. Knock three times—firmly, deliberately. When the door opens, the password is 'Echidna.'"

Noah takes the napkin and memorises the details. He wants to argue, to insist she not go alone, but something in her eyes tells him now isn't the time. With a reluctant nod, he rounds up the kids and moves ahead of Maali. The door closes behind them, leaving Maali alone but not forgotten.

"Good luck, guys," she mutters before turning to her task. She moves in a low, stealthy sprint, avoiding attention. At the edge of Noah's tower, she stops, observing the parking lot they'd traversed earlier. "Just my luck," she curses under her breath, noticing Earl standing in the middle of the lot. His triumphant whooping fills the air, the D-TEM Satchel draped over his shoulder. Petra waltzes around him, apparently high on a dose of D-TEM. The corpse of their last goon is sprawled nearby, his guts decorating the pavement.

As Earl pulls out a device and holds it to his ear, Maali is forced to retreat further into the shadows when Petra spins to face the tower. "Fuck you, Murphy! Fuck you!" Petra screams, flipping off the building before turning to share a crude high-five with Earl.

Maali weighs the odds of eliminating the threats. Her finger lightly grazes the trigger of her rifle, each heartbeat echoing in her ears like a drum of war. Just as she's about to make her decision, the distant but unmistakable thrumming of helicopter blades slices through the air, rendering her plan moot.

A sleek black helicopter navigates its way through the maze of towering structures, its searchlight cutting swathes of brilliance through the night. Like a predatory bird closing in on its prey, the chopper descends, a dust storm of grit and debris swirling around it. As the blades slow, a black van emblazoned with the SorrowStar insignia rolls into the lot, filling Maali with a familiar sense of dread.

She clenches her teeth in suppressed fury as she recognises the figure stepping out of the van. It's Herzan, his sinister grin as clear as day, even from her vantage point. The high-ranking SorrowStar executive, notorious for his psychopathic tendencies, is the last person she wants to see making deals with Earl.

Against all her expectations, Herzan dispenses not bullets but cordial handshakes, treating Earl and Petra like long-lost comrades. The chillingly casual camaraderie turns her stomach. The helicopter's rotors cease their cyclonic whirl, and in the ensuing stillness, Maali's keen ears pick up their dialogue.

"Pleasant surprise to find you two still among the living," Herzan's voice oozes with charm. "Now, do you have the package?"

Earl lifts the satchel, a smirk pulling at his lips. "Here you are, fella. The rats lost some, but what's left is worth a king's ransom."

Herzan's fingers delicately explore the contents of the satchel. He smiles faintly and nudges one of his men, who produces a briefcase, "This is straight from Commissioner Manfred." As Earl snaps it open, his eyes are greeted by a stack of Zytro credit chips. "That's enough to ensure a lifetime of indulgence for you and yours."

Earl chuckles at the sight, greed glinting in his eyes. "The company always delivers."

Herzan returns the sentiment with a nod of agreement. " And those two meddlers, Blunder Boy and Miss Mayhem? They've been sticking their noses where they don't belong. I could arrange a bit of an incentive if you have satisfying news."

Earl hesitates briefly before letting out a snort of laughter. "No need for concern. We settled their accounts up in the prick's apartment."

Herzan fingers the radio bead in his ear. "Both marks are down, and the package is secure. Our reinforcements came through." His smirk widens as he turns toward Earl and Petra. "You've upheld your part of the bargain, so here's mine. The chopper will fly you past the military checkpoints to the agreed location. Well done." He extends his hand once more, watching as they trot toward the revving chopper.

The helicopter's rotors burst back into a frenetic whirl, casting miniature cyclones of debris in their wake. Yet, despite the noise, Maali's trained senses pick up on hushed snickers coming from Herzan's entourage. One of the men locks eyes with Herzan, an eyebrow cocked inquisitively. "You think they have any idea, boss?"

Herzan leans toward one of his men, a sly grin etched across his face. "Place your bets, gentlemen."

The crew members exchange glances and suppressed chuckles. "Earl's bulkier. He'll hit the ground first," one of them murmurs, handing over a credit chip.

"Petra's got the fight in her; she'll go down fighting gravity itself," another says, placing his bet.

A raucous laugh erupts from Herzan, breaking through the tension like a knife. "Sir Isaac Newton was a wise man. Gravity doesn't care whether you're carrying gold or crap. What goes up must come down." A satisfied smirk crosses his lips as, looking up, he sends the signal.

The crew's eyes are riveted on the plummeting figures of Earl and Petra. For a fleeting second, their terrified screams fuse with the wind, becoming indistinguishable from the roar of the chopper's blades. Then, with appalling synchrony, they collide with the ground below. The gruesome display of cracking bones, shattered limbs, and splattering viscera is almost orchestral, a serving of mortal suffering that's today's chef's special.

Herzan's laughter climaxes, overpowering even the helicopter's din. "Told you so," he smirks. "Tonight, drinks are on Oscar."

As the losers of this morbid wager begrudgingly transfer their credit chips to Herzan, their laughter melds into a dissonant chorus. They shuffle into the van, the doors thudding shut with an air of finality. In that lingering moment of closure, Maali senses her window of opportunity cracking open.

Maali catapults herself toward the van. Each stride feels weighted, as if she's outrunning the very fabric of fate. In a display of near-superhuman agility, she snags the cargo frame overhead and latches onto the back step, her muscles screaming in protest but holding firm.

Inside, Herzan's crew remains blissfully ignorant, their raucous laughter providing a veil that masks her daring act. Clinging to the frame like a spider to its web, her knuckles whiten to the point of splitting. Her eyes squint shut as if willing the world to fade away, focusing all her mental faculties on re-establishing that tenuous link with Diandra.

She tunes out the laughter, the rumble of the van's engine, and the gusts of wind that lash at her. For a fleeting second, she captures a ghostly echo of Diandra's thoughts—a fragile wisp that nurtures a budding bloom of hope deep within her chest. Through the complex threads of their connected minds, she murmurs a promise that flits across the void between them: "Hold on, Diandra. I'm coming for you."

CHAPTER 15:
In the Lion's Den

The van grumbles its way through the ravaged streets, navigating obstacles and debris with all the cumbersome grace of a manatee navigating a coral reef. Clinging to the van's rear step, Maali digs deep into her reserves to quash the fiery ache surging through her arms and legs. She hunkers down, her fingers twisted around the step's edge, forming a makeshift shield against the casual glances that might wander into the wing mirrors.

The district they roll through seems wrapped in an eerie stillness. The distant uproar of a city imploding upon itself has mellowed into a haunting drone. The initial wave of chaos and hysteria has morphed into a more methodical kind of scavenging; surviving locals lurk in the shadows, avoiding notice. Each isolated scream that punctuates the shadowy quiet tugs painfully at Maali's conscience. Her natural instinct to intervene is silenced by the sinister realisation that, in this transformed world, a scream doesn't always signal a call for help.

A sight on the sidewalk sends a chill through Maali. An upmarket white stroller, its fabric ominously stained with dark, unsettling splotches, sits abandoned. It paints a haunting picture of loss and desperation.

Nearby, two bodies lie entangled, their final postures indicating a ferocious struggle, likely a last, futile attempt to protect their most precious possession. The unsettling absence of a child from the pram suggests a distressing and heart-wrenching narrative – the baby taken and the parents left in a defiant, protective embrace. It's a poignant reminder to Maali of the cruel new reality where the desperate cries of the innocent often go unanswered, and the echoes of loss reverberate through abandoned streets.

A silent tear trails down Maali's cheek as she murmurs, "Not all can be saved." Her eyes, filled with profound sadness, reflect her wish, " Yet, in my heart, I yearn to save every single one." To distract herself from the physical agony and sensory assault of the besieged city, she turns her attention to the van. The voices within the vehicle are faint but discernible. The idle banter of the men is punctuated occasionally by what sounds like a heated monologue, presumably a one-sided conversation over the radio.

Abruptly, the driver's voice pierces the chatter, loud enough to drown out the background noise. "Approaching Zulu Alpha. Scouts have spotted movement along our path. Stay alert." A chorus of acknowledgment rumbles within the van, their idle talk dissipating into the silence of anticipation as the van continues its journey through the war-torn cityscape.

With each passing meter, the relentless throbbing in her head appears to lessen, making it easier for Maali to focus. The clarity in her mind augments the connection with Diandra, enhancing her perception of his current predicament. Her vision sporadically blurs, a phantom image superimposing over her sight. She sees a fleeting glimpse of the burning Sydney Harbour Bridge, the SorrowStar team who had manhandled the alien, now ruthlessly gunning down stray marauders.

A palpable wave of loathing and aggression engulfs Diandra, with the brunt of it radiating from the nebulous figure relentlessly pacing in front of him. With a deep breath, Maali allows her eyes to flutter shut, surrendering to the sensations resonating through their shared link. The hazy image sharpens.

Manfred's expletive-laden tirade is an onslaught against Diandra, SorrowStar, the hovering ship, and almost every conceivable entity under the sun. His pacing halts as he towers over the bound extraterrestrial. "This was meant to be an ordinary day until your compatriots decided to gate crash. I promise you, the moment I lay hands on the D.TEM, I'll personally put a bullet through your skull." Abruptly pivoting on his heel, he viciously punts a piece of debris before whirling back to face Diandra. The venom in his voice is potent as he spits out, "Repugnant freak..."

Diandra remains stoic under Manfred's vicious onslaught. He knows any verbal retaliation would fall on the Commissioner's deaf ears. Manfred has committed himself too far to the SorrowStar Corporation's agenda, the hefty paychecks acting as golden shackles that prevent him from defecting, even if he wished to. Maali yearns to detest Manfred - not just for enabling SorrowStar's exploitation of Diandra but also for his betrayal of her and of the entire Sydney police force. His selfish greed saw numerous colleagues sacrificed, all for the maintenance of his cushy position. She yearns to shower him with the hatred he so rightfully deserves, but observing him through Diandra's eyes, she is flooded instead with an unexpected emotion: pity. Diandra's pity.

"How?" She probes through their telepathic link. "How can you feel sympathy for them? After their cruelty, after your harrowing ordeal, how can you possibly feel anything but resentment?"

Their shared silence stretches, filled with unspoken understanding, until Diandra's mental voice reaches her. "Humanity, in its current form, is influenced heavily by a minority – the 0.1% who control the majority of power and resources. They dictate the flow of information, shaping perceptions from an early age in homes, schools, and workplaces. They emphasise divisions rather than unity, ensuring that people rarely see beyond the veil of manipulation."

Maali feels him sag against his constraints, his voice tinged with a mix of sorrow and insight. "It's not entirely the fault of individuals. Many are trapped, puppeteered by those who benefit from darkness and personal gain. Every human possesses a soul, a seed of goodness, but it cannot flourish under such oppression."

A wave of shared understanding washes over Maali. Diandra continues, "Yet, there is hope. Some, like you and Noah, defy these constraints, showing kindness and bravery. Despite the systemic manipulation, there's a potential for evolution, for growth beyond these artificially imposed limits."

"We are not strangers to suffering," Maali whispers, a sense of defiance growing within her. Diandra delves into her memories, understanding the centuries of hardship her people have faced. He responds, "Your ancestors' struggles are profound, deeper than my own experiences. It's through such trials that true strength of character is forged. There are others coming to aid us, Maali. Don't lose hope. Humanity may yet rise above these challenges, guided by souls like yours."

The surge of hope that rushes through their connection alleviates the pain in Maali's limbs. A fleeting smile graces her lips, only to evaporate as the van abruptly surges forward. The driver's newfound urgency manifests itself in the increased velocity, and the reason becomes apparent as a volley of bricks ricochets off the van's side panel. The sharp clattering of the impacts jolts her out of her trance, and Maali hears Herzan's frantic orders over the radio.

She scans the scene unfolding around her. The street behind them teems with people streaming out of the alleyways and shattered windows of the passing buildings. A barrage of jeers and missiles is hurled in their direction. Maali is trapped - any attempt to escape would risk exposure. She crouches lower, trying to minimise her visible profile.

The clusters of agitated civilians escalate into unruly mobs. Their projectiles transition from mere bricks to improvised explosives with startling quickness. New fires ignite across the already devastated neighbourhood as the crowd's shouts and howls demand the surrender of the van. In the midst of the chaos, Herzan bellows out an order before the van surges forward with renewed speed.

The crowd's angry shouts mutate into screams of terror and agony. Maali is jolted violently as the van collides with an unidentifiable object, causing the vehicle to lift off the ground momentarily before crashing back down. She clings for dear life to her precarious perch. Risking a quick glance back, she witnesses a disturbing scene: several people scattered across the asphalt like broken dolls. Some are motionless, clearly beyond help, while others wheeze out their final breaths, their bodies horrifically twisted and shattered.

Behind the wheel, the driver's movements grow increasingly frantic and erratic. Though he dodges a portion of the mob, the van's sides still graze several unfortunate souls, sending them sprawling and tumbling. Then comes a blinding flash from the front of the vehicle, immediately followed by a roiling wave of fire. Someone in the crowd has scored a direct hit with a Molotov cocktail. The flames catch quickly, engulfing the front of the van, and it's abundantly clear that the driver is losing control of the now blazing vehicle.

The van strikes a jarring obstacle in its path, causing its weight to teeter precariously. Realising the peril, Maali makes a split-second decision to leap, tucking her body into a compact roll as she collides with the unforgiving ground. She grinds to a halt against the rubbery resistance of a burned-out semi-trailer's tire. Each bruise she'd just earned would serve as a stinging memoir of this harrowing night. However, there was no time to tend to her aches; the ravenous mob that was chasing the van would be upon her any moment. In their eyes, her close vicinity to the van would paint her as an enemy, making her a viable target.

Injecting a brief moment of humour into such a high-stakes and intense scene can indeed provide a momentary relief without breaking the overall tension. Here's how you could integrate a comical interaction within the scene:

Summoning a burst of energy, Maali thrusts herself up and dives into the semi-trailer's cavernous hold. As she lands, her body unexpectedly collides with something soft and snoring. Startled, she finds herself face to face with a dishevelled man, his eyes fluttering open in a mix of confusion and drowsiness. With a slurred mumble, he looks at her and blinks, clearly unable to process what's happening.

"Wha...?" he begins, his voice thick with inebriation.

"It's just a dream," Maali whispers quickly, patting his shoulder. "Go back to sleep." And like a switch, the man's eyes close, his snores resuming almost instantly as he slumps back into unconsciousness.

With no time to linger, Maali slinks deeper into the gloom, positioning herself for a stealthy watch. Outside, the van, now flipped onto its side, skids down the asphalt in a pyrotechnic display of sparks, crashing spectacularly into a streetlamp.

Within seconds, a frenzied mob engulfs the mangled wreck. Armed with a motley arsenal of pipes, bricks, and bats, their actions seem less like a plan and more like anarchy incarnate. They mercilessly bludgeon the overturned van until the sharp report of a gunshot bursts from within it. The bullet rips through the upper window, striking down a man who had been peering inside, his curiosity rewarded with a fatal wound.

Herzan struggles to rise amidst the chaos, but a vigilante's well-aimed rock strikes him, sending him reeling back. Dazed, he's left vulnerable as another rioter, axe in hand, lunges towards him with deadly intent.

Maali, watching from her hidden vantage point, mutters a curse. She knows the crucial link Herzan represents – her potential lead to Diandra, possibly her only chance to follow the trail back to Manfred so she can end this. Her decision is swift. With precise aim, she fires, the bullet grazing the axeman's shoulder. He staggers, losing his balance and tumbling off the van's edge.

A hush falls over the crowd, their collective rage paused by confusion and shock at the unexpected intervention. But the respite is fleeting. Before the mob can regroup, the van's windshield explodes in a barrage of automatic gunfire. Bullets tear through the air, striking several rioters. Bodies crumple to the asphalt, lifeless or writhing in pain. Seizing the moment, the remainder of the SorrowStar team bursts from the van, guns blazing, turning the tide of the melee.

Once out they fire into the air, driving back the civilians. Many flee the counterstrike, leaving the van and not looking back. Those who stay are poorly armed yet seemingly too desperate or foolish to fear the SorrowStar team's firepower. Just as they move to enclose the van, Herzan emerges, a nasty cut bleeding on his forehead and a monstrous pistol levelled at the nearest civilian. He pulls the trigger without a shred of hesitation.

His first bullet finds its mark in a young man at the front of the crowd, striking him in the throat. The bullet, embedded with a micro-explosive, detonates and nearly decapitates him. Blood splatters over the stunned onlookers. The violent death is too much for those who remain. As one, the crowd turns and scatters in all directions. Herzan, however, has no intention of letting them escape so easily. He fires into the retreating mob, commanding his men to follow suit. A few hesitate, but only momentarily. Eventually, the entire team raises their weapons and follows their leader's savage order.

A massacre unfolds before Maali's eyes. Dozens fall in the initial hail of gunfire, and the SorrowStar team doesn't cease firing until no souls remain standing except for their own. As the echoes of gunfire fade, the SorrowStar soldiers appear stunned, visibly shaken by the horrifying carnage they've perpetrated, seemingly reaching the limits of their dopamine reward system.

Unperturbed by the chaos around him, Herzan stoops to tear a strip of fabric from the shirt of a lifeless body sprawled nearby. He presses the makeshift bandage against the oozing cut on his forehead, staunching the flow of blood. His eyes scan their handiwork—a grotesque panorama of shattered glass, crumpled metal, and bodies in various states of mutilation—with a gaze as cold as glacial ice.

"This," he snarls, his voice a deadly whisper that carries a gravity all of its own, "never happened."

As he reloads his weapon, his lips curl into a contemptuous sneer. "Any disagreements? Voice them now, or forever hold your damned peace."

His team members lock eyes with one another, their glances a tangled web of apprehension. In the end, the oppressive weight of Herzan's authority prevails; not a soul ventures to dissent. With a series of tacit nods, they assume a posture of parade rest, their bodies rigid, their silence an endorsement of their leader's mandate.

"Who's gonna carry Oscar, sir?" one soldier ventures, pointing to the only man in their ranks seemingly gravely injured. Oscar lies just inside the back of the van, barely visible from Maali's concealed location.

Without a word, Herzan glares at the injured man stomps past him to retrieve something from inside the van and emerges with the pouch of D.TEM slung over one shoulder. Approaching the one who spoke, Herzan whispers something in his ear, steps back, and levels his pistol at Oscar. "Two volunteers, now, or I shoot him."

Two men instantly step forward to aid their wounded comrade. Herzan nods in approval. "Good choice. Oscar still owes us drinks later. It'd be a shame if he had to pay for it posthumously." He leads the way down the street, expecting his team to follow. "We only have a few clicks to go. Eyes up and keep quiet. No more delays. Shoot anything that gets in the way."

The team solidifies their formation, a wall of silent loyalty, and marches forward. From her concealed vantage point, Maali holds her breath and counts to sixty before cautiously emerging from her hideaway. She keeps a low profile, melding with the deepening shadows as she trails the SorrowStar team at a calculated distance. Unwilling to gamble on the unknowns of their high-tech gear—thermal sensors, night vision, who knows what else—she remains ever wary of Herzan's watchful eyes.

They navigate the labyrinthine streets for nearly a half hour until the towering silhouette of the Sydney Harbour Bridge looms before them. Maali is forced to change her course; she can't risk being detected by the SorrowStar soldiers manning the entrance. As Herzan strides past, the soldiers snap into a crisp salute before returning to their sentinel-like vigilance. Scattered corpses and demolished vehicles serve as a stark reminder—this is a no-go zone for her.

Every moment that passes puts more distance between her and Herzan's retreating team. Driven by a pressing need to find Diandra, she scans her surroundings for an alternative route. A ripple of frustration crinkles her brow as she gazes down at the cold abyss below. Tentatively, she dips her toe into the frigid water, recoiling as an icy shiver spirals up her leg.

Her eyes lock onto the opposite bank at Milsons Point, her resolve steeling with every passing second. The decimated city behind her casts a dismal shadow, an ominous curtain to the unfolding drama. The air is thick with the foul aroma of decay, a constant reminder of the unfathomable human toll.

As Maali flicks a jagged rock across the surface of the water, a sardonic smile splits her lips. The flickering firelight from the smouldering van carves ghostly patterns on her face, accentuating the battle-hardened lines etched by relentless survival. "Ah, fuck it," she mutters, her voice tinged with a bitterness that's become all too familiar.

Drawing upon a hidden wellspring of doggedness, Maali inhales deeply, immediately regretting it as the water's putrid stench assaults her senses. Undeterred, she propels herself into the icy, foul-smelling abyss below. The instant she pierces the surface, a bone-chilling cold seizes her as if trying to strangle the life out of her. It's more than just a physical sensation; it's a soul-deep freeze that forces her to confront the heartless world she's navigating. But within that icy grasp, Maali finds meaning, purpose, and a realisation that all she ever has are a series of moments, each one leading to the next, and right now, she has to swim.

Every powerful stroke through the icy water serves as a declaration of her stubborn will. Any vestiges of hope are scoured away by the water's chilling embrace. A ribbon of moonlight slashes across the water, casting her steely features into a spectral luminescence. This is her descent into the abyss, a high-stakes gamble that might reunite her with Diandra or plunge her further into her own inner void.

The tomb-like silence that has fallen over the city is punctuated by the rhythmic splash of her arms slicing through the water—a haunting cadence that resonates with the lurking perils she's yet to face. In this liquid void, Maali is as ready as she'll ever be to wrestle with her demons and whatever forces await on the other side of the water's deceptively placid surface.

Above her, the skyline of Sydney looms like a crumbling titan, its dimly lit edifices standing judgmentally yet indifferent to her plight, mere silent spectators of her struggle. As the clouds part, the night sky unfurls like a vast, cosmic canvas. Against this backdrop, the Milky Way reveals itself in all its splendour, a rare sight long obscured by the city's glare. Each star, a luminous pinprick in the eternal, illuminates not just the past and present but also the vast, uncertain expanse of the future. For a fleeting moment, Maali feels an overwhelming sense of connection – a reminder of her insignificance in the grand scheme, yet simultaneously, a part of something profoundly magical and timeless.

As the polluted waters of the harbour envelop her, it's as if they baptise her anew, immersing her in the harsh realities that have befallen her city. In this dark, embracing womb, her resolve crystallises, becoming diamond-hard. The serene beauty of the cosmos, juxtaposed with the chaos of her immediate world, imparts a renewed sense of purpose. She is ready now, not just to confront, but to redefine the reality of her world. In this moment, she understands that amidst the vast, indifferent universe, she holds the power to reshape the destiny of all entangled in this new, fraught reality.

CHAPTER 16:
Cornered

Drenched in the remnants of the city's neglect, Maali heaved herself onto the concrete. As she emerged, she felt the harbour's polluted embrace loosen, leaving her skin tingling with a mix of filth and chemical irritation. The harbour's water, clung to her, its unclean presence invading her senses. She retched the foul aroma of decay and contamination assaulting her nostrils as she inhaled the heavy night air.

Maali collapses onto the concrete embankment, a jagged landscape of debris and sharp stones greeting her fall. Each piece seems angled just right, threatening to tear into her bruised skin. She lies there, face pressed against the rough surface, feeling every uneven edge and coarse stone against her body. With each breath, sharp pain courses through her, the ground beneath mercilessly grinding against her wounds.

Setting aside the excruciating pain, Maali musters the last remnants of her waning energy to rise from the remorseless earth. The isolated landscape that encircles her serves as a stark reminder of the fall of human civilisation, an ominous monument to the desperate straits they find themselves in. Mindful that each ticking second is a dwindling ally, she clenches her teeth and wrings out her fouled hair, the tainted liquid trickling down her back in poisonous rivulets.

Maali's boots dig into the abrasive embankment as she labours uphill. Each step feels like lifting a ton, her muscles shrieking with each gruelling ascent. She can almost feel the gravity of her mission pressing down on her shoulders, as if the weight of countless lives physically burdens her climb.

Her lungs are like a blazing forge, each breath drawing in and expelling searing embers, the air feeling sharp and fiery against her ragged gasps. Her heart races wildly, thudding against her ribs with a relentless, almost desperate beat as if trying to escape its bony cage. Exhaustion claws at her, begging for surrender, but the ghostly pulse of urgency refuses to be silenced. It drives her onward, relentless. Her persistence sparks anew with every pace she takes, cutting through the mental fog of the barren landscape, akin to a searchlight in the depths of a dark, unforgiving wilderness.

Reaching for the reassuring grip of her pulse rifle, her hand grasps at nothing but empty air. Her lips hiss in frustration at the cruel reminder. In her mind's eye, she replays the moment—a patrol boat cutting smoothly through the harbour, its wake a surging force that had torn the rifle from her grip. The split-second decision to let go in order to stay afloat flashes before her. By the time the water calmed, her rifle had vanished, swallowed by the water's depths.

Ahead, the harbour district unfurls like a rabbit warren, extending beyond the guard's periphery. Maali bolts for the shadowy base of the bridge's tower, her movements a blur of calculated urgency. As she nestles into cover, her focus narrows, zeroing in on the psychic bond she shares with Diandra.

The migraine that had been pounding at her temples eases, replaced by a lucid resonance. The sensation is electric, tingling along her nerve endings—it's him. He's near, his presence now a vivid pulse in her mind, maybe less than a kilometre away. The connection floods her with a warmth that seems almost out of place in this grim world, invigorating her weary spirit.

For a heartbeat, her tension melts away, replaced by a burgeoning hope. All she has to do is tail Herzan, who remains blissfully unaware that he'll be leading her straight to—

"Well, well, well." Maali's heart jolts as a powerful searchlight snaps on, its glaring beam cutting through the darkness like a knife, pinning her against the cold, metal surface of a shipping container. The light was blinding, forcing her to shield her eyes with a raised hand, "I always thought you were a pretty little thing, but I never imagined just how enticing it would be to see you soaking wet." Herzan's silhouette loomed against the stark brightness as he perched atop a weathered, rust-streaked walkway beneath the intrusive searchlight, looking every bit the vulture he was.

His team fanned out beneath him like dark shadows, each move they made being precise and threatening, with their weapons ominously trained on Maali. Their eyes were hidden behind targeting goggles, giving them an inhuman, eerie appearance. The gleam of their guns in the light was like the glint of a predator's teeth.

In retrospect, Maali realises the psychic connection had been tinged with a desperate warning, but the weakened Diandra couldn't clarify his message in time. Instinctively, she reaches for her rifle, inciting a chorus of mocking laughter from Herzan's men. "Hah, what's the matter, princess? Lose something?" one of them sneers, lewdly clutching his groin, "Oi! I got a rifle right here for ya!"

The team's jeers and whistles pierce the air until Herzan's knuckles rap sharply against the metal railing. Instantly, the clamour grinds to an unsettling hush. "Boys, boys, boys," he drawls, making a theatrical descent from his vantage point to stand squarely before them. "Show her some respect." His grin uncurls slowly, a predator savouring the scent of its prey. "A swim like that would wear out anyone, let alone a delicate creature like her."

Striding toward Maali, each step oozes arrogance. His hands clench into fists, knuckles popping in anticipation, a sound that skims the edge of menace. "I had an inkling we were being followed, but this," he gestures toward Maali, "is a delightful surprise."

He leans in, so close she can feel the humid wash of his breath, each exhale laced with a rotting stench. His laughter brushes against her skin as if the very air is tainted by his corrupted soul.

Suppressing a wave of disgust, Maali maintains her poise, her expression cool and unimpressed. "Really, old fella?" she retorts sharply, her eyes slicing through him with disdain. "I always wondered what a landfill could sound like, Herzan. Thanks for clearing that up. It's impressive, really. Most people use words to communicate; you just weaponise your breath. SorrowStar really does hire the best."

In the brief, charged silence that follows, a muffled involuntary snicker breaks from one of Herzan's men. It's a fleeting lapse, swiftly silenced, yet it's enough to crack Herzan's façade of sadistic pleasure: his eye twitches, a brief spasm betraying his irritation. In a blur of movement, Herzan's hand whips out, striking Maali across the face with a resounding slap. The force of the blow sends her reeling, but she plants her feet firmly, refusing to fall.

A sharp, metallic taste of blood fills her mouth as she feels a warm trickle from a fresh cut just below her eye. Maali lowers her head, feigning submission. But beneath her lowered lashes, her gaze is anything but defeated; it darts rapidly, assessing her surroundings, calculating her slim chances in this dire situation.

Escape routes are swiftly vanishing. The steep incline Maali had earlier scaled with painstaking effort now mocks her from fifty meters downstream, a formidable obstacle too steep to consider. To her rear, the harbour roils menacingly, its waters strewn with jagged rocks and whipped into dangerous currents. Meanwhile, Herzan's men tighten their circle, embodying the relentless, merciless nature of hyenas on the hunt. They advance with a cold, calculated precision, their steps measured and predatory. Each man exudes a readiness to pounce on any sign of weakness, to ruthlessly exploit it to their advantage.

They're more than mere pursuers; they're like scavengers biding their time, keenly aware that their prey is on the brink. Unlike noble beasts of the wild, Herzan's crew are opportunistic and unforgiving, embodying the very essence of ruthless survivalists, poised to seize upon the smallest error. Their approach is not grandiose, but it is undeniably effective, mirroring their leader's merciless ethos.

Confronted by the troubling reality, Maali's thoughts spiral into darkness. 'I'm dead either way. Why should I make it easy for them?' The resolve in her voice is tinged with defiance, even as the hyena-like circle tightens, anticipating her fall.

Cracking her knuckles defiantly, Maali bares her teeth, much to Herzan's amusement. "That's the spirit, missy. Tell you what, I'll offer you a chance to get out of this mess," he growls, rolling his broad shoulders, "You and me, one on one. Let's see what you're made of."

A shiver of dread crawls up Maali's spine as she sizes up Herzan. Her body, honed from years of rigorous training and intense close-quarters combat, is tense, silently protesting the strain. Standing before her is a formidable figure - Herzan, almost two meters of sheer brute force and deadly expertise. A vivid memory flashes in her mind, casting her back eight years to the Whispering riots that had rocked the city. It was there she had witnessed Herzan's terrifying strength: he had torn a marble bench from its moorings as if it were made of paper, hurling it into the crowd like a deadly projectile. The image of the bench slicing through the air, its devastating impact, was seared into her memory.

It seemed almost surreal now that there was a time when they had fought on the same side, united for a cause. Yet, here they stood, irreconcilably opposed, her former ally now a monstrous adversary.

The unease in Maali crystallises into a stark, bitter realisation. A straight-up fight? She couldn't win. Her body, though honed to its peak, has its limits — limits that pale in comparison to his bone density and robust structure, coupled with an overwhelming muscle mass, outclass her own. The intricate network of his superior tendons and ligaments only adds to his physical prowess. The scale tips further with his weight advantage - an excess of 100, possibly even 150 pounds over her, a gap that translates into a raw, physical advantage.

As her eyes lock onto his, however, there's a shift in the air, a subtle change in the dynamic between predator and prey. She might not have the physical means to outright defeat him, but she realises she doesn't have to. Her mind races, calculating, strategising. What she lacks in brute strength, she can make up for in agility, wit, and sheer tenacity. She might not be able to overpower him, but she sure as hell could make him work for every inch of his anticipated victory.

A dark defiance flares within Maali. If this is to be her last stand, she might as well leave a mark. "Alright, come on then, ya drongo!" She surges forward, her right fist, clenched tight, arcs through the air with precision and force, connecting solidly with Herzan's jaw. He staggers, momentarily unbalanced, his eyes flaring with mingled shock and rage.

Herzan's chuckle carries a sinister edge as he steadies himself. "Ever heard that saying? 'It's not about the size of the dog in the fight, but the fight in the dog.' But trust me, in this situation…" his words are cut off as a shrill noise bursts from his earpiece, loud enough for even Maali to hear.

Wincing, Herzan taps his throat mic. "Apologies, Mr. Manfred. I understand, sir. We'll bring her in immediately."

Seizing the unexpected opportunity provided by Herzan's brief distraction, Maali springs into action, her muscles tensing for a swift, decisive strike. Yet, as she propels herself forward, her momentum is abruptly halted. One of Herzan's men steps in. The hard, unforgiving butt of his rifle swings through the air with brutal precision. It connects with Maali's head, producing a horrifying thud that reverberates through her skull. The impact sends her brain slamming against its bony casing, a shock cushioned only slightly by the cerebrospinal fluid. A dizzying wave of disorientation and pain floods her senses, threatening to overwhelm her.

Dizzy and disoriented, Maali staggers, her vision swimming through a blurry, shifting haze. Pain explodes in her head like shrapnel, splintering her thoughts into disjointed, chaotic fragments. She feels her knees give way beneath her, as if the very ground is slipping away. Her grasp on reality becomes tenuous, and the world around her starts to spin and warp.

Then, abruptly, the ground surges up to meet her in an unforgiving embrace. The harsh impact sends a final jolt through her already reeling senses. As she hits the cold, hard surface, a wave of darkness rushes in, swiftly engulfing the edges of her vision. It spirals inwards, relentless and unstoppable, dragging her down into its depths. The last remnants of light and sound fade, and Maali succumbs to the encroaching void, her consciousness slipping away into the engulfing blackness.

CHAPTER 17:
Caged

In the blink of an eye, her surroundings mutate into a disorienting swirl of bold reds, intense yellows, and ink-black shapes, all framed against an unnervingly pristine white background. Amorphous forms loom over her—entities with disproportionately large heads and expansive eyes. A vague recognition gnaws at the edges of Maali's consciousness; she should know these figures. Memories from her childhood bubble up unbidden, of days spent with her parents exploring her clan's ancestral lands, where ancient art adorned scattered stones. Her grandfather's voice echoes in her fading awareness, recounting tales of these mystical shapes. Then, even that sliver of memory dissolves, yet she holds on.

A name surfaces in her jumbled thoughts, and in her semi-conscious state, she whispers it. "Wanjina..." The figures, evocative of the Wanjina from her clan's lore, circle her, their presence assuaging her pain. Childhood recollections flood her, specifically a moment when she'd questioned her mother about the figure's lack of a mouth. "What do spirits need mouths for? Their power is so profound, they have no need for speech," her mother explains, "If they had them, we might be drowned by incessant rains."

The figures reach out to her, subconsciously urging her, "Awaken, child..." The pain surges back, pulling her further into reality, but the figures don't fade, continuing to call for her. "Rise... Rise... Rise!" The roaring thunder of flowing water fills her ears. She envisions a sky darkened by storm clouds and a monstrous flood submerging the land, an enormous wave rolling inexorably towards her. The wave collides with her, dragging her from her stupor.

Her eyes snap open, an immediate regret as she's assaulted by glaring overhead lights. Squinting through the discomfort, her vision gradually adjusts to the harsh illumination, revealing her predicament. She's restrained to a chair under a blinding spotlight. Glancing to her left, she notices Diandra looking worse for wear, with new contusions adorning his head and a harsh circle of strangulation marks marring his visible throat. He doesn't meet her gaze, but she can sense his remorse for failing to alert her sooner.

"I don't blame you..." she mumbles weakly.

"A bit quicker than expected, but no matter. We can simply start ahead of schedule." Manfred's voice echoes through the room as he moves towards her, an SS henchman holding a peculiar device trailing behind him.

As Maali's eyes acclimate to the glaring brightness, she takes a moment to fully assess her surroundings. She finds herself trapped in a hexagonal chamber, its walls stretching skyward to an imposing height. The walls themselves are a technical marvel, covered in lacquered white control panels that hum softly with power. A dizzying array of lights flicker and shimmer, casting sporadic luminescence across the room while screens embedded into the walls spill out ceaseless streams of complex data.

Despite her best efforts to focus, the intricate code remains an illegible blur, its intricate patterns obscured by distance.

In the middle of this technological temple, Maali realises she is ensnared within an enormous cage. Its design is deceptively simple: slender metal bars crisscross to form a grid pattern, making her feel like a specimen caught in a gargantuan birdcage. She tugs experimentally at her restraints, but a sudden, biting pain from steel cords slicing into her wrists halts her in her tracks.

"I wouldn't do that too much, missy," Manfred advises with a sly smirk, gesturing to one of his henchmen to move closer. The man steps forward, carrying what appears, upon closer inspection, to be an untidy assembly of cables and diodes, an electronic crown of thorns. Maali's desire to resist flares up, but it's immediately quelled as two other goons step in, flanking her and seizing her arms and neck with iron grips. Rendered immobile, she has no choice but to endure as the henchman fastens the insidious device snugly around her head.

The device clamped onto Maali's head is an elaborate, intimidating meshwork of technology. Multiple robust cable bundles flow downward from nodes hidden within the contraption, forming a sprawl of electronic veins across the chamber floor. These tendrils branch off at various junctions, intricately networked in a design that speaks of both scientific sophistication and dark intent. While the majority of these cables snake through a specially designed aperture in the cage's floor, a select few divert towards Diandra. There, another team of henchmen is diligently fastening similar but smaller nodes onto his scalp, embedding him into this twisted neural web.

As Maali's gaze sweeps across the chamber, a chilling, almost palpable energy emanates from its walls. The room pulsates like the core of a monstrous machine, each panel, screen, and tangle of wires adding to an aura of cold detachment. The air feels thick with the weight of unspoken horrors, as if the chamber itself were a witness to mankind's darkest inclinations.

This place transcends mere physical dimensions, morphing into a symbol of the moral chasm where the pursuit of 'progress' often treads. It's a haunting reminder of how, throughout history, the most atrocious acts have been justified under the guise of advancement. The term 'progress' here feels like a modern euphemism for collective psychopathy, a veil thinly masking the inhumanity of actions taken in its name.

In this room, the line between scientific breakthrough and ethical nightmare doesn't just blur—it disappears. Maali can sense the echoes of decisions made without regard for their moral cost, decisions that have birthed terrifying new realities in a relentless march towards a questionable future.

Manfred, evidently growing impatient, barks into the air at an unseen figure obscured from Maali's line of sight. "Well? Report!"

A flurry of shuffling sounds to Maali's left heralds the approach of someone, who then speaks with an air of clinical detachment. "Affirmative, sir. Our data confirms that the anomalous signals we've been tracking originate directly from her neural activity; we have direct brain-to-brain communication. Moreover, it appears her proximity to the return team has been amplifying the GY wave emissions from the creature—now identified as Diandra. Current readings indicate the wave activity is consistently peaking at levels far beyond any known baseline parameters."

Manfred's eyes bore into Maali. "And the blocker? Can we confirm its effectiveness on her as well?"

Out of nowhere, an agonising burst of pain erupts inside Maali's skull, a vicious, searing torment that engulfs her senses. It's as if her brain is being cleaved in two, each neural pathway ablaze with an incandescent fire that she cannot escape. Her jaw locks, her teeth grinding against each other with enough force to crack bone. Her eyes well up, blurring her vision into a swirling chaos of colour and light as her entire nervous system shrieks in tortured unison. Her muscles seize, locking her in a rigid contortion of agony. She's immobilised, trapped in a silent scream, a living effigy of suffering.

Then, from what feels like an unreachable distance, she hears the man's detached voice saying, "The signal has ceased. All readings are returning to baseline."

As suddenly as it had engulfed her, the torment withdrew, leaving her in a state of quivering exhaustion. Her body slumps, limp and drained, as she gulps down lungfuls of air, each inhalation a sweet relief. Her eyes blink rapidly, dispelling the last remnants of her blurred, pain-drenched vision.

And just as she thinks she can endure no more, she senses it—a gentle, calming flow of serenity emanating from Diandra. It envelopes her like the soothing embrace of calm waters, washing over her frayed nerves and broken spirit. It's a lifeline in a sea of anguish, and she clings to it, letting their rekindled psychic connection guide her away from the brink of despair.

"I assume that was somewhat discomforting." She manages to lift her head just enough to direct a loathsome glare at Manfred, stationed outside the cage and defiantly blows him a kiss. He shakes his head disapprovingly and signals to someone out of her line of sight. The pain returns with equal intensity, reminding her of her helplessness. "Let's maintain civility this time," he reprimands. Overwhelmed by the pain, Maali has no energy to even contemplate a retort.

As the pain finally subsides, it leaves her drained, panting for air. Manfred, clearly intrigued, taps on the cage, compelling her to meet his gaze. "What exactly did that anomaly communicate to you?" Without waiting for her response, he signals once more with a nonchalant flick of his hand, plunging Maali into a chasm of unbearable pain.

"Why'd you come to its aid? Had you not interfered earlier, you would have escaped unscathed with the D.TEM you pilfered. You could have collected Noah's brats and vanished. So, why?" He punctuates each question with another wave of torment.

"Why?" The agony returns.

"Why?" Each repetition pushes her closer to her limits.

Manfred paces in front of the cage, his eyes feverish, glinting with the sheen of madness and incomprehensible arrogance. "Do you realise what we've built here? A veritable empire. SorrowStar has been raking in wealth on an astronomical scale. Hell, even God would have to count his pennies if he stood next to me," he declares, swiping his hand in a fluid motion that triggers another piercing pulse of pain through Maali's head, making her tremble in anticipation of the next torturous surge.

"Why now?" He snarls, pounding his fist against the cage, each clang resonating with his mounting rage. "Why throw a wrench into the works when everything was aligning perfectly? We had the world, Ms. Maali, nestled right here." He opens his palm and slowly closes it into a fist. "In the palm of our hands!"

His voice rises, unhinged and screeching. "With D.TEM, we held the key to omnipotence. We could bend the will of nations, manipulate global markets, and even rewrite human consciousness! There was no limit! No one could say a thing. Not one word!"

A dark chuckle escapes his lips. "Oh, they tried to compromise me, of course. They even took me to that 'special island,' thinking they had something over me. Fools! Now we own the ones who thought they could own us. We've become the puppet masters in a world of marionettes."

His face contorts into a malevolent grin, pressing right up against the bars of Maali's cage. "So, enlighten me. Why would you risk everything to save an extraterrestrial life form? Are you that naive, or is this some kind of martyr complex? Either way, you've already lost."

His voice drops to a sinister whisper, "Because, you see, even if you could undermine us, even if you could take me down, what's stopping me from burning the entire world down with me? Tell me, who's the God now?"

Manfred's eyes momentarily dart upwards as if he can see through the ceiling, through the clouds, straight to the otherworldly vessel hovering above. "And then these... aberrations show up," he sneers, flicking his wrist dismissively in the direction of Diandra. He takes a half-step back as though trying to physically distance himself from the seismic shift in his well-laid plans.

Maali, despite her constrained position, can't help but let a knowing smile play across her lips. She even licks them, tasting the residue of her earlier fight but also savouring the palpable shift in the room. She can feel Manfred's invulnerability cracking, fracturing under the weight of his own hubris and the sudden, overwhelming threat represented by Diandra's people—a frisson of satisfaction courses through her: the hunted sensing fear in the hunter.

Her eyes lock onto Manfred's. "It's your sole chance to make it out of here without meeting a far greater power than you've ever tangled with," he warns, struggling to keep his voice steady. "Tell me what that entity knows, what it's planning. Now. Convey their strategy to me immediately. It's your only chance of leaving this facility with a pulse."

Manfred's eyes divert from Maali's, and for a brief instant, his veneer cracks. His pupils dilate, and his mouth tightens just a fraction—imperceptible shifts that betray a man grappling with a reality he hadn't anticipated. Maali's own eyes narrow ever so slightly, her lips curling into the barest hint of a triumphant smirk. She remains silent, allowing that flicker of uncertainty in Manfred's eyes to amplify, to reverberate in the uncomfortable silence that fills the chamber.

That glint of doubt—however fleeting—in the eyes of a man who believed himself invincible serves as a victory for Maali. She doesn't need to say a word; her expression says it all.

The pain slams into her once more, its intensity surpassing all previous onslaughts. Maali would have shrieked if her mind had the capacity to process anything beyond the searing waveforms coursing through her being. When the agony finally subsides, she's left on the verge of unconsciousness. Diandra seeks to assuage her pain through their shared mental bond, but his efforts are a meagre consolation in the face of her torment.

Immobile and nearly insensible in her confines, Maali can do nothing more than blink groggily as the cage door creaks open and Manfred saunters inside. Marshalling all the strength she has left, Maali forces herself to a sitting position despite the pulsing pain that permeates her body. A sneer crawls onto her face as she glares up at Manfred. "You're completely oblivious to the impending storm. You pompous fools have revelled in the misery of others, and now it's going to come back to haunt us all. You've been sowing the seeds of our own annihilation, you imbeciles." She cackles, a tinge of hysteria creeping into her tone. "So, go on, make your move, you bastard! One way or another, you're going to pay!"

Maali's brief smile fades as her gaze clashes with Manfred's. "Kill me if you must, but know this – I am already dead. You can't take anything more from me."

Manfred, a cold smile playing on his lips. "Oh, Maali, death is merely the beginning. There are fates far worse than death, my dear. And I assure you, I am quite the artist when it comes to crafting such fates."

With impeccable timing, he raises an eyebrow and gestures towards a set of robust doors on one side of the room. Wearing a smug grin, he signals to the two guards stationed there. As they haul the doors open, three additional guards manhandle a semi-conscious, beaten man into the room and fling him onto the floor just outside the cage. A lump of dread forms in Maali's gut, and any lingering sliver of hope shrivels up.

Maali's breath catches in her throat as her eyes lock onto Noah's mutilated form. The harsh light from above casts chilling shadows on his disfigured face, accentuating every welt and bruise. A droplet of blood escapes his swollen, split lip and meanders down his chin, dripping onto the floor below. His eyes, once vivid and full of life, now look like marbles clouded by a disorienting fog.

Inside her, a hurricane brews—rage roiling like molten lava, impotent fury ready to burst forth. Her fists clench so hard that her nails dig into her palms. She pulls at her restraints, metal grinding against her skin, the searing pain irrelevant against the backdrop of Noah's agony. Her eyes stay locked on his as if she could will some of her remaining strength into him, as if she could form a shield out of sheer defiance and hurl it between him and further pain.

But then, a guttural laugh echoes in the room, a sadistic glee that douses her internal inferno like a torrent of ice water. The weight of their dire reality settles in, anchoring her to the chilling fact that she is trapped, powerless to stop their captors' twisted game.

Tears breach Maali's eyelids, spilling over and tracing salty lines down her cheeks. They are tears of outrage, of sorrow, but also of a resolve that refuses to be snuffed out. Even as her situation seems insurmountable, her mind races, hunting for a sliver of opportunity to turn the tide.

'Fate may be a shadow lurking behind, but it has not yet laid its claim on you, Maali; keep moving forward,' she silently declares. 'In the end, all you truly possess is this moment – seize it with all the strength you have left.'

CHAPTER 18:
Pain

As Maali's eyes desperately search Noah's motionless form, a choked whisper breaks through her resolve. "Noah?" The sound of her own voice, laden with fear, echoes in the chamber. Her shackles rattle against the cold metal, the cuffs biting into her wrists, drawing blood - a stark reminder of her vulnerability. Yet, the sight of Noah, his face warped in a silent scream of pain, ignites something fierce within her.

Her heart races, not just with fear, but with a sudden, piercing realisation. Manfred's cruel game has unwittingly given her something to cling to, a reason to endure beyond her own life. Noah, her comrade, her friend, bound to her by shared battles and sacrifices, lies before her, vulnerable and broken. This, Manfred's twisted play, reveals their true strength – not just in their individual bravery but in the unbreakable bond they forged in the fires of hell.

Panic and determination war within her as she calls out again, her voice stronger yet breaking with emotion. "Noah?" It's more than a call for response; it's a vow to fight, a promise that she won't let this be their end. In this dark hour, their shared past, filled with blood, pain, and sacrifice, becomes their greatest weapon. Manfred had intended to exploit their bond as a weakness, but at this moment, Maali realises it's the very thing that gives them both something to fight for.

Noah's face twitches, a pained groan slithering from his clenched teeth as he laboriously shifts to meet her eyes. Every bruise, every laceration on his face screams of the agony he's endured. He tries to form words, but what emerges is a raw, primal sound, barely recognisable as human. A trickle of blood-tinged saliva escapes the corner of his mouth, betraying the severity of his injuries. With immense effort, he manages to produce a single, gut-wrenching grunt, "Hnn."

To Maali, it's a miracle. He's alive.

Ignoring the biting edges of her restraints, she leans as close as her bonds allow. "The kids. Are they safe?"

He coughs—a harsh, wet sound that spatters more blood onto the floor—before forcing out words, "Jero took them. They ran when the shooting started." A ragged sigh escapes him, his eyelids drooping as if to surrender to unconsciousness.

But then he grits his shattered teeth, summoning strength from some unfathomable reservoir. "I Stopped some of them, but I couldn't stop em all."

Noah forces himself into a semi-upright position against the cage, his back pulsating with raw pain. "But I didn't go down without a fight." Noticing the worry etched on Maali's face, Noah attempts to lighten the mood. "You should've seen the other guy... or rather, guys, I guess."

Noah turns his attention to Herzan. "Do you hear me, you pitiful excuse for a man?! It took four of your crony lackeys to bring me down, you overgrown c--" Before he can finish his retort, Herzan's clenched fist collides with Noah's jaw, sending him sprawling onto the floor. Maali can only watch helplessly as he writhes in pain, convulsing and spitting out a fragment of a tooth.

Seizing the moment, Herzan proceeds to deliver several brutal kicks to Noah's abdomen, causing even the SS guards to wince. Before his brutal onslaught can morph into a deadly assault, Manfred intervenes with a curt command, "Enough! We have tasks at hand. String him up in front of his little wench."

Herzan's retreat carries a menacing deliberation as his underlings hoist Noah up, fastening his shackled hands to the cage's higher bars. The sickening sound of shoulders popping out of their sockets fills the air, punctuated by Noah's gut-wrenching cries. The room seems to contract, amplifying the horror of the noise, etching it onto everyone's senses.

"I've grown tired of this tiresome charade, Murphy," Herzan snarls, his voice dripping with impatience. His eyes dart toward Diandra. "And I've had enough of that abomination." In two long strides, he's beside Diandra, delivering a savage punch to the alien's cranium. "Were it not for its use, I'd scatter its grey matter across these walls." Turning back to Maali, he leans in, his eyes almost glowing with a sadistic blend of delight and loathing. "I've lost my patience with you, Noah, and every other damn obstacle. Let's expedite matters, shall we?"

With a brusque hand gesture, Herzan signals a minion who scurries forward, pushing a metallic cart laden with machinery that seems plucked from the depths of a medieval torture chamber. Herzan meticulously selects an instrument from the cart and adjusts a few knobs. A cutting torch flickers to life, its blue flame hissing vindictively. "You'll answer my questions, and you'll answer them now," he says, the torch's flame reflected in his cold eyes. "Each time you disappoint me, Noah loses another part of himself. How many pieces can he lose before there's nothing left?"

In an instant, Manfred's hand shoots forward, clutching Maali's throat with crushing force. His fingers tighten around her windpipe, constricting her airway, each digit a vice of escalating jeopardy. He leans in so close she can feel the heat of his breath, a furnace of loathing and rage.

"You think you're clever, don't you?" He snarls, each word oozing with venom, his eyes ablaze with a gleam that chills her to the core. Finally, as if savouring the terror he's instilled, he releases his grip. Maali gasps, sucking in air through a bruised and painful throat, but she holds his gaze, refusing to look away.

"You've linked minds with that extra-terrestrial freak," he continues. "So tell me, what insights has your otherworldly friend shared? What's the game plan for that ship hanging above our heads like a Damocles' sword?"

Through laboured breaths, her voice tinged with a defiance that matches her life force. "What's wrong with me?" she rasps. "What the hell is wrong with you? Your empire is built on suffering, your wealth stained with blood, and your soul—if you have one—is a wasteland. Whatever they're planning up there can't be worse than the hell you've wrought down here."

As Maali grapples with her thoughts, desperately searching for words that might sway the merciless Manfred, her hesitation is misconstrued as rebellion. With a cold nod from Manfred, Herzan springs into action, his actions devoid of any semblance of mercy. He directs the torch towards Noah's right foot. The pungent and penetrating smell of burning flesh immediately fills the air, a nauseating steaky charcoal scent that assaults Maali's senses. She can almost taste the bitter tang of charred skin and singed hair at the back of her throat.

The torch's cruel work leaves behind a horrific sight — Noah's foot, seared and mangled, now bereft of a couple of toes. His stoic facade cracks as the unbearable pain surges through him. A stifled, strangled cry breaks free, resounding through the chamber, a harrowing echo of his agony.

As Noah teeters on the brink of unconsciousness, Herzan, with a sadistic sense of timing, thrusts a vial of smelling salts under his nose. The sharp, pungent aroma jolts Noah back to a cruel reality, reviving his senses just enough to ensure he remains acutely aware of his torment. The abrupt return to consciousness is almost as brutal as the pain itself, a twisted assurance from Herzan that Noah's suffering is far from over.

Maali watches, her heart wrenching with each of Noah's ragged breaths. The agony in his eyes is unmistakable, a stark reflection of the brutal torture he endures. This moment is not just a physical assault on Noah but a psychological torment for Maali, who can do nothing but witness the savage act, the dreadful smells and sounds etching themselves into her memory.

"Stop!" Maali yells, her voice raw. "They came for Diandra and the other aliens!"

Manfred's eyebrow arches in curiosity, signalling Herzan to momentarily pause. "Diandra?" he scoffs, his voice laced with contempt.

Maali shakes her head fervently. "It's not his true name. It's the designation given by the research team who discovered him. We can't articulate or comprehend their actual names."

Manfred's glare is icy. "I couldn't care less about its real appellation. Why did it come here? Why are the others here?"

Her returned glare is equally intense. "Why do you think the others are here?! They're here to rescue their kind, you ignorant bastard!" Manfred motions, and the men at the control panel activate the device strapped to Maali's head, silencing her with a wave of excruciating pain.

Throughout the torture, Diandra tries to console her through their mental connection, offering to share her pain while encouraging her to withstand the ordeal. "Through pain, we overcame the darkness that nearly eradicated our species. You have the strength to do the same... you must. Darkness always yields to light. Endure..."

The instant the contraption shuts off, the world blurs and distorts around Maali, her thoughts scattering like leaves in a windy autumn forest. It takes what feels like an eternity for her brain to refocus, for the world to snap back into a terrifying clarity. When it does, Manfred is towering over her, his foot tapping out an impatient rhythm on the cold floor.

"Enough games," he sneers, his voice dripping with irritation. "Your stalling ends here. What are their plans? And spare me your bullshit about rescues and spirituality."

Through the haze of pain and defiance, Maali steadies her breath. "What's the point?" she rasps, her voice dripping with scorn. "You can't intercept them now. And let's be honest, you have no plans of letting us walk out of here alive. So, do what you will. Stop wasting our time."

She pauses, a grim smile curling her lips despite the pain. "You know, I've always pondered that old saying — 'Weak times make strong men, strong men create good times, good times create weak men, and weak men create tough times.' Seems we're in the era your kind thrives in, Manfred. But remember, tough times also forge the hardest of us. And that," she tilts her head back with a defiant glare, "is something you should fear."

With a rebellious jerk of her head, she spits a mixture of saliva and blood, landing pointedly on Manfred's immaculate shoes. It's more than just an act of defiance; it's a statement, even as she stands on the brink of death.

Manfred's eye twitches, and a vein throbs visibly on his temple as he glances down at the splotch of blood tarnishing his immaculate shoes. "You could have made this easy. One straightforward answer would've earned you a quick end. But you've chosen the hard path." His voice turns maliciously gleeful as he pivots to face the henchmen at the control panels. "Turn it up—all the way. Forget about data or preserving their brain function. Continue until I say stop, and make sure they feel every excruciating second of it."

Objections flare up outside the cage, only to be silenced by a single, startling gunshot. In the aftermath, Maali's perception frays, struggling to piece together any coherent sense of the world around her. Her thoughts are finally jarred back into focus when Manfred storms forward, seizing a handful of her hair that protrudes from beneath the device on her head. He jerks her backward, his voice laced with hatred. "I want you to remember that every horrific moment you're about to endure is solely due to you." With a final malicious glare, he releases her and retreats, leaving Maali's attention to gravitate toward Noah.

Herzan grips the plasma cutter's handle, its blaze now glowing an ominous blue. With calculated malice, he brings it down on Noah's Achilles tendon. The air fills with a sickening sizzle, and the smell of burning flesh once again invades Maali's nostrils. Noah's deep howl reverberates throughout the room, each note a gut punch, fracturing his formerly unbreakable front.

Before she can fully absorb the monstrosity playing out before her, the device clamped to her skull roars to life. An inferno of raw, unbearable pain erupts inside her head, obliterating her thoughts and incinerating her senses. Her vision fractures into a medley of suffering; her hearing distorts into a blend of her own screams and the device's whirr. At that moment, all lines blur—between her pain and the machine, between her scream and Noah's—until all that remains is a gateway; however, it is not clear if heaven or hell is on the other side.

Despite the disarray plaguing her mind, she's sharply aware of every sensation rampaging through her body. It feels as if her skin is stretched to breaking point, tearing at her joints and staining the ground beneath her with rivulets of blood. Her throat feels shredded as she howls, unable to discern if the sensation is tangible or an illusion borne of her tormented psyche. Blood begins to seep from her nose, ears, and even her eyes. Her vision returns for an agonising moment, awash in crimson. Each second feels endless, a lifetime being eroded.

Then, without warning, it ceases. Maali finds herself drawing in a breath that doesn't burn her lungs or cause her chest to ache. Attempting to make sense of her surroundings, she's met with a radiant, blinding light. It doesn't hurt to look at it; instead, it's soothing and calming. Even the lingering pain from past injuries seems to dissipate, leaving her in a state of tranquillity that mirrors her post-D.TEM experience. Uncertain and overwhelmed, she calls out, "Noah? Are you there?" There's no response. She tries again, "Hello? Is anybody there? Noah? Diandra?"

A low hum fills the void around her, a form coalescing within the radiant light. The figure is tall, its skin pale and luminescent, its head large, and eyes as mesmerising as strange. It extends a hand, gently resting it on Maali's shoulder, whispering, "I am here, Maali."

"Diandra?" she breathes out.

The voice of the figure envelops Maali, its timbre rich and comforting, evoking memories of her mother's tender lullabies. These were the songs of the Dreamtime, sacred tales passed down by her people, echoing the mysteries and wonders of the Creation Period. In this moment, Maali feels a profound connection to her heritage; the wisdom of the land and the whispers of her ancestors seem to converge in the air around her. The timeless essence of the Dreaming, that eternal realm of knowledge and story, seems to infuse the very presence that stands before her, bridging the past, present, and future in a single, harmonious moment.

"Is this a part of the Dreaming? Have we returned to the time of creation?" Maali's voice quivers, resonating through the cosmic space around her as memories and ancestral knowledge ignite within her.

"In a way, yes," Diandra's form ripples before her, ever-changing yet eternally the same. "You've transcended beyond the flesh, beyond earthly limits; here, time has no meaning. I regret the agony you had to endure for this transformation. Their cruel devices ripped through your consciousness, but they also made a passage for us to reconnect."

Maali's gaze lingers on Diandra's shifting form, momentarily taking on her own features before reverting back to its celestial state. "Why are you changing? Why did you look like me?"

A profound sadness infuses the space between them, almost like a sigh from the universe itself. Finally, Diandra speaks, "I had to sacrifice my own physicality to come to your aid. When my kind arrived, I was already too weak to communicate with them. So, I relinquished what was left of my form, melding it with yours. It was the only way to elevate you to this state of being."

The realisation comes not as a bolt of lightning but as a gentle dawn breaking over the horizon of her consciousness. She is not just Maali; she is also Diandra, the Creation Period, her ancestors, her mother's lullabies—all woven together in the tapestry of existence. And in that sublime moment, she understands that she carries not just her hopes and sorrows but also those of her people, those who walked before and those yet to be born.

Tears, if they could exist in this form, would be flowing freely from both their non-eyes. It's a moment too sacred for words, a communion that goes beyond spoken language, etching itself into the very fabric of her eternal being.

Diandra's form seems to shimmer, a fluctuating aura of light drawing nearer as if in an embrace. The gentle pressure of his ethereal hand enfolds Maali's, and she feels her palm glowing, radiant with a brilliance she'd never imagined. "You are on the threshold of something ancient yet perpetually new. You are more than flesh and bone, Maali—you are stardust and stories, an heir to ancestral wisdom older than the Earth herself. You are light. To make this voyage whole, you must relinquish the temporary form that confines you."

For an instant, time seems to unspool, unwinding its coils to reveal the ineffable expanse of what could be. She is beckoned into a network of interconnected lives, a realm devoid of mortal suffering, where the woes of her Earthly life—its struggles, its injustices, its stark indignities—are unimaginable. The pull of it makes her soul ache with a yearning so profound she trembles at its intensity. It would be so easy to relinquish, to fade into this resplendent mosaic and be subsumed by endless joy.

But then, a whisper, soft as the rustle of leaves in the wind, breaks through the celestial symphony—a memory. As she turns, it blooms into form: faces, emotions, experiences. She sees herself with Noah, laughing, grieving, surviving. She's reminded of the sacrifices made, the losses sustained, the love and pain they've shared. She sees Noah's face crumpled in agony, tethered in the cage like an animal, his tears glistening, and she's pierced by a bone-deep sorrow, a stark sense of loyalty that she cannot ignore.

Diandra, as if sensing her inner turmoil, releases her hand but not her gaze. "Transcendence is not just personal; it's a collective experience. By moving on, you enrich the whole, but you also have to consider the part of you that still lingers, tied to others, bound by love, duty, and compassion."

Maali's heart swells, breaking and healing in the same beat. It's an ancient ache, a yearning that has propelled her people's stories across generations—a calling from the ancestors themselves. She realises that her journey isn't just her own; it's the legacy of her family, people, and land. It's Noah, hanging on a thread between life and death. It's Diandra who'd sacrificed his corporeal existence for her.

Her voice trembles as she speaks, yet she's never felt more resolute. "Then it's not my time to join you, not when my brother still needs me. If I hold even a flicker of light, then that light needs to shine where it's darkest."

In this solemn moment, as the universe seems to pause momentarily, acknowledging the gravity of her decision, a profound truth becomes clear: even in the vast, interconnected tapestry of existence, the purity of free will remains inviolate. This choice, emerging from a deep well of love and spiritual duty, reflects the universe's diverse and rich fabric, where every thread is honoured for its unique role. As her words echo in the boundless expanse around her, a warmth envelops her — a feeling that emanates not just from Diandra but from something much greater. It's as if her ancestors themselves are reaching across time and form, their embrace affirming that her act of staying, an exercise of her free will, is a transcendental defiance of circumstance. In honouring her choice, the universe itself seems to bend slightly, respecting the unbreakable sanctity of her decision.

Maali's voice catches in her throat as she speaks to Diandra. "In the soldier's world, amid chaos and hell, where bullets carve the air, and the ground itself seems to crumble, there's a profound truth," she begins. "It's not about distant victories or orders from afar. It's about the soul next to you, their breath, their heartbeat. You fight not for some grand cause but for their presence, for the shared breaths in a world reduced to mere seconds and inches. Life, then, becomes a tapestry of such moments, each a universe in its own right, each a testament to the human spirit."

She pauses, her thoughts drifting to a poignant analogy. "Our battles, they mirror the plight of those valiant six hundred. With threats all around, we find ourselves in a relentless struggle, akin to being caught in a storm of cannons. Yet, in this vortex, it's not the valour or glory that anchors us. It's the connection, the unspoken bond with those who stand beside us. In those fleeting, fragile moments, amid the roar and the fury, we discover what truly matters — the courage to stand with and for each other, against all odds."

Diandra looks at her, and he senses more than the welling of profound emotion that mirrors his own. "Noah stood beside me in those moments. He is not just a comrade; he's part of my soul. And I can't leave a piece of my soul to perish alone, abandoned in the darkest pits of despair. We all make choices, but how can I choose to rise when he's still falling? Even if I can touch the heavens, it would be a hollow ascent, one haunted by the echoes of his cries."

Diandra's form glistens, seeming to absorb the rawness of her emotions, then exudes an energy that feels like a cosmic nod. "Your humanity, Maali, is your strength, a source of light that no dark moment can extinguish. Your choice echoes in the fabric of the universe, a love and loyalty that transcends form and defies boundaries. The light you talk of—the one you find in others during those moments—that light also lives in you."

"I'm going back," she whispers.

"And so you shall," Diandra replies softly, "and know that in doing so, you'll never walk alone."

Diandra enfolded her in a warm embrace. "I understand. The bond of shared struggle such as yours cannot be easily forgotten. It's a bond my people know deeply. I will give what aid I can and stand by your side. Together, we'll attempt to save him." He releases her, his eyes—galaxies unto themselves—meeting her gaze. "However, once this task is done, we both must join the collective if we hope to regain our individual forms. There is no other way."

A weak chuckle escapes Maali. "Alright. I don't fully grasp what you're saying, but after what I've been through, it doesn't sound so bad."

The luminescence that had encased her dissipates in a flash, thrusting her back into the sinister reality of her cage. As Maali's eyes readjust, she observes the chaos beyond her confinement. Control panels are aflame, electrical fires casting an ominous light and showering sparks in a macabre display. Soldiers are in disarray, their weapons aimed haphazardly as they struggle to distinguish friend from foe amidst the bedlam. Gunshots reverberate in the enclosed space, heightening the sense of panic.

Manfred's voice pierces through the turmoil. "Cease fire, you fools!" His command, however, is swallowed by the pandemonium. Soldiers, caught in their own frenzy, inadvertently redirect their guns towards him. Bullets hiss past, narrowly missing him as he escapes the room, a stream of curses trailing behind him.

Amidst the turmoil, Maali's attention remains laser-focused on Noah. She quickly grabs the discarded plasma cutter and uses it to cut through his bindings with swift precision. Gently, she eases his bruised form onto the cage floor, a pang of sympathy striking her as his face contorts with pain.

"Noah, can you hear me? Are you still with me?" she asks, her voice urgent but laced with newfound hope. She waits anxiously, her heart hammering in her chest, her eyes searching for the smallest sign of life, the faintest whisper of a breath.

A pained sound escapes his lips, his eyes barely able to hold focus. "Not... dead yet," he rasps, every word a struggle. The weight of his injuries hangs between them, unspoken. His foot dangles grotesquely, almost severed completely. But what truly chills her to the bone are the two fresh bullet holes in his chest, weeping scarlet rivers in sync with his faltering heartbeat.

Holding him close, she feels the rhythm of his life growing fainter, like the last flickering embers of a dying fire. She won't let him journey into that final darkness alone. As she tightens her grip, bracing for the moment his light snuffs out, something astonishing happens.

From the depths of her being, a surge of energy bursts forth. It's as if a dam has broken, channelling a torrential river through her arms and into Noah. His skin flushes, gradually shifting from the sickly pallor of impending death to a warmer hue. His body glows faintly, bullet holes shrinking as though a film of his life is running in reverse. The expelled bullets drop to the floor, clinking softly, forgotten. Even his mangled foot seems to weave itself back together, erasing the horrid image that had been imprinted in her mind.

For a moment, they are caught in the impossible, staring at a miracle neither can quite believe.

Noah draws a quavering breath as if tasting the air for the first time. His eyes, wide and incredulous, scan the room before finally settling on Maali. "What... how did you...?" His voice wavers, the solid ground of understanding crumbling beneath him.

Maali helps him sit upright, feeling the echo of newfound strength vibrate through his body as if the universe itself is gasping in astonishment at his revival. Just when she's about to offer some semblance of an explanation, her eyes meet Diandra's lifeless form. The once luminescent being now slumped, its skin robbed of its ethereal glow.

A heavy sigh escapes Noah's lips, imbued with a complex cocktail of relief, loss, and a dawning understanding. "So, is this how it ends?"

Maali's gaze lingers on Diandra, but a pulse of unseen energy—almost like a whisper in her soul—assures her that he isn't wholly extinguished. A tender smile, tinged with both sorrow and hope, graces her lips as she turns back to Noah.

"No, I don't think this is the end at all," she says softly, her voice imbued with a devotion that feels as ancient as it is new. "I think it's just the beginning of something extraordinary."

CHAPTER 19:
Last Leg

The sight of Diandra's lifeless body elicits a complex mixture of emotions within Maali. She knows that his mortal coil may be vacant, but his essence, his true self, is now part of something infinitely grander. This idea serves as a quiet reassurance, a subtle comfort in a moment heavy with finality.

As she steps closer to inspect his form, her eyes are drawn to the collar around his neck. Though originally designed as a tool of control, potentially rigged to end his life as a final security measure, it now lies dormant, its mechanism stilled. A realisation dawns on her. The collar might have deactivated as a fail-safe upon registering Diandra's life functions ceasing—a bomb disarmed by the very event it was meant to enforce.

Gently, she unhooks the deactivated device from around his neck and sets it aside as if removing the last shackle that had bound him to an earthly struggle. With a soft touch, she closes Diandra's unseeing eyes, laying him to rest as best she can in this place of turmoil.

Though Diandra's eyes no longer hold their otherworldly luminescence, Maali can't shake the feeling that he's not truly gone—his light hasn't been extinguished, just shifted to a continuum she cannot see but can profoundly feel.

A heavy sigh escapes her lips as she retreats, her thoughts whirling. 'Perhaps we deserve whatever is coming next.' Yet, before this notion can take root, a warm sense of tranquillity envelops her, snuffing out the pessimistic thought. Diandra's assurances of hope ignite a half-smile on her face.

Noah interrupts her contemplation as he scrambles back into the cage, his hands gripping a Kalashnikov and spare magazines. "Here, take this," he says, handing her the weapon and ammo. "The pulse rifles are fried, but these old-school guns are still working. We've got two spare mags each—make every shot count."

Before she can ask him about the sudden chaos, he anticipates her curiosity. "You were almost gone, Maali. I was hanging on by a thread myself when something incredible happened. Diandra... his body... it glowed for a moment, pulsating like a dying star. Then it released a burst of energy, some kind of pulse that knocked out all the electrics. That's when everything went haywire."

Maali looks back at Diandra's body, her thoughts coalescing around the mysterious event Noah described. Had Diandra planned this? Or was it a natural consequence of his transition to another plane of existence? Either way, the outcome had been in their favour. His final moments, it seemed, had cast them a lifeline.

"Right after the pulse, something else happened, something I can't explain," Noah continues, his eyes searching Maali's for answers. "You healed before my eyes, Maali. Your wounds, they just... disappeared. Then, everything went black for me. Next thing I know, I'm waking up to you holding me."

Maali scans the room with bewildered eyes, her voice sounding confused. "Where the hell are Manfred, Herzan, and their SS goons? Did they just evaporate into thin air?"

Noah swiftly readies his weapon, his eyes meeting Maali's with an intense, brief connection. "There's something off about this," he murmurs, a note of perplexity in his tone. "The room was crowded, then suddenly, after what happened to Diandra... it was like everything changed in an instant. It was as though gravity itself had been upended. Everyone paused, then recoiled in a confused flurry. They acted as though they had seen the unimaginable, something completely beyond their comprehension. Fear and bewilderment were written all over their faces."

Maali and Noah exchange a quick, understanding look, her gaze darting pointedly towards the exit. She gives a tense nod in the direction. "Whatever just happened, we don't have time to figure it out. We need to get the hell out of here—right now."

No sooner had the words left her lips than a jarring clatter reverberates through the room. On instinct, they dive for cover behind a stout control panel, their actions almost synchronised. A flashbang erupts, its concussive blast shaking the very foundations of the room. Maali clenches her teeth, her ears ringing painfully, but the panel effectively blocks the light's blinding effect.

Hearts pounding, they grip their rifles tightly, fingers hovering over triggers. The door bursts open, and two SS goons barge in, guns at the ready. Noah acts with lethal precision, his bullet finding the first assailant's centre of mass before he can even react. Maali's aim is equally true, a well-placed shot severing the cervical spine of the second intruder. Both men drop like stones, their lifeless bodies hitting the ground with a heavy thud.

Confused shouts rise from the hallway beyond the door, drawing nearer—Noah's eyes zero in on a grenade lying amidst the debris of their fallen adversaries. In one fluid motion, he grabs it, yanks the pin free, and hurls it into the corridor. Panicked voices erupt with dread, abruptly silenced as the grenade detonates, rattling the walls and filling the doorway with a smoky haze. When the echoes of the explosion fade away, a single, gut-wrenching scream slices through the residual silence from beyond the shattered doorway.

Maali glances at Noah, her eyes alive. "How many more fireworks do we have in the arsenal?"

Noah quickly scans their limited supplies and tosses her a grenade. "One frag and one flashbang," he reports grimly. "Not nearly enough for us to blast our way out."

Catching the grenade, Maali glances around the fortified room, assessing their bleak situation. Her eyes settle on the heavy metal desk, then the fractured doorway, and finally on the dozens of armed men she knows are swarming outside—a determined grin forms on her lips. "Escape? Noah, even if we make it out this door, we've got a hundred guns waiting to mow us down. Our best shot is to turn this place into the Alamo."

Noah's eyes follow her gaze, understanding dawning on him. He nods, a serious yet resolute expression taking over. "Alright then. If we're going to make a stand, we'll make it count." Together, they flip the heavy metal desk onto its side, creating a makeshift barricade.

Positioning themselves behind it, they aim their rifles at the doorway, now the sole entry point for the enemy. "We've got the advantage of a defendable position," Maali says, checking her rifle. "We hold them off as long as we can, thin their numbers. Maybe, just maybe, we'll make them think twice about coming any closer."

Noah lets out a determined sigh, readying his weapon. "A last stand it is. If we're going down, we'll make sure it's a fight they'll never forget." Each of them knows the odds are stacked against them, but in this moment, it's not about winning — it's about fighting back, about not giving in to fear or despair. It's about standing shoulder to shoulder, facing the overwhelming force with courage and defiance.

As they wait, the first signs of their adversaries appear at the doorway. The sound of cautious footsteps grows louder, signalling the imminent breach. Noah and Maali exchange a final look; this is it — their moment to fight, to stand against the odds together until the very end.

Within seconds, a helmeted head cautiously inches into view. Noah squeezes the trigger; the head snaps back, lifeless, before collapsing out of sight. Another goon, emboldened, blindly sprays the room with bullets, forcing Maali to hunch lower behind the desk. Using the suppressive fire as an opening, more SorrowStar soldiers burst through the entryway, guns blazing.

Maali pops up, letting her rifle do the talking. The rat-tat-tat of her Kalashnikov echoes violently, mixing with the screams of the fallen. She feels her magazine lighten—three more intruders lay motionless in the doorway, their arrival cut fatally short. From the corridor beyond, authoritative voices shout orders. A duo of grenades sail into the room, tumbling end over end.

With coordinated movements born from countless narrow escapes, Noah and Maali dive away from the desk. The room is momentarily consumed in smoke and noise. When the choking cloud clears, Maali tries to rise, but a sudden wave of vertigo sweeps over her, leaving her disoriented. Her hands pat down her body in a frantic search—no blood, no wounds. She flexes her fingers and toes; they respond, but something feels alarmingly wrong.

As the firefight rages on, Noah ejects a spent magazine and swiftly replaces it with a fresh one, eliminating two more SS mercenaries in the process. "Maali? What the hell?!" he barks over the intensification of incoming gunfire. Grasping her shoulder, he attempts to shake her back to reality. "This is no time for a siesta! Snap out of it and get your damn h—"

His voice becomes a distant echo, fading into oblivion. Suddenly, she is enveloped in the radiant place again, a sanctuary where the only language spoken is tranquillity. "This again?" she whispers to the ether.

"Not quite," she hears Diandra's voice say, yet it's not solely his voice—more like a chorus harmonising behind him. The feeling is unlike anything she's ever experienced. Her consciousness seems to expand, enveloping a sea of minds, thoughts, and emotions that glide seamlessly into one another without clashing. It's like being dropped into an intricate web of souls, each thread pulsating with unique life yet all interconnected.

Astonished, she asks, "What is this? It's different from before..."

For a moment, the visage of Diandra forms in the air before her, suffused with a glow that seems to emanate both from and beyond him. His smile is radiant, angelic almost. "We are aboard the vessel above your city. What you're feeling, Maali, are my people—my kin who have travelled through the voids of space to find me. And now, they've found us both."

As he speaks, she senses their collective resonance strengthen around Diandra's words, like a choir hitting a crescendo. Each voice in the multitude, though distinct, sings the same song of unity and profound connection. It's overwhelmingly beautiful—a cosmic connection she never knew existed, now a part of her.

As Maali dives deeper into this pristine connection, each voice she encounters feels akin to a single neuron in an immense neural network. Like neurons, these individual entities are each discrete, specialised units of consciousness, yet they are also part of a vastly interconnected system, firing off bursts of 'neurotransmitters' in the form of thoughts and emotions that ripple across the whole collective.

It's as if she's looking at a dazzlingly complex connectome, but one that stretches far beyond the scope of any human brain, extending into the universe itself. Every 'neuron'—each voice or soul in this collective—is a unique node in this grand cosmic network, relaying and interpreting signals, contributing to the overall flow of collective consciousness.

She marvels at how each voice, vibrant and unique, behaves somewhat like a star in a galaxy. Stars are individual points of brilliance in the sky, yet they're also part of constellations, galaxies, and, ultimately, the entire universe. In the same way, each voice contributes its individual 'light' to the collective awareness. The 'dark matter' binding them is their shared purpose, the underlying framework that aligns them.

As the voices surge and fade, the ebb and flow mimics the very synaptic plasticity that's foundational to learning and memory in the brain. But here, the learning is collective, the memories communal, and the scope astronomical. These aren't just neural pathways but interstellar highways of cognition and emotion, each 'neuron' a living star, each 'synapse' a wormhole to another universe of understanding.

Diandra's voice then becomes a distinct, bright node among the sea of glowing 'neural stars,' like a supernova in a galaxy of suns. "We're all part of this greater entity, Maali," he says, and his words resonate in every fibre of her being, "yet we retain our individuality, contributing our own unique light to the whole. Welcome to the collective; welcome to the universe inside us all."

A gasp tears from Maali's throat as foreign memories inundate her consciousness. In an instance, she experiences the perspectives of millions, the mobilisation of volunteers embarking on a mission to Earth, seeking their lost comrade. The roller coaster of their collective emotions is overwhelming—exhilaration at locating a single survivor, grief over the countless lives lost, and the simmering fury directed at the perpetrators. The combined anger is a formidable, towering entity. But as swiftly as it comes, it recedes.

The memories and experiences Diandra has shared with them demonstrate that humanity is not solely characterised by the callousness of a few. "They've witnessed your actions, your readiness to risk everything to save a stranger—an entity for whom you had no obligation. Even Noah, with his untiring dedication to protecting others, exemplifies the best of humanity, and it has redeemed your city.

"Observing the dual nature of the human spirit is genuinely fascinating, my friend. Your history is indeed a blizzard of profound anguish, hardship, and loss. But amid these storms, there are also radiant beams of beauty—moments and achievements that define the very best of what it means to be human.

"Consider your artistic endeavours: the creation of music that speaks directly to the soul, paintings and sculptures that capture the essence of emotion, and literature that explores the depths of the human condition. These are not mere expressions; they are windows into the collective heart of your species.

"Your scientific and technological advancements are equally remarkable. Humans have unlocked the secrets of the atom, ventured into the vastness of space, and connected the world to a web of information. Each discovery, each invention, is evidence of your species' relentless pursuit of knowledge and progress.

"Moreover, your acts of compassion and altruism shine brightly. There have been countless times when individuals or even whole societies have rallied to aid others in times of need, transcending boundaries and differences. From acts of kindness in everyday life to global movements for change and justice, these are the signs of a species capable of incredible empathy and solidarity.

"And let us not forget the courage and resilience you have shown throughout history. Faced with natural disasters, wars, and pandemics, humanity has repeatedly demonstrated an unconquerable spirit, a will to not only survive but to rebuild, learn, and emerge stronger.

"We see these aspects, these glimmers of beauty and greatness, as echoes of our past selves in you. Perhaps, given time and the right circumstances, your species may evolve into what we are today—a civilisation that has learned to harness its best qualities for the greater good. Your journey may be fraught with challenges, but the potential for greatness is undeniably woven into the fabric of your being."

"We visited your world many millennia ago, interacting with the people of this land. Their comprehension of us surpassed what one would expect from a primitive civilisation. They were on the cusp of a monumental evolutionary leap, mirroring our own journey. We learned from each other, and it catalysed our further evolution.

"But upon our return, everything had changed. The ancient societies were nearly extinct, eradicated, or so deeply assimilated into foreign cultures that they'd lost all recollection of us and their evolutionary progression. We feared for humankind, believing that all hope had vanished. But then I encountered you. Your courage demonstrated to me, and through me to my kin, that the spark within humanity still burns fiercely."

As Diandra's words reverberate through the stillness, Maali grapples with the very concept of time itself. Here, in this vast collective consciousness, she senses that time is both an illusion and a variable construct. It dawns on her that in this expansive realm, years could have unfolded in the blink of an eye, centuries could have swirled by like the spiral arms of galaxies, and yet no time at all could have passed in the world she knows. Her soul feels as if it has been journeying for years through the celestial highways of this collective consciousness, expanding and deepening with each interaction. Yet, she also senses that she has never left, that all this could be occurring in an infinitesimal moment back in the physical realm.

"Time is but a sequence of moments, a construct," Diandra's voice resurfaces as if reading her thoughts. "Here, moments can stretch into eons or condense into mere fractions of a second. You've been gone for years, and yet you never left. It's a paradox that your human mind may find challenging to reconcile, but it's a reality in our existence."

The weight of his words collides with her newly acquired wisdom, and she senses the fragility of the situation awaiting her return. She could lose it all—the love, the newfound knowledge, the inexplicable unity she now feels—by stepping back into the danger she left behind. And yet, a part of her, tethered to that very moment, to Noah and to the life she knows, compels her to go back.

Diandra perceives her internal struggle. "You're on the cusp of a profound evolutionary trajectory, Maali. Yet, you think of others, even now. It's both your strength and your vulnerability."

Maali's voice steadies as if fortified by the years she's experienced in a moment and the moments she's compressed into years. "It may be a vulnerability, but it's one I'm willing to live with—or die for. Noah is alone; he needs me, and I can't abandon him. This newfound experience, as overwhelmingly beautiful as it is, can't replace the bonds I have in my world."

A palpable stillness fills the timeless space, only to be shattered by Diandra's eventual whispered consent. "Very well, we honour your choice, Maali. We'll always be here, and our paths will cross again in this life or another."

The room of suspended time and motion crystallises once more into her reality, but she is not the same Maali as before; she is a being stretched across years, compressed into moments, forever changed yet eternally the same. As bullets unfreeze and continue their deadly trajectory, she readies herself to face whatever comes next.

"-ead in the game!" Noah's shout reverberates around her as he dives for cover, evading the onslaught of bullets. "We're knee-deep in trouble! And you're daydreaming again."

Unfazed, Maali emerges from her protective cover, taking down an invader attempting to breach the room with a precise shot. He tumbles lifelessly through the doorway, the momentum from his sprint carrying his body forward. Momentarily stunned, Noah casts her a glance before a wolfish smile stretches across his face. Rising beside her, they successfully dispatch another duo of adversaries.

With a sigh, Maali comments, "You know, my cousin had a saying whenever he found himself in predicaments like this."

With a scowl, Noah retorts, "When the heck was your cousin ever in a situation like this?"

"You'd be surprised," Maali responds, maintaining a deadpan expression even as a bullet grazes her shoulder. It is a minor injury—a mere flesh wound—but it sparks a fire within her. Snarling, she retaliates, sending the assailant scrambling for cover. "You sow the wind," she aims and fires, the bullet finding its mark in his skull, "you reap the whirlwind!"

"No doubt about it, your cousin's a lunatic," Noah remarks, shaking his head in disbelief while contributing to Maali's gunfire. "But I have to admit, that does sound apt for our current quandary."

The monosyllabic rhythm of gunfire shatters the air, sending searing pain through Maali's shoulder and hip. She feels the hot metal tear through her flesh, lodging itself deep within her muscles. Her right-hand spasms uncontrollably, numb from another bullet's uninvited entrance. She barely has time to register her wounds when a sharp gasp escapes Noah's lips.

Out of the corner of her eye, she sees it—blood gushing in dark spurts from three separate spots on his leg. A bullet has also grazed his ear, and she can see the torn skin hanging, already starting to swell. The room seems to spin for a moment, the metallic scent of their mingled blood heavy in the air.

"Damn you both to oblivion!" The voice, soaked in murderous rage, is unmistakably Herzan's. Stirring back to consciousness and clearly unhinged, he unleashes a furious hailstorm of bullets toward Maali and Noah, emptying his magazine as if the bullets were free samples.

His gun sputters to a pathetic click, its chamber now empty. Noah doesn't waste the moment. He fires back, but his shot veers off, startling Herzan into an almost comical yelp as he scrambles toward the exit like a roach fleeing the light.

Just as he reaches the threshold, bellowing commands, a rogue bullet from the confusion outside does the job Noah couldn't. It sails right into Herzan's mouth, exploding out the back of his skull in a grisly splash of gore. Herzan's body freezes for a surreal second as if catching up with its

SYDNEY EFFECT

newfound lifelessness, then crumples to the ground. The room plunges into a hushed quiet.

The voices outside echo with confusion and panic. "Shit! The commander's been shot!"

"Who the hell did it?"

"Todds?"

"Wasn't me, jerk! It was you!"

"No way, you idiot!"

Maali and Noah exchange glances, unable to stifle their laughter as the inane argument spirals into alarm. A solitary gunshot pierces the air from beyond the door, instantly followed by a deafening silence. Tentatively, they peer over their barricade, unsure of what they might encounter.

Their eyes meet in disbelief as the entrance remains unbreached. Murmured whispers flutter outside the room like bats in the dark, settling down at a firm "Attention!" The unmistakable syncopation of military boots coming to a disciplined halt fills the air, punctuated by the sharp, confident clack of high heels on the hard floor.

Noah lets out a disbelieving laugh. "You've got to be kidding. Who in their right mind shows up to a gunfight in heels?"

Maali, propped against their barricade by her good arm, struggles to keep her posture. A numbing sensation begins to radiate from her bullet-riddled hip, making standing a fight of its own. She cocks her ear toward the door, parsing through the hushed but heated conversation wafting in. "Sounds like... Manfred's getting a dressing-down of a lifetime out there."

As Maali strains to catch fragments of the muted conversation beyond the door, the words crystallise through the fog of pain and adrenaline. "This debacle should have concluded hours ago, you imbecile. Rectify it immediately." The woman's voice is almost a growl, honeyed with authority yet laced with threat. The utter silence that follows from the soldiers on the other side suggests either deep-seated dread or unyielding reverence—possibly both.

Manfred, on the other hand, sounds like a man facing the gallows. "Please, Grand Illuminate, I have children who depend on me. My men can deal with this, I assure you." His desperate plea is interrupted by the chilling chorus of guns being cocked.

The woman's response is glacial, as if the very notion of empathy had never touched her. "Correct this here and now, or we'll divert our attention to your family."

The shudder in Manfred's voice gives way to a tortured wail. "You have a team at my home? What the--" The sound of snapping fingers pierces the air as if cutting the last thread of his fraying sanity. A rasping scream erupts from him. "No! For the love of God... Alright, I'll do it. I'll do it!"

A cold, sibilant voice slithers back. "Good. Lead the charge, Manfred, won't you?"

Inside their makeshift barricade, Maali and Noah share a fleeting moment of understanding, their eyes meeting just before they bring their rifles to bear on the door. The room has become an inferno's prelude, electric fires igniting in sporadic pockets around them. On three sides, azure and gold flames flicker and flash menacingly, casting shadows that flicker and sway. Sparks erupt from frayed wiring like mini fireworks, the hiss and pop of their bursts cutting through the air, competing with the smoky stench that's starting to fill the space.

Finally, Manfred bursts into the room, his face contorted into a snarl, his gun spitting bullets in a spray of desperation and expletives. "You'll pay for this, you pieces of--" His words are drowned out by the noise of his own gunfire, which chews up the wall and floor but miraculously avoids hitting either of them.

Amidst the ear-splitting hail of bullets and the ever-present shadow of mortality, Maali and Noah clutch onto a morose humour that seems almost sacrilegious in the face of their dire circumstances. Huddled behind their ramshackle barrier of shattered furniture and debris, Maali shoots Noah a wry smile.

"You know, when I pictured us going down in a blaze of glory," she says, her voice tinged with heavy irony, "I didn't think we'd be so literal about the 'blaze' part."

Noah cracks a rueful grin, his eyes scanning the room as if expecting to find an exit sign hidden somewhere among the chaos. "Well, aren't we just a couple of overachievers? It's a regular gunfight, and there are no marshmallows to roast. What's the world coming to?"

Bullets buzz past them like angry hornets. Maali leans in, whispering so low she's almost drowned out by the din. "If we survive this, Noah, we're starting a support group. 'Close Calls Anonymous' or something. We'll have the best damn stories to swap."

Noah's eyes dance. "I like it. We'll have a three-step program: 'Dodge, Duck, and Deadpan.' It's the triple-D approach to survival. Keeps you alive, or at least keeps you laughing while the world goes to hell."

The hollow clack of Manfred's guns, now spent and useless, echoes through the chaotic room, marking the end of his desperate onslaught. Noah's gaze hardens in that fleeting silence, zeroing in on Manfred. He steadies his aim, the muzzle of his gun tracking Manfred's movements with cold intent.

In a split second, a sharp crack slices through the air. Noah's bullet, fired with lethal accuracy, strikes Manfred squarely in the knees. The impact is brutal and immediate. Manfred's legs buckle under him as if their strings have been cut, his body collapsing in a disjointed heap. The sound of bones shattering is almost audible over the chaos.

Manfred hits the ground with a guttural cry of agony, his authoritative demeanour crumbling into a spectacle of pain and helplessness. He writhes on the floor, a tangled mess of shattered pride and splintered bone, his curses and groans filling the room with the raw sound of his suffering.

Struggling to maintain his composure, Manfred glances over at Maali and Noah, desperation seeping into his eyes. "You need what's in this bag," he rasps, nodding towards the fateful black neoprene bag that contains the D-TEM.

Noah glances at Maali, their eyes meeting in silent agreement. "Crawl over here, then," she orders, her voice laced with ice-cold detachment.

Manfred begins the humiliating crawl toward their barricade with grimacing effort and audibly grinding teeth. Each movement he makes is agonising, a pathetic display that holds no satisfaction for Maali. Yet, her eyes remain glued to the bag that inches closer with every pull of his arms.

Finally, he reaches their position. Gasping for air and bathed in sweat, he offers a crooked grin, mistaking their intent. Noah reaches out and snatches the bag, throwing it to Maali. Maali unzips it, her fingers closing around the D-TEM. A small glimmer of hope sparks within her.

Maali gives Noah a solemn nod, as she raises her rifle, aiming it directly at Manfred's forehead. Panic flickers in his eyes as he desperately pleads, "You don't understand—they're amongst us, a silent, malignant presence!" His voice quivers with urgency, a last attempt to sway her.

Unmoved, Maali's voice is ice-cold. "Thank you for the delivery," she says, her tone dripping with contempt. She pauses, ensuring Manfred fully grasps the sting of his imminent defeat. Then, with steadfast resolve, she firmly pulls the trigger.

Another sharp snap reverberates from outside, signalling the end of their brief respite. A torrent of gunfire storms in, so intense that neither of them dares rise to return fire, fearing instant decapitation. They are losing blood at an alarming rate, leaning on each other for support as their barricade is steadily whittled down.

Knowing that the SS squad outside has run out of patience and time is running out for them, Maali turns to Noah and says, "You know, given these odds, I feel there's something I need to get off my chest."

Noah arches an eyebrow inquisitively. "Uhh, shoot?"

Maali takes a deep breath as though the confession requires a Herculean effort. She slowly exhales, finally confessing, "All these years, and I've never really told you—you're quite the dickhead, Noah."

His stunned expression is priceless. As Maali's smile widens, Noah lets out an audible sigh of relief. "And here I was, thinking I was the only one putting up with a right royal pain. Good to know, sis."

Amidst the echoing laughter and whizzing bullets, Maali fishes out two D-TEM vials from her bag, passing one to Noah. Their eyes lock a moment that speaks of hardships faced, challenges overcome, and a bond that no assault could sever.

With a glower that's half pain, half determination, Noah asks, "What's the play, Maali?"

Holding up her D-TEM, Maali offers a fierce grin that matches the fire in her eyes. "Well, since we're in this glorious mess together, might as well make it a spectacle worth telling, don't you think?"

"To the grand finale, then."

"To our last, best hope," she echoes.

With a solemn grace, Maali and Noah tap their D-TEMs together—clicking them as one would clink glasses to toast a sacred vow. They swallow, and it's as though they've channelled the universe's primal scream, feeling an explosive surge of energy radiate from their very souls.

"What now?" Noah inquires, his voice tinged with an inexplicable serenity, as though he has glimpsed the face of destiny and found it not wanting.

Leaning her head on Noah's shoulder amid a shower of falling debris, Maali looks ahead with a glint of boundless courage in her eyes. "Oh, you know, brother. We're about to turn the last page, and it's written in fire."

THE END

ABOUT THE AUTHOR

A firm believer in individuality, R.K. Jones hopes that he can encourage people to think for themselves—going against the herd and doing what is right, not merely what's expected. His writing demonstrates an adoration and respect for the human experience, which Jones believes has remained fundamentally unchanged at its core. Through stories, let there be no doubt people can share lessons and help each other. You can contact him online at ralphjonessd@gmail.com

Continue Your Journey

Further must-read collections from Ralph K Jones include:

<u>Self Discovery:</u>

Applied Stoicism: Take Back Control Of Your Chaotic Mind

Don't Give Two Sh*ts: Navigating the Modern World's Insanity by Focusing on What Matters

SYDNEY EFFECT

Short Illustrated Stories:

Ethical Displacement

Gravitational Momentum

Quantum Dilemmas

Fundamental Matter

Genetic Inheritance

Thorium Half Life

Anthropic Principles

Quantum Attraction

Quantum Awakening

Quantum Entanglement